Secessia

Also by Kent Wascom

The Blood of Heaven

Secessia

Kent Wascom

Grove Press
New York

Published simultaneously in Canada
Printed in the United States of America

FIRST EDITION

ISBN 978-0-8021-2361-9
eISBN 978-0-8021-9133-5

Grove Press
an imprint of Grove Atlantic
154 West 14th Street
New York, NY 10011

Distributed by Publishers Group West

groveatlantic.com

15 16 17 18   10 9 8 7 6 5 4 3 2 1

And much of Madness, and more of Sin,
And Horror the soul of the plot.
—Edgar Allan Poe

New Orleans is a settlement of the dregs of the French bohème, in
the truest sense of the word a French convict colony—and never,
with the changes of time, has it belied its origin.
—Karl Marx, *Die Presse*, May 20, 1862

For Alise

Characters

Prologue
1844

Elise Durel . . . age fourteen, a suburban girl
Emile Sabatier . . . age seventeen, a boy of prospects

Parts 1–5
1862–1863

New Orleans
Joseph Woolsack . . . a slaver's son
Angel Woolsack . . . his father
Elise Woolsack . . . wife of Angel, mother of Joseph
Inés Pichon . . . her friend and neighbor, a free woman of color
Ligeia . . . handmaid, human property of Elise Woolsack
Dr. Emile Sabatier . . . scientist, physician, agent to Angel Woolsack
Lydia Sabatier . . . his wife, a spiritualist

New England
General Benjamin F. Butler . . . Massachusetts jurist, politician,
commander Union Forces, Department of the Gulf
Sarah Butler . . . his wife
Major George Strong . . . a Vermonter, Butler's adjutant

The Golden Circle
Marina Fandal . . . an orphan, late of Cuba

Prologue

1844

Blood runs from the corners of her mouth, down babyfat ridges in twin red arcs that meet and pool at the jut of her chin. The waltz halts with a gut-string shriek; the masqueraders stop mid-step and turn to see. She wavers on the dance-floor, hands limp at her sides. A spare fourteen but ancient by her gaze and carriage, she stumbles through the awestruck crowd. Myriad costumed youth, gathered here in the Théâtre d'Orléans guised as clowns and devils and beasts. This nightmare cast, among whom she moves, is endlessly imaged in the ballroom's mirrored walls. Horror likewise multiplied in the specula of their souls.

She reaches for her lips, one trembling hand, wrist braced in a corsage of hawthorn branch, according to custom. Saw-toothed leaves clustered with berries red as the blood that drips onto her satin cuffs, purpling the midnight blue. Her sleeves are rumpled and torn, her dress mauled as is her person. The beginnings of bruises clot along her

1

pale throat, stud her bare shoulders. Her only unmarred article is her mask, and within the bone-white pits of her Columbine the girl's eyes are crazed and wide. Silent as the grave, she wades the stilled dancers. Our Lady of Mutilation. She is hardly of this world.

In the galleries, those of finer family drop fans and their gasps fall to meet the murmurs rising from the stunned below. Questions dart among the bewildered young. Who is she? Even were the girl unmasked none would know her face. Her name is hers alone and it is barely that, a mean tether by which she keeps a slim hold to the real.

Elise Durel, here tonight for her first dance. She's come from the outskirts of Lafayette City to New Orleans, a place no more her own than this blood. She cranes her neck and searches the crowd and the galleries above. Where is her mother? Nowhere. Chaperone gone off, enacting her own dalliances elsewhere. Mother who, in her day, would never have been able to attend such a ball. Mother who whispers of droplets of blackness and who raised her lily Elise in suburban hothouse so that she could make her entrance into the city unfettered by questions of race. Mother, drunk and disappeared. She chokes; there is something in her mouth. A gristly chaw, a gob. Her throat revolts.

Members of the band call out, an unmusical thud of a fallen violin. Black voices from the stage, but none will interfere in this whitefolks' madness.

She feels the dancers shiver at her passage, stiffened half-wrought armatures of adulthood imbued with needs beyond their years. Needs presently shriven at the sight of her. Needs she felt earlier in the night, taken giggling and wine-drunk into one of the shadowed anterooms where suppers had been held before the ball began, by a boy with tawny hair and hands that doubled round her wrists, his face strong and handsome, his leonine mask athwart. Those first touches among the snuffed tapers and greasy plates. Needs suddenly nearing fulfillment that heretofore had only held night-hour purchase in her mind or at such times as when she'd watch from her porch the sons of shopkeepers carrying crates down the street, their sweat-clung shirts and rolling muscle. Needs never made flesh until now there it was, his arms round her, spinning her as lightly as he had when they'd danced, as though she were nothing. His gleaming straight teeth and his strong smooth jaw, this same countenance, laughing as he pinned her to the creaking table, and when she tried, laughing too, to wriggle out, hustled her against the wall and knocked the laughter from her. As though she were nothing. One hand holding her fast by the neck and shoulders while the other spidered fruitlessly down and fought against her layers of clothes as though she were nothing, nothing more than an *itchy little slit* he said in that same bright strong voice with which he'd asked her hours before to dance; those same hands that had slipped the bracelet of hawthorn branches round her wrist, the berries red as blood, now dug into her neck and pulled her close, his mouth on hers then lapping at her throat like some mockery of lovers, his head pressed against her cheek, the reek of pomade and cologne. Occupied, his grip loosed and her neck was free; and there in the dark it was as though a mantle of rage broke over her head. When her mouth closed over the sweating ellipse of his ear, he groaned glad for a moment, much mistaken. She felt her teeth, her pearled salvation, growing long and sharp as cockspurs, and she sank them into the flesh of the boy whose screams now form her train.

Elise steps to the pitch of his peal, a childlike cry issuing in belated agony from the dark doorway of the dining room. All around her masks are lifted, flung aside. Those boys not rushing towards the scream stand with jaws agape, stunned by the incongruity of beauty and gore. The girls, for their part, give her sickened looks as though the blood on her face was that of their own revealed menarches. The very pit of mortification.

Shouts and wails, the rescuers call out the bitten boy's name and what has happened, the boy himself howling about *the bitch* who's done this to him. The crowd stirs and the gobbet is jammed to the roof of her mouth. She hears the bitten boy and his helpers nearing, and now the crowd is stirring into tumult.

A lone face bears her a kind expression, appearing from out of the horrified mass. Sallow, sunken-cheeked, with hair the same shade as the bags beneath his wide green eyes, he clutches to his chest a Harlequin mask and edges improbably towards her, gathering the strength for words. He might be mistaken for the corpse of a handsome lad. He holds out his hand and she jolts back from him, a wretch mounting in her gorge.

She is the most beautiful girl he has ever seen. No matter the blood, no matter her bobbing throat and the shouts and chaos now ensuing all about. Emile Sabatier, Harlequin mask dropped jangling at his feet, stands in awe of this stark creature. He pendles on the edge of doubt. One of those children too often wrapped in the clammy arms of illness, he retains a survivor's wasted aspect. He wears his mortal coil loose. Vitality as ill fitting as the new-sewn suit made especially for tonight, his advent into the world of the well, when this boy who studies books of medicine and collects crime clippings from the paper was supposed to dance for the first time with girls who weren't his cousins or the waylaid daughters of family friends, and meet in person those matchless ladies of his imaginings. Finding instead fragile beauties tacked like tapestries to the walls and flocks of mincing shrikes waiting for the chance to pin the unwary on the tines of their disregard. A dull and sorrowful vision now shattered and dispatched by the girl in blood-decked blue. A pagan queen arrived at her barbaric coronation.

The wildness, he sees, is gone from her eyes and now they are fired with an awful poise. The assurance of the damned. She raises a cupped hand to her face, parts her lips and there a white whorl of flesh rests like some foul sacrament upon her tongue. When she gags the gnawed bit into her upturned palm, it seems the entire hall, all but she and him, is screaming.

Maledictions, an explosion of hands and the dancers erupt into treacherous snares. They swarm her and their collective voice is that of a hive as they grab and snatch and try to hold her still. Her mask is tugged tight against her face by some wrenching grip and the ribbon breaks from her Columbine, the mask torn away to no revelation but that of her full fury.

A girl with florid hair and pimples at her doubled chin appears, lipping cusses. Elise flings the twist of ear in her face. A piercing squeal. She rakes herself free from one and another, but there are more and she thrashes against them, battering shanks and clawing troughs of skin. She will have them all bloodied; she will have them all in rags before they can bring her down. Voices cry out for police, some tenderhearted girls on the periphery weep. And she sees, weaving in their midst, the boy she bit: dabbed with handkerchiefs, his wailing abated to an angry mewl.

She has clawed herself a gap when from out of the heaving mass shoots the arm of the green-eyed sickly boy. Emile Sabatier, hand not proffered now, takes hers, and his move is so sudden that when he tugs she is hauled out like a tooth, spit bloody from the crowd and they are loosed and beating for the door.

He kicks it free, strength in his legs as he's never before known, and they spill out into the chill January night. He grips her tight and they tumble from the banquette onto Bourbon Street. Rude suck of mud and he must struggle to maintain his feet, wondering how she possibly can and whether that sound is the snapping of her heels. Still she keeps his pace, a prize beside him. Running, holding her, he is something great and brave and beyond himself. A sudden burst of glory in what was heretofore a twilit life of broth and book-dust.

They run through the fog of their concert breath. Damp air on the verge of ice, like powdered glass to these children of summer heat. She feels her arm near tugged from its socket the boy pulls so hard. She can say nothing for her lungs are blasted out. She lags a little, shakes her arm to make him stop. She doesn't need this boy to drag her on; she wants nothing but to be alone and far from here. She wants to say I'm grateful and now let go my hand. But on they sprint and he will not let her go.

He takes aim by the white cupolas of the church, turning riverward and in hopes of a cab, a cart, anything. The thought of sending her off rises hateful in his mind, but there's no place for him to put her. He cannot hide a full-grown girl the way he can the objects of his nightly self-abuse. And he is suddenly painfully aware of his youth, his homebound state. Mother and father waiting up with tea. They will be furious. But for now, in these black blocks, he can be different. Something more than the boy who pastes murder-clippings in a journal, who pores over the nightmare history of his native city. He can run forever, casting aside clutches of drunks and hurtling vendors asleep beneath their carts, avoiding scabrous old madwomen who yowl of children decades lost or that perhaps never existed in the first place. And who's to say what ghosts walk or crawl or scrabble in these streets. He feels their fingers at his heels and he doesn't care; he is faster than them all and he will never let her go.

Her face is burning; the wind claws tears from her eyes. Her feet are sacks of battered bone. With haggard breath she calls for him to stop. He doesn't listen and, heedless, squeezes harder, and they come to the alleyway beside the vestry, beneath the shadows of the church. Faster now, and she says *stop* over and again. The boy doesn't listen but some other power does. A jut of street-flotsam reaches for his legs and he's upended; arms outflung he tumbles to the ground. And she, upright and running on, is free.

Hammered out of a waking dream, he rises aching from the ground in time enough to see her disappear into the great black swath of the Square, where once men were broken on the wheel or cooped in barrels and sawn in half alive.

The wind seethes, the bleak chill enclosing like an iron casket. The moon seems no less cold a place. Pale falcate mirror of the city's shape, swiftly hidden by unraveled bolts of cloud.

Dark city, winter shorn, witness to the courses of this pair tonight and in all the nights to come. A wicked span in which youth is continually broken and remade until the day arrives when they will meet again. Children of the Damned Crescent, a place whose gates in older days were piked with the heads of criminals and freedom-hungry slaves. Leering skulls rather than ward evil off, which bid it entrance. So all the souls who people this sunken shore must have their moment at the gates. Even a furious girl with bloody lips or a boy beholden to disease.

Now the gates and skulls are gone to dust, but their invitation remains. The watchword is the same.

PART 1

"And All the Devils Are Here"

1862

One

A Witness

Days of fire now but smoldering ash; the smoke of burnt bales and barrels and ship upon ship has the boy enwrapped. He chokes on drifts of blackened cotton fibers, on the caramel stench of immolated sugar, and peers out at the shrouded river. And there might be no sun above, no river before, no city behind, so thickly billows New Orleans's self-destroyed commerce. Joseph Woolsack, lank and fair, crouches in the oystershell of the levee-back and aches to breathe, aches to see the meaning of today's alarm. The bell-peals echoed by church and school, firehouse and watchtower, a tocsin chorus tolling since the pair of blue sailors strode stiffly ashore to demand the surrender of the city. So through brawl and bemoan and the chaos of the raging grown, he has come to watch the end of the world.

He waits for what the wind reveals in snatches among the charred remnants of platform, piling, and sleeper—a ruinscape made paltry foreground when a norther blows and presents him the river in full:

11

the pincushion masts of Federal sloops at anchor off Slaughter; squat steamers add their measure to the fog, and from their rope-slung hulls dispatch men among the scuttled defenses. Fire-barges, doused and impotent, wheel by, unfinished ironclads and rams drift hopeless, abandoned of crews who day by day stumble mosquito-bitten and choleric back into the city to join the teeming ranks of the bewildered and enraged, a detachment of which stands above him—milling and growling, pocket spyglasses glinting—at the head of the levee the city claims it will cut to flood the progress of the Northern troops. But still the earthworks remain and with a change of winds the ash and smoke pass over him and like storm surge slips the crown. Men hack and say they will fight, women that they will drink poison.

He pulls his knees to his chest, enfolding in the curvature of his bowed boy's ribs the birthday pistol. Given this year for his twelfth, the revolver is sized for a child's hand but of sufficient caliber to kill whatever comes, so his father says. It weighs him, presses with a side-stitch strain as he bats at the smoke. Above him, on the levee's crest, loyalties are bandied, declaimed, and if any voice bears hint of joy the offender is quickly corrected. A thwack, the rustling of boots, the thud of collapse. Cheers. Joseph settles in the churn of shell. The smoke parts.

Skiffs have rowed ahead, lurching towards the landing. The crowd calls for the current to grow muscle, for waves to swamp the men within. The sailors are flecks of blue not so bright as he'd imagined. Before the school term was cancelled he'd been instructed that gray is the noblest of shades, and grayness is what swallows the sailors when a smokebank overtakes them. Staring for when they will reappear, he feels the impulse to take the pistol out and—as he's practiced so many times with his father—hold steady, level, and fire.

He is an inveterate murderer of bottles, mortal wounder of fence-posts. But these do not scream, as he knows a man would—an enemy's scream soon drowned by the cheers of the people who would lift him up and in a flower-flung parade hoist him on their shoulders round Jackson Square. He would be like the 'Ti Poucet of his mother's stories: the clever little boy who cuts off ogre's heads, who tricks wolves into traps, and returns home heroic and legendary.

He is already partway into legend, having made a broad-daylight escape from his house. The clever boy who waited until Ligeia came to fix the mosquito bar at his bed for a *sieste* unthinkable with the craze of bells and the riot in the streets, waited until he heard her go to his mother's room to do the same, and for an anxiously dull afterward before he rose, put on his clothes, took the pistol from its wooden case, and, with all the quiet he could muster, unlatched the door and slipped out onto the balcony. There he leaned at the corner of the jasmine-coiled railing, looking down the spiraled column leading to the street—a leap of bone-breaking distance—considering the blunt threats of curb and iron horsehead hitch, the carts and 'buses trundling by with hoofs and wheels to pulp the skull, the gutter to catch the spillage, and above all the silent threat of his father, not party to the enforcement of afternoon sleep (or any sleep at all, it seemed), locked away in his office where the walls are hung with antique guns and from beneath the door issue periodic puffs of cigar smoke and mumbled curses. So he waited in the tangle of jasmine, their smell as dizzying as the height and his fear, until he could wait no longer and pulled himself up, clinging to the railing, legs slung to the expanse. He might've made the climb headfirst and rapid, as do the sons of Spanish fruit-vendors. No orange-hawker's son, he; the descent would be more careful. And it would have been were it not for the sudden appearance of the shipwrecked girl. In the alley-side window of Mlle Pichon's was Marina Fandal—pale hair pinned, pink barége like a stage-ghost's cowl, arms folded at the sill. They share the age of twelve in common, but here the similarities end, for she is a girl, and this means that she's outpaced him in growth by half a foot—a distance as terrifying as that from the balcony to the street. They have met only once, two weeks ago, a brief and sputtering introduction on the day she was brought to live at the home of Mlle Pichon, the woman of her uncle, Willie Fandal, who maintains an irregular residence there. What little of her story he knows comes from the overheard talk of his mother and Pichon: Marina and her parents aboard a Havana blockade-runner bound for New Orleans, their ship pursued by a Federal gunboat into one of the sudden squalls so common to our coast, the fury of the storm, a shipwreck, and she the sole survivor. Whether she was rescued at sea or floated to Ship Island, home of the invading fleet, it is an accepted and bitter fact that her saviors had been the same Yanks who sent her parents to their deaths. So there she was, shipwrecked Marina, Marina of the island, watching him as gravity took hold and he had to lock his feet round the column to slow his streetward slide.

The smoke thins as the first skiff nears, its officers directing oarsmen towards the dockwork most intact. Huddled now in his spying place, Joseph cannot help but feel that between Marina and himself has been strung a silver thread of complicity. And, feeling the birthday pistol at his chest, he wonders if she wouldn't be happiest of all to hear he'd plugged one of the invaders.

The watchers jeer and keen; gentlemen jostle; ladies spear unruly children with their parasols. The struggling sailors in their small and harried craft go spinning again, and he imagines Marina dashed among black waves, hair windblown and lit by lightning, calling out from some scrap of wreckage for her parents; the rage passes and she suffers now days of calm in the immensity of the Gulf, her hair dried and rimed with salt; sunrise, she awakens on white sands, there builds herself a hut of driftwood and bamboo, befriending birds who chirrup her awake and proffer gifts of fruit; she goes about in banana leaf and palm-frond clothes; blazing afternoon, she holds a bamboo spear and dives into the surf, emerging with a wriggling snapper impaled on the tine; this she eats raw, her cheeks flecked with varicolored scales, her lips part revealing teeth grown sharp, a savage prettiness.

A grunt, a scratch of boot heels sliding down the oystershell, and before Joseph can turn he is overcome by the accustomed terror of the grip of his father's hand, which does the job for him, jarring the birthday pistol from its hiding place so that he must fumble and snatch for it, cupping it close as if it were an egg as he is brought round to face the single blue eye, the patch worked with a gilded cross like a gun-sight, a coda, fixed on him, the features a frozen maelstrom of scarring. The true eye glowers, from Joseph's to what he holds; the hand does not let go; it is strong from overuse, for his father has no other; the stump of his right twitches at its pinning of folded sleeve as though it seeks also to possess him. Joseph feels spectral fingers at his throat, staunching his yelp at the sight of the pistol he points now at his father's chest.

"And what'll you do with that?" The old man bends, his lone eye thins. A laugh escapes his lips like an inmate from the madhouse. "Boy, I've killed men whose spilled guts were bigger than you."

His father speaks with more than words but the doubling of pale cudgel-splits, the indentations of rifle butts where his white hair claws far back on his scalp.

"Go on. Go on and fire like I taught you."

So many times they have gone to the outskirts at Jefferson City with the old bottles and jars picked up along the way to set on fenceposts for marks, his father at his shoulder, saying in a way this same regular and terrible voice to *fire*. Now Joseph no longer winces at the loudness of the pistol's report, loving always the moment when, if his aim was true, his father would grin approval through the blue tufts of powdersmoke, clap his shoulder. *Again*.

Joseph's arm is trembling, shook by the long-gone hand while his father takes the living from his neck, presses it to heaving hollow chest now caught in fit of coughs. The boats must be righted, for the people howl louder. His father cages a final hack within his ribs, throws out his chest.

"Not every boy gets a chance to kill his father," he says. "Though every man might should."

Now Joseph's arm is not his own; the ghost hand has unpeeled the flesh from his wrists and sewn it to the pistol's grip. And what he wants is to rear back and pitch the pistol out into the Father of Floods, far from the father whose hand darts now for the barrel. And for a moment their fingers knot across the trigger guard, but when Joseph, stumbling back, tears his hand away, the pistol is still there.

His name hollered after him like a curse and punctuated by coughs, he goes slipping down the shell into the wreckage of the landing. His footfalls stir the ash-heaps back to smoking life, so that when he looks back his father is a dim thing thrashing through the clouds of his departure. He runs from his name, from the chorus of those along the levee now screaming for the end, from ruin to ruin, heaving himself over pilings whose crystallized turpentine glints like spiders' eyes, into pits of cotton-ash and caves of fire-baked sugar that shatter like glass. He does not hold the pistol; the thing holds to him. He runs, under a suddenly fallen curtain of rain and through endless wreckage, scrabbling at slickened boards and going on, in the interminable, halting progress of nightmare.

Two

Cyanosis

New Orleans has a new disease, more virulent than the yellow fever they say will decimate the invaders, more insidious than cholera. A sickness of society, an affliction of the body politic. The doctor has foreseen it; he knows affliction well. He can bottle death and draw disease up the barrel of a syringe and by cannula and needle-tip distribute desolation. Of course, his skill applies to cures as well. But sickness, whether corporeal or not, always has the shorter odds.

New Orleans's heart is malformed, and as new blood invades the old, what was gray will bit by bit turn blue. A cyanosis of the spirit, as the Confederate gray is overtaken by the Federal blue. And what will be the symptoms, what forms will this new sickness take? First he must give a name to the societal disease, to the effects of invasion and the coming occupation on the populace: cyanosis. In medicine, the bluing of the skin as a result of the mixing of venous and arterial bloods; in New Orleans, invasion, occupation, capitulation.

He has seen the miasma of this contagion gathering in the sky, at treetops and gaswork rosettes, at the roofs of houses and above the foul canals he has for years petitioned the council to dredge, and sees it now passed in stunning virulence between the retreating soldiers gathered at the Jackson and Great Northern depot.

For four days the Confederate regulars have been seeping steadily out, bled from the city in despairing rivulets of gray and occasional clots of bright Zouaves by the great fool General Lovell. This last clutch of the defeated await a train two hours late, themselves traversed by vendors bearing coffee, biscuits, bedrolls, half-cobbled boots with lolling soles. Messengers bark their prices and rainfall seethes at the great ceiling of vaulted glass. Rain, insipid as on the day of a funeral, elicits bewilderingly banal comments about how right it is, how even Heaven weeps for us.

The doctor leans on his cane, brocade of a lieutenant of the Crescent Grays awkwardly bunched at his shoulder, and regards this exhibition of futility. Men of his own well-heeled troop throw out their chins, doff kepis, share solemn tips of Armagnac, all the while affecting veterans' stares as though they are powderburned and flecked with dried blood, as though their weapons are not ornaments, as though they were something more than a gentleman's marching society. Some pass paper and pen, their footmen slaves attendant with jars of India, and, forming a hop-frog line, use each other's backs for writing tables as they scribble out a pair of letters each—one for wife and one for mistress. So in bowed shoulder and furious hand the chain of fidelity and infidelity forms, interlocks, the doctor being the only link missing.

The doctor takes no pleasure in occupying a supposed moral high ground; he simply hasn't the time. And with an end to this Confederate business at hand, what time he has surrendered to the formality of allegiance will be his own again. For months he has ornamented himself as an officer of his company made up of the finer men of the city, having joined for the same reasons he might a supper club or the city council.

In the line, Willie Fandal, young corporal, shipping agent, rake, raises up from his missive and meets the doctor's eye. "None for you, Sabatier? Not even to the wife?"

Tall and blonde, of the strain of recent Teutonic arrivals, aspirant to the baroque mélange of New Orleans gentility though more interested in the baser aspects of life than his importations from Cuba, Fandal is precisely the sort of fool the Confederacy requires.

"I'm afraid I'm only here to see all of you off," he says. "And you, my friend, only one sheet?"

Amid jeers and grumbling, Fandal grins and shakes his head. Were he to write each of his women a letter, he'd keep the stationer in business for some time.

"Don't be crude, Sabatier," he says. "This one's to my niece, my little Marina!"

His niece, of course. Not a member of the Grays hasn't heard the bachelor bemoan how, two weeks past, he was saddled with the burden of the orphaned girl, installed her among one of his many women. Now child and woman both will be abandoned for the flagging haggard cause.

Let others weep for the stillborn South, incipient fetal prodigy now jarred and bobbing in the formaldehyde of eventual defeat; he wheedles possibility. And like so many intrepid students of epidemic, he will seek no escape; he will infect himself in order to understand.

Disease invades. Sickness is a process of capture. The Mongols flung plague-ridden corpses over the walls of Constantinople and let buboes do the work of siege; and so by way of rats and commerce the scourge fans from port to port in Europe, touching lands the Khans would never know. Body to body, sore to sore, so much more elegant than tramping boots and cannonades.

"So you're staying," says Fandal, leveling his broad jaw with distaste. "A shame. We'll need good physicians."

The doctor shakes his head. "For you, my friend, the shots will make hard turns." He envisions Fandal with hollow cheeks, sockets black, churned in a pile of the fellow dead. "And besides"—he gestures down the platform—"you'll have Dr. Trilling."

Fandal assents to the quality of the good surgeon Trilling, a man who keeps a pair of slippers made from the breasts of his first dissection. Fools and madmen, the cause deserves them. He, the doctor, will stay.

Shriek and rumble of the train's approach, letters slip, the authors struggle to hold their offices of love in place. And in the clamor will the addresses be confused? Will the names of *placée* and materfamilias find their way into missives intended for the other? Of course, the doctor thinks, to receive the wrong letter would unsettle no New Orleans society wife. They know where their husbands go on Sunday evenings; they saw their fathers do the same.

Lydia, his own wife, would know already, for she trades in spirits and their secrets—hosts table readings where the chair legs nightly wiggle and the summoned voice their needs from ruffled curtains, knocked tabletops, or in leaves of tea. The perfect work for a woman, so he thinks: to try the supposed other world you must be attuned to the smallest things, the slips and differences in benign domestic happenings, and find in them the import of the universe. For her the war has been a boon, so many ladies with ghosts they wish to call upon—spirits both living and dead, for a husband, though extant, may be as spectral to his wife as any Negro's haint. And such husbands, perhaps gone off to war, may be contacted by spiritual means. An ancient method, Lydia assured him. Have a glass set on your table, a bridal goblet preferably, slip the wedding ring from your finger, and tie it with a lock of his hair; now dangle the ring within the glass and his transmitted thoughts will cause the ring to *tap-tap* against the sides. The husband should, of course, have set down a code before he left—two for "yes," one for "no," and so forth—to prevent the intrusion of her own thoughts.

A tangent. A distraction. He dismisses her for now along with thoughts of how the abolitionists will ruin his business and he will have to find other financing for his work. But so goes cyanosis, and he will adapt to the disease, not struggle like these fools now pressing past him towards the slowing cars. He continues with his thesis. He must formulate the conditions and controls.

Fandal, flushed and buoyant, claps the doctor's shoulder as the train comes to brake, an unexpected gesture he graciously endures until the man is gone, absorbed into the crowd of fellow gentlemen struggling haughtily for primacy in seating. *Descending rank, front to rear!*

Disease infects and infection is invasion. A healthy body may fight invasion, only to succumb for the toll resistance took. So disease must be an occupier, too, overtake and divert the body's functions after its own purpose. Invasion is simple, flesh a million gaping porous mouths accepting of infection, never mind the other orifices. What sickness cannot breach the flesh will be invited in by filthy hands jammed in every available hole. The paths of invasion are endless; the battlements of health are weak and as poorly manned as our pitiful forts; but the trick, yes, is to occupy the body, the neighborhoods of organ and ventricle byways. The invader must become an occupier, turn the functions of the body to his own ends. Make lungs believe they should be filled with mucous; make bowels believe they should be filled with blood. Find venal veins; retrofit glands into factories of bile; adapt the industry of health to the commerce of contagion.

Watch them go. The dead and soon to be, singing, drinking, bent over volumes of Hammil's *Tactics* and Caesar's bloviations on Gaul. And, turning, the doctor finds himself suddenly alone on the platform.

He strides off through the last gasps of coalsmoke from the departing engine, wearing an irrepressible grin, a student's glint at the prospect of a fabulous experiment.

21

The thought of returning home makes him linger at the exit, and he is struck by the image of Lydia in their bed, at the culmination of one of their infrequent and always unfruitful couplings. Her hand keeps the bedpost from the wall; she doesn't want this kind of tapping.

To know the mind of her husband, a wife must abandon the rational world. And he wonders now will she use her pendled ring to seek his thoughts in the everyday. She knows so few of them in life. For the time being, let her keep company with his ghost. He will go into the streets, immerse himself in the city's furious reactions to the new disease.

He is jaunty, cocks his cane, the weighted tip ready for the skulls of the affronting, the mewling crowds who scream at him that he's a coward. Down Carrolton, his prospects seem only to grow sunnier. So the Yankees will ruin his business; he will find one they prefer. Among his projects is the proving, scientifically, the inferiority of the Negro; he can just as easily modify his work to illuminate the Negro's humanity. Laughable, of course—and he does, unbuttoning his tunic as he goes—but such are the reversals forced upon us by circumstance. He whistles, a tune of his own invention. Give him a way and he will take it; give him an ear and he will ingratiate; give him those who govern—all occupiers of one kind or another—and like specimens he will carve them up, their plans panned like so much spleen and useless appendix.

Shopwindows glossed by slackened rain give him back his reflection. He wears his flesh well; and, admiring himself, so too does he admire the resilience of disease, the indomitability of infection. So they will put the slave trade down, remove the disloyal, the recalcitrant, from governmental posts. Fine. The amputation of a gangrenous arm proves often useless; by the time the sawyer's work is done, the patient mourning loss of limb, ingenious infection will have found another home.

Marina

Three

Far Off, and Rather like a Dream

The storm is a shear of blackness out of which descends a winged demon. His fingers aim lightning at the frightened faces of the mariners who cling to ropes, to their sinking topmast, to each other—some looking to Heaven and others to the rocks where they will soon be dashed. Upon this outcropping stands the father, dark as the storm he regards; with one hand he clutches to his chest a staff and book of spells, holding in the other the pale upturned palm of his cowering daughter. Dressed in white, her hair crowned with sea lilies and weed-pods like the Virgin of Cobre, the daughter kneels at his robes and gapes in horror at the scene. The only darkness she admits is the hash-stroke outline of her figure; so blanched is her person that she fades from the engraving to the blank borders of the page, the foot of which reads *The Tempest*, words themselves obscured by foam and storm clouds.

Leafing past INTRODUCTORY REMARKS—she has little use for these—Marina comes to the engravings at the beginning of the play. Beneath a clear and starry sky father and daughter huddle in their lifeboat while a large ship with wind-filled sails abandons them to the sea. Below this, a sea nymph reclines in her clamshell, ACT I stated on the inner pearling. She is naked, the nymph, and gives a smile of coy invitation, for this is, according to the volume's title, one of the author's Comedies.

Though Marina has read the play now many times, she has yet to find much humor in it. Instead it seems awfully oracular, twinning her life with the men who suffer shipwreck, with the daughter previously marooned, attempting to recall her past—Miranda of the weed-bedecked hair and fine features, Miranda who fades into the page just as Marina feels herself fading into the dullness of this room, having resumed her station as gossamer vagary behind walls of mosquito netting after watching the boy scale down his balcony. She'd enjoyed spying his deliberations, the lovely feeling of being unseen ruined the instant he caught sight of her and slipped away as though drawn by the incessant bells, themselves sending the house where she stays into a furor—Uncle Willie's zamba shrieking that *they are coming*—so that when she looked back to the street where he should have landed all that met her eyes was an empty stretch fogged over by her breath on the glass, this too soon departing, leaving her to return to bed and book.

The red leather binding is alive; the gilded filigrees pulse beneath her fingertips. She turns the pages, lingers on a line she favors: Miranda's remembrance of the time before she came to the island, what Prospero, her father, calls "the dark backward." And so Marina has tried, at the behest of the seemingly endless array of incredulous adults through whose hands she's passed, to render plain the particulars of her past. But she would rather seek her story here in ink, in the

24

company of conjurors, princes, and monsters. Of a girl restored to her rightful, royal station after a long and torturous exile. In this way, the play has become not only an embellished analog for her past but also an object for the divination of her future. Still, not all aspects correspond. Her father was not so lucky as Prospero; he did not survive to exhort his daughter's memory, to instruct her on what to make of a castaway existence and life after the storm.

She remembers this: thunder, rain, and wave-crash meld, her father drenched so deeply that with every gust of wind his clothes give off a mist of droplets. He shouts her mother's name, but they are so far from the other boats, so far from the abandoned, sinking *Sarabande*, so far from the warmth of Cuba and San Antonio de los Baños, where a storm meant only that the coffee blossoms would smell sweeter at its end. Father clings to the gunnels and bears the waves that hammer the bow in endless and terrible succession while she crouches in the decking at his feet, water welling at her wrists. Stung by brine, lashed with froth and the fluttering tails of his soaked nightshirt as he crouches lower and lower, crushed. Then all her breaths are water and she is drowning though she hasn't met the sea. Rising to her knees, she clings to his bent waist and looks up: father's face is turned, his mouth hisses rain and her mother's name one last time before they are borne upward, spun, and he shoves her down beneath the thwart and a wave slashes from starboard and sweeps her father so cleanly away she might have never had one.

And the storm has yet to pass. We are never rid of storms. The alarms have ceased, but the house—she cannot call it hers; her house still stands in a grove of green lemon and the shuddering limbs of avocado—has acquired its high-pitched peal. The whore has descended the stairs, jabbering in French with the voice of another woman, even more frantic. Marina is not so strong with French as she is with German, Spanish, English. The women go on squeaking until the door slams and there comes the petty thunder of the zamba's heels up the stairs.

When the door opens, Marina has composed herself in an attitude of sleep, Shakespeare arm-slung and snuggled like a favored doll. Behind her eyelids the storm rages.

"Don't play with me." Mlle Inés Pichon tears aside the netting. "I said, 'Don't play with me,' girl."

Marina snaps upright, facing this woman whose caked makeup cannot hide her color, whose wide eyes speak of terror. There are so many more blacks here than in Cuba, so numerous that the half-castes themselves are innumerable and you must take your mark by their declining shades as you would by shadows note the time of day.

Mademoiselle's nostrils flare. "The Woolsack boy, next door, is missing."

"Oh?" Marina tilts her head. "And who is that?"

"Fresh," she says. "You met him last Sunday."

"So he's missing. Is that why the bells are ringing?"

"Don't be stupid. We are invaded. A disaster . . ."

She knows disaster, and this one seems rather tame by comparison.

"His mother is downstairs. She wants to know if you saw anything."

His mother: Marina has seen the lady on occasion, when Mme Woolsack has come to visit the zamba. They are friends it seems, despite their differences of color and form. The boy's mother is fine and razory and pale, whereas Pichon is thickset, dusky, opulently fleshed. When Marina considers the latter woman's curves in contrast to her own puffy, slattern form, she is troubled in a way she can't yet name.

"Nothing?" The wrinkles stand out in the zamba's face.

"I wasn't at the window," says Marina. "I was reading."

Mademoiselle winces knowledgeably. "Too much reading stunts a girl's mind. Thins the blood, bends the backbone into ugly shapes."

Illustrating, she makes an arthritic snake of her arm. "A woman's book is the world."

Downstairs the boy's mother is shouting, playing tenor to the basso howls of the people in the street.

"You picked a fine time to come to New Orleans," says Mlle Pichon, letting go the netting and stomping from the room and down the stairs.

A sudden snipe of guilt. But what could she have told? Even if she'd seen where he'd been headed, she wouldn't tell it to this woman, to this zamba who acts as though she had some choice in the matter of coming here.

Wrong or right, she will reconcile it in her prayers tonight.

She will pray for her sins, pray to be back in Cuba, where she could of an evening follow the banks of the Ariguanabo, carrying with her a basket of gifts from a visit to the Faustino cafetal—coral beans, short-cut cane stalks, bitter oranges—to the great ceiba tree through whose ancient roots the river disappears into the mouth of a cavern whose walls are slick with moss, not the brittle hag's hair that drapes the oaks here but soft and green and imprintable, where the bones of trapped creatures rest in the eddies, and if you are attentive and sharp eyed might find a tortoise shell of enormous size, faded plates polished smooth from years of submersion, or a knife blade that disintegrates with a touch.

And despite a smattering of Spanish voices, the presence of a cabildo, and of the familiar sight of Indians sitting cross-legged in its colonnade with their baskets of roots and wares, New Orleans is alien. Great stone buildings oppress the dull houses, which are without the welcoming grilles and bright *vitrales* of Havana, where they would go when her father had business at the chandlery or the exchange, taking the new train from San Antonio: happy evenings spent seated in a hired carriage, pressed between her parents while they listened to the plaza band play the rondo. Her mother had said that the markets in New Orleans would dwarf any she'd seen in Cuba, carrying not only the produce of Louisiana, but the hemisphere entire. But the war, now in their laps, has rendered the markets bare, not even a head of lettuce to kick down the empty stalls. And what would her mother have said about that mudhole in Mississippi? Biloxi, where she was deposited by Major Strong when her convalescence on Ship Island was at an end, where the filthy gawking people on the wharf fired at him as he departed even though he flew a flag of truce. That there's for you, missy, the Mississippians said, in an English more similar to that of the Negro sutlers she'd met on the island. And she was too shocked, her fists too infuriatingly small to do the damage she'd have liked, thrashing at them until she was dragged away; she remembers the pleasure she forced herself to hide when Major Strong returned next day to demand an apology or else he would shell their sorry town to pieces. Their cowed and corrected state had been a great comfort to her in the week that followed, while they waited on a response from the wire to Uncle Willie in New Orleans. There, just as she has done with Mlle Pichon and Uncle Willie and a reporter from one of the city newspapers, whenever the Mississippi people would prod her for details of the Yankees and their island encampment, she would play the role of the fainty, sunstruck girl. *How many ships? How many men? What did you overhear? Come now, you must've been listening!* To these she would give Miranda's answer: *Oh*, she'd say, clutching her book tightly and affecting a wrist thrown over her eyes. *It seems so far off and like a dream*!

Shrieks from the ground floor, cries that they are landing, and Uncle Willie nowhere to be found. Marina smiles, settles back with her book. She parts the thin paper from the smooth page of illustrated plate: the demon Ariel is rendered in half descent of a crag grown with tufts of palm and fern, peering down at bathing, ever-fading Miranda. Ariel's pose is not unlike that of the boy Joseph when he teetered at the edge of his balcony. And the image of him grows in her mind like a climbing vine through shingles, unseating her thoughts as the cries of what *they*, *they*, *they* will do grow shriller.

Marina turns the page.

Elise

Four

Mother of Sorrows

She seeks son and husband in the streets. Untrussed hair flailing her back, she parts the crowds on Royal, heading east. Guided by her fear past upturned stalls and drays, beneath an oak fettered with soaked Confederate notes strung amid the moss adrip with remnant rain, passing under a lamppost at the corner of Iberville dangled with a length of noose whose intended victim, a Unionist, was cut down alive last night by the European Brigade.

Cast aside by a gang of Germans charging who knows where, Elise catches hold to the bars of a gate—about the width of the barrel of the damned pistol her son now carries. A six-chambered revolver damascened with stars, its gutta-percha handle beveled and carved with his initials. And she remembers exactly what she thought the moment he unwrapped it: *Dear God, not another gun.*

The city has long bristled with arms, just as the walls of Angel's office are hung with ornaments of slaughter, weapons acquired in the long and brutish life before he knew her; there, in his cachot, smelling of powder and steel and oil and lead, where a pallet bed stands in one corner like a dusty afterthought, and for a year of nights her husband has imprisoned himself in the writing of his life—walled in not brick by brick but page by page—pages she has never read, for the yield of those hours he keeps locked away in a drawer. Walls of shotgun, bas-reliefs of dragoon pistol, an Aztec calendar of barrels and tamps and shot, retaining for the last thirteen years the same awful threat as they had on the day she first moved in, when, stumbling into the office, then only half-festooned with its hideous decorations, she'd felt as one impressed into a very private army. As it stood, the only wars he had left to fight were with himself, with his past, the surrounding collection less a trophy room than a stark reminder that he'd lived so long that the tools and mechanisms of his better lifetime have become obsolete.

But Joseph is not like him. Joseph won't shoot anyone, so she thinks, prays, growing dizzy and holding fast to the bars of the gate as gasping overtakes her.

Her lungs are the feet of a Chinese princess, made small by years of compression. Beneath the boning of her corset they feel weak as crepe paper when she tries to draw air, needing time to regain what little breath she is allowed by fashion.

Now her mind is filled with possible fates. The many ways in which the city can end her son's life. There are twisted men who snatch up errant lads; there are bricks thrown from windows; there are ditches to drown him, beasts to maul him, accidents and cataclysms untold. Not three days ago a nine-year-old child was blown to bits passing a boiler-works off Carondelet. The poor thing happened to be strolling by.

The shadow of a rain cloud passes overhead and the street is for the moment empty, save for herself and a grinder's ape sipping water from a trough. His tiny clothes, Italianate, his hands—now prodding dully at his own reflection—are missing their thumbs. Both turn their heads at the roar from the river. Another riot, another stinking row for flags. So many days of banners, arguments, and postures over standards, the mayor prattling with the commander of the Federal fleet about which strip of cloth would be removed and by whom until he was gelded by the threat of bombardment. A disaster narrowly dodged, for some fools had scaled the Mint and torn down the conquering flag and caused a zealous Yankee captain on the river to fire off a single round of cannon that sailed, so she's heard, past the patriots atop the Mint and smashed into a nearby bawdy house. When this happened, she was in her sitting room surrounded by friends asking would she accompany them to City Hall to sign a petition against the reinstatement of the hated flag. But Elise has no love for flags, and much for roofs and those within them, particularly her own. And at the moment of the shot, the piercing whine of the shell, the *clap-crash* of crumpling brick, she saw the terror on her friends' faces, knowing then that when the bombs fall all the talk in the world amounts to nothing more than piss-stained culottes.

The ape harangues her with a chirp as she starts off again, up past Chartres and into the riot of citizenry amassed at the Bienville landing. They empty bottles down their throats, and soon bottles become bludgeons and here they are, the vanguard, outrage-artists decorating this overturned basilica dome of a city with impotent transgression.

Among them she seeks the redeemer of her blood, the child who has reclaimed the place forsaken by her family long ago. For lust or love, she doesn't know—only that generations back, on Saint-Domingue, an island soon to be consumed in flames fed by human flesh, white and black and myriad intermediary shades equally reduced to soot-gray—a woman had lain with a man and sometime thereafter was set in motion a familial mission, undertaken by succeeding generations to reverse what the pair had done. Whether it was an Adam or an Eve who caused the Durels to be cast out of Eden Blanc, all that matters now is that she accomplished the return. Her mother, who tolerably passed but whose own mother had to be called Auntie, told her as much on the day Joseph was born, her hand wound with an ochre-stone rosary, praying for his eyes to remain blue like his father's, for hair like his father's would have been when he was young, praying for little of themselves to remain, though Elise could see even in the wrinkled reddened face the shape of her own eyes, her brow, her nose, her cheeks. So she seeks herself as well among the crowded hips and the scampering children picking the pockets of the unwary, casting aside the cussers and those spitting jets of rum, and is met instead with the sight of the flailing form of his father.

Angel is in his natural state: he fights. Thrown back upon the hands that have him hoisted high, an officiate of a ceremony of extraordinary violence, with boot heel he pulps one face, then another whose spouted teeth fall like wedding rice on her husband's black coat; two of his bearers drop at Elise's feet, and she has rushed too soon, come too close, must spin and duck the whirligig of mayhem of which her husband is master component. Three remain, broad-chested and swag-bellied dandies of the gambler type, jabbing at his ribs with ringed fists until by thumbed eye, elbow-bladed nose, and finally the lone hand closed around one's throat so that he sinks with bizarre gentleness to the ground; his bearers are dispatched. Her husband is, by his own reckoning, seventy-eight years old.

The crowd redirects to the river, parts as he staggers a handful of haggard paces towards her and collapses to one knee. She is at his side, and any onlooker might think she is whispering wifely dotage rather than what she gives him now, venomous, seeking:

"What have you done, goddamn you? Where is he?"

Angel spits blood with casual savor, the way some do tobacco. He clutches his ribs and jars loose the words:

"Gone"— he mocks—"*goddamn it.*"

His patch has been torn off and when he looks up she sees for the first time in full daylight her husband's ruined left eye. A puckered swirl, not unlike the nub of his arm, to which she applies nightly salves. A battle took the eye; his first wife took the arm. And she, Elise, has ahold of the remaining, clasping his hand. And what price can she exact? What is left but withered flesh and bone imprinted with fury? Fury, hers now, she will break his hand; she will tear the eye from his skull if he doesn't tell her.

She is shouting, demanding to know, when the age-lined lips part, the mouth she has endured so long that his decrepit desires transfigured into a kind of comfort—mausoleum love, to lie beside the never-dead—speaks.

"He ran from me." Angel reaches out, lifting her hand with his, and points a crooked finger north and west. "It doesn't make a damn now."

She damns him, hissing, spitting, feeling herself tear apart. Joseph still has the gun? You couldn't at least get the gun you horrible old bastard with your hair horrid white in long thin strands I must pick from my clothes and the awful withered haunches and parts I have endured for thirteen years since my mother—damn her—pawned me off and me just past nineteen matched to you already ancient and I hoped, yes, I hoped dearly, that such an old man couldn't be long for this world but then you gave me Joseph and I reasoned you might stay alive a little longer but now I wish with all my heart you were dead as dirt.

What she speaks and what she thinks go twined and confused in the hammering rage of her thoughts, in the yelps of the crowd and flair of martial drum-rattle as now, see, the Northerners come ashore with teams hauling a pair of brass cannon of such luster that Elise sees her face and that of Angel remembered in the sheen.

He straightens, gains both his feet and some vampiric composure, the serenity of a man most comfortable in Gehenna. But tired, very tired.

"It doesn't make a damn now," he says. "It's done."

She casts his arm aside and steps back crumpling with rage. And what is she supposed to do? What can she—goddamn you—do? Angel's eye never leaves the soldiers; he sucks back blood from the corners of his lips and croaks, "Whatever in Hell you like. It's his life now."

Her slap is hard enough to make him pause, but only for a moment, fixing her with a gravestone grin before he shambles off into the Quarter.

By Canal she's wiped her face so many times for sweat that her husband's blood is a thin red mask across her face, smeared like the shirt-fronts of the hanged men she'd seen as a child, whose neck-veins swole and burst. She does not care that to those she stops, to those whose hands she takes and tells of her son who has disappeared into this city even the police have abandoned, she must seem a ghoul, just as they called her when she was a girl, after the night she sealed her fate, the night of the spring ball. The night that reduced her to marrying an old and wicked man. She sees that wide-eyed girl, feels the blood dribbling at the corner of her mouth. But she is no more girl than ghoul; she is no longer anything but mother, on the hunt for all to her that matters.

Butler

Five

His Old Complaint

Hooded eyes jammed shut with pain, he lurches to the railing of the steamer *Saxon* and vomits gouts of orangeish froth into the Mississippi. His old complaint, an ailment of the stomach contracted four years ago at the National Hotel in Washington. Some blamed poison for the illness of the Democratic representatives, others unsanitary water. All General Butler knows is that at varying times in the month he will be visited in the morning by burning diarrheal evacuations, in the afternoon by throatfuls of froth, with the mean of the day occupied by pain from groin to jaw as if he were being strangled from within.

Here on the quarterdeck there is only one witness to his shame. Will Clary, 2nd officer of the ship, whose young wife has come under Mrs. Butler's wing. Sarah with her theatrical need for an understudy, she's likely playing whist with the woman at this moment.

Now comes Clary clopping across the deck, asking him between his retches whether he is all right. Butler holds up his hand, watches the river carry away his bile, and tries to regain his breath. "Go," he says.

He listens to the clop of Clary's boots, his murmured apologies, and when he is gone lets loose another surge of froth. Finished, he dabs at his cheeks and blinks at the city in the smoky distance. He brings the marine glasses to his eyes, to better see the prize. And in the haze of smoke the city's vegetal encroachments of tree and tropical undergrowth and mold give off a uniform gangrenous glow, as will a putrefying body left afield. Now we have come to tidy up the corpse. More than that, to clean it, dress it, bring it back to life.

His eyes cannot hold upon one sight for long without left or right going to wander; their lids have lowered as he's aged, drooped now at the age of forty to such an extent that his regard is a sleeper's squint; and without surgery he will be, one day, effectively blind. All his life he has been known by his eyes. Lobster-eyed, walleyed, goggle and wild and unmoored. He chews the inside of a not inconsiderable cheek, for he is a man of wealth and well-fed beyond the sickly gangle of his youth, allowing himself only the slightest smart at the recollection of some childhood hurt. He wonders what appellations the people of New Orleans will find for him. See them now in ant-lines along the levees that keep their preposterous city from inundation. They wished to escape from America; she will redeem them in the dark. If all goes well, they'll have to wait until morning to get a proper look at him.

He lurches, throat burning, his viscera twisted as though divined by an unkind haruspex. This must have been how his father felt on St. Kitts, when he was first overtaken by the sickness that would end his life, his crew's, and his dreams of Latin glory. He sees his father hanging over the gunwales of the quarantined ship, searching blearily for the coast of Venezuela, where Bolívar had crossed the Andes. All the promise in the world, for fortune and fame, passing between Captain John Butler's lips.

poor French soldiers whose bones turned up in the occasional storm. He remembers a Connecticut private bringing him a pair of bleached wristbones still yoked with shriveled lengths of rope.

He fishes in his tunic, finds his watch, and takes the time. One o'clock. Hours before he assembles the detachment, before the signal flags are run and across his armada the men will debark and make ready for their landing.

"Are you well, General?"

"The National's come calling," he says over the cup-rim. "If that's what you mean."

The orderly sighs. He is a man, not unlike the general himself, of a somewhat disconcerting countenance. Tibbets keeps his cap tucked almost to his eyes for the fact his brows are entirely hairless, the result of a babyhood abandoned to the Tewksbury almshouse, where infant Tibbets was bathed in some communal cesspool, and thus christened with a syphilitic infection of the eyes, saved only by a caring uncle who rescued him some weeks later, who administered a cure that took his eyebrows but saved the eyes themselves. Butler thinks of the man now standing beside him as he once must have been: a baby with its eyes boiled shut. And he knows the whispers that the general only keeps Tibbets around so that he isn't the oddest-looking man in the room.

Starboard, a transport hoves into view. The men on deck wave and halloo; Butler waves back. Their uniforms are made at his mill; their supplies come from factories in which he or some family member owns a controlling interest.

"Last cheers we'll hear for some time, I'm afraid," says Tibbets.

Clearly. Ah, but he is used to basking in the warmth of others' anger—worth ten times their weight in approbation—for each overturned case, each back-wage paid to some girl with cotton fibers growing through her fingertips, each bill pushed through, each radical reinvention of military procedure. So he is hated: decried, shunned, despised to such an extent that the War Cabinet had to pass a special resolution in order to deny him, ranking officer, promotion to the station now attained by Grant, McClellan, and Hooker—these fellows who were still being measured for their uniforms when he was hearing the guns at Bethel.

Whistle-pipe and there appears from off the bow a plug little steamer, hauling an immense black ruin of a ship. Colossal, towering, and gun-bristled, this must be the *Louisiana*, the rebel hope dragged unfinished downriver to meet Farragut's fleet in futile combat. The only industries these people have mastered are ineptitude and destruction. He smells the goods they were foolish enough to burn, the coalsmoke of engines spiriting banks' specie from the city, hears the cartwheel creak as bullion is secreted to foreign consulates. He will right it all. He has been learning the figures of the city, and he will wield them like a sabre. But first he will visit them in the dark, send forerunners to search ahead and snuff the streetlamps along their predetermined route; and should his troops be sniped at from above the muzzle-flash will illuminate the culprit's window and seal his fate; should mobs form, their devices will be stymied by the blackness of the night, their communications impossible from one block to the next. Citizens awakening the next morning to find themselves occupied will be far more inclined towards acceptance than if he came storming through in the middle of the day. They will have simply woken to a new world, and must reconcile themselves to it as they would looking out the window of a frosty morning and seeing the ground covered in snow.

Of course, this place has never known snow.

Well, he thinks, soon enough they'll feel the chill.

Six

The Submarine

Late afternoon, clouds dried up for a moment, mist rising from the rain-drenched ground. He has come out of the city proper, into neighborhoods and groves of orange and magnolia, past tiny garden beds where ladies looked up from their hyacinths and asked where he was going, to this waterway that has no bank but wooden floodwalls hemming placid murk. Blown and stumbling, he has wandered from the Carondelet Canal into the grassy fields about Bayou St. Jean and what appears to be a gang of men in throes of worship at a massive black and ovoid idol. Propped on trestles of enormous size, bolstered by sacks of shell, the idol towers over the reverent.

And this might be a ceremony of voudou, though he counts no blacks among the worshippers. Still, who knows how things are done so far from home. Farther than he's ever been on his own feet. He wants a sunny place to let his clothes dry; he wants water to drink and to sit. He wants, more than anything, to hear a grown voice say that it will be all right.

Closer, he finds the idol is built of iron, riveted from back to belly in the shape of a great black eye bearing down on him and on the men hereabouts. He sees now they have their hands in its side, prying away parts and loosening mechanical organs while other fellows lean on mauls, their backs to him, waiting.

Settled in the moist ground, Joseph thinks his mother will be angry that he's muddied his pants.

Apart from the workmen stand a pair of gentlemen. One, spade bearded, coat unbuttoned, cups his hands upon his hips and surveys the work while his companion cuffs his eyes and sobs. The latter's hair is wild, his beard grown to his chest. And he actually sobs, as Joseph has never seen a man do.

"God," says the wild-haired man. "That she'd never see the sea!"

"Easy, Burton," says the other, then to the workers: "All right, boys, when you've got the engine out we'll have her in one go."

The sobber, Burton: "This damned world. Another week and she'd have been ready—"

"Mind where you strike. We don't want her falling backward."

"—and she'd slip under the water and then we'd have the bastards smashed!"

So it's a ship, this iron eye. Now he sees how it favors a fish in fin and tapered tail. Joseph listens: the crying man talks of broken block-ades and his great invention powering beneath the waves even as the spade-beard directs its dismemberment.

The pistol jabs at his lap and so he shifts, imagining what kind of men would go into the dark belly of this ship, like riding in a roving coalbin, the press of the pistol recalling his father's anger, the stories he tells of the punishments of his youth. How, when he raised the ire of his own father, he'd been made to eat coals burning hot. Joseph knows the story rote, and he would rather eat coals than do what his father asked today. Better to be beaten, better to burn. Better yet to run.

Egrets light ahead in the bug-humming grass, and clouds have regrouped to overtake the sky. The maul-bearing men approach the ship, strike the braces at the end nearest the water as others pitch engine guts over the side. A propeller goes windmilling, followed by handles and crankshafts, each mourned aloud by the weeping man. Joseph thinks of himself and Marina, far below a surface battle, hearing the muted sounds of cannon fire as errant shots sink harmlessly like marbles in a bath, stealthily threading their bulky enemies in this sleek wonder on their way to her island home. Alone with her in the dark.

But the time for wonders is past: the pegs and braces break; the workmen stagger back, as with a ferrous groan the ship slips its mooring and slides forward, splintering the floodwall as it topples end over end into the bayou, sending up a spray that doesn't cease. He looks up; the clouds have broken and the rain begun again.

He is at the floodwall, unable to resist the sight of this doomed christening. The submarine rights itself, bobs, throwing wake above the boards. A churning gurgle as water fills its bowels; froth builds to a boil and the wonder sinks lower, until the last patch of iron is subsumed and the wonder gives no hint of its existence save bubbles. He fights down a hitching at his chest. This sight is somehow sadder than the city's fall, or his own fate, whatever that might be. He wants to weep as the inventor, Burton, weeps. He has wandered from a nightmare into something worse—the dismantling of a dream.

He is lifted up to a face wet with tears, eyes red-rimmed. The inventor rasps, "What do you think you're doing here, boy?"

He has no answer.

The spade-beard calmly approaches, easing Joseph from the grip of his quivering friend.

"Don't you know what's happening today?"

"We've lost the war," says Joseph.

The calm man seems for a moment to agree but, seeing Burton wander off a ways, shakes his head. "We haven't lost," the man says, as much to himself as Joseph.

"Lost!" cries Burton.

The calm man's face is a soggy mask of reassurance. "Only one city," he says, bending to eye-level. "One city and one weapon."

"Lost everything! I should've gone down with her!"

The workmen pitch their tools away and go for shelter. The spade-beard stands, looks to his friend: "Come now, man. It's time we went." Then crouching back to child-height, and with a voice meant for advice of great importance, he says, "And you should get home and out of the rain." With this wisdom imparted, he starts off in pursuit of his friend, who goes writhing and stomping through the field.

One last look to the bayou. From the scuttled marvel rise bubbles, now almost indistinguishable from the rainfall on the water's surface. He sends fingers to the pistol at his waist, as though it might spring out on its own and seek a place down there in the dark, among the failures of this world. He will not throw the gun away, just as he will not give himself to the roads but heads through rain and sucking mud for home.

When he regains the streets, he finds New Orleans speaks in hastily scrawled signage affixed to shopwindow and storefront. A clapboard adumbration of municipal outrage, bluster, and confusion. Joseph reads them as running conversation between the mute buildings.

THEFES WILL BE SHOT!

ETATS-UNIS—MERDE

LOOT AND DIE

OWNER ARMED—II CLUBS, I SHOTGUN, III MAD DOGS

DEATH AWAITS WITHIN

Seven

Encounter on
Girod Street

One dog tears out another's throat, and, whining softly, mounts the fallen, tugging almost playfully at its limbs. A shovel-headed pit, the victor's darkened muzzle spreads in the murder-grin peculiar to its breed.

He tamps his cane in feigned indignation at the loss, flips a coin to this corner's bookman, and starts off. A few women follow, whom popular argot knows as frails, though their freckled hands—not long removed from the plows and lye-tubs of Hibernia—could wrench the life from most men's necks. Catcalls and songs; they call him Captain, declaim their attributes, and when he does not respond they call him queer, thinking in their workingwomen's brains that such dares will send a gentleman between their legs just as surely as calling a boy a chicken will send him up a lamppost or into a bull's pen. They hustle in their heels to match his pace, joined by sisters, en déshabillé displays of jiggling cleft, or what the American wits call a "Georgia Colonel's

Uniform"—a shirt-collar and spurs. Uniformly young, Irish, and drunk, their company is not unwelcome this apocalyptic afternoon. He is no more a Dionysian than a man of blood sport, but the opportunity so rarely presents itself: to hear the snarl and jaw-clamp, see the fur float gently above the thrashing beasts, to catch flecks of blood on one's cuffs. And more importantly, to see how the lower orders react to invasion.

Belligerent indifference, exhausted sarcasm: blinding, Bacchusian disregard coupled with an obscene opportunism as peculiar to New Orleans as the chop-house grin is to the pit bulldog. The levee is broken? Hitch your breeches and your skirts. The fever season is upon us? I've had my round with yellow jack. Murderers are turned out of the jail for nights on the town? So what, this is New Orleans!

Such thoughts run clear through from lowest whore to richest cottoneer, garnished with stupendous self-obsession. Soon he'll see the rising nodules of cyanosis at work on the faces of the high and mighty who remain. He will see them when what is left of the City Council reconvenes; he will see them at the Medical Society, and at the meetings of the Mystik Krewe of Orcus.

As for the women of the street, these who were despoiled by deckhands on immigrant ships or farmed out by parents to feed the fruit of their own mindless and inexorable rut, cyanosis will also prove a boon. Corner to corner, hear its praises sung: the Yankees are here, with mechanic's dispositions, pockets full of savings girding pale pubic entuftments, and we will make them *pay*. So they sing of a vengeance long protracted on the male sex, a blood price measured in money.

Make for the office. There is real work to be done, work impossible at home, where Lydia will come bounding to the door screeching in grating wifely glee that she just knew he would return, that he wouldn't go away from her and to the battlefields and camps and . . .

A few more blocks to the dry confines of his office, where he will shake off the rain and this actor's uniform, fold it away in the drawer where he keeps the bones of his first dissection. Onward, the doctor's gaze dulls as though he must conserve his faculties for what lies ahead, and he goes on by native instinct, stepping over drunks and gutpiles and garbage, an indistinct swirl of waste.

The whores have fallen back, their chanson ceased. Then who is calling him now? And why does she call him by name? Not monsieur or sir or doctor, but Emile. His vision answers to surname shrieked and codifies the street. Down a twisting mud-vein turned a slough by rain she comes, waving and calling.

Elise. Her dress shows a waterline almost to the hip; her face is smeared with a thin mask of blood.

Blood as trickled at the corners of Elise's mouth on the night he first saw her. The night of the ball, almost twenty years ago. Blood bright as hawthorn berries.

"Emile! Emile!" She comes on, slow progress through the mud, to no catcall, no chuckled threat. Hoodlum voices are dried up. She is a visitation, a messenger from another world. Men who normally would have dragged her screaming into alleys can only stare bemused, doubting the convictions of their perversities.

She is still saying his name when he takes her by the shoulders, asking what in God's name she's doing here. And he can remember the last time she called him so: the day that, years after the ball, when he was newly married and had taken over his father-in-law's speculation business, she came to his door, respondent to an ad placed by his client, Angel Woolsack, for a companion woman. A place reserved for women who still bore darkness, those sufferers of varying unspoken degrees of Negro blood who fashion for themselves the lives of fairy-tale princesses afflicted with a curse of color, a station far below one such as Elise, whose descent to all appearances seems unshakably white. Were it not for what happened on the night of the ball, she, with her thin nose and hair smooth enough to wind in fabulous plaits, by consequence would have never had to resort to an arrangement. She might never have had to reveal the particulars of her descent. But that day, thirteen years ago, she'd come into the office that still wore the name of his father-in-law, accompanied by the mother who meant to pawn her off. He remembers the look of startled recognition that came over her the instant she entered: a gasp escaping her lips, then withering within her to be battened down in knotty reaches of contempt as he, calmly, coolly, put to her mother the racial questionnaire. *It never needs to be mentioned on censuses or the like, but my client must know the absolute truth.* And so he'd found her out, this girl of his childhood, the one who had run from him, sent him skulking off to Paris and into the arms of Lydia, uncovered her very core, noted her delineations. Her fate in his hands. Recall her face in bitter pout as the knowledge broke upon her that she was, for his aged and decrepit client, the ideal match. He has never again felt so utterly in control, his mastery so absolute. And never, since that day, has he made any but the most professional of overtures to her. Another form of torment. Ignoring her and their former lives. For thirteen years he has given her bows and scrupulous courtesy, examined her son, never once exchanging words on the subject of themselves. It was, after all, nothing of import. And perhaps they have both enjoyed holding polarities of power the existence of which required their shared burial of the past.

But look here, in your arms, weeping and moaning to you that her son, her precious boy, is gone, run off, and Angel, that bastard, he won't help her any more than the police—and where are *they*, Emile?—Cowards! Everyone! Dear God, she has been everywhere and his is the first kind face she's seen.

Holding her, electric with her fear and exhaustion, Dr. Sabatier wonders if he has ever before been accused of having a kind face.

Thus far he has said nothing comprehensible, mindless cooing and assuagement, finding that he is making the same sounds as he does when Lydia is upset. He counts the ellipses he rubs on her back and speaks. "Elise," he says. Her eyes flutter, sharpen—the beginnings of a scowl. He tells her foolish things. Not to worry, for instance. So the boy has a gun? Then he's far safer, yes? The boy will come home. It is, he assures her, only a symptom of the day, this terrible day's events. Now what about Mr. Woolsack?

"To Hell with him," says Elise, punctuating, unimaginably, with spit.

Shirked of refinements and niceties, crowned once more in madness, she is herself. Or, at least, as he once knew her. As, for years, she was known in the neighborhood, her own special oubliette in the labyrinth of gossip. A small, dark space he shared with her in the bygone slanders of others.

They called her the Ghoul. 'Ti Vampire. Mademoiselle le Cannibale. The girl who spit out Claude Arnaud's ear and went dumbly into the arms of that pale little bookworm, Emile—whatshisname?—Sabatier! That's the one. Took Mlle le Cannibale in his arms like a bizarre gallant and spirited her away.

Just as he now leads her from Girod, from the smattering of hoots and jeers and the dangers of the drunken, drugged, and poor. He makes use of his practiced grip, his hand no longer husband's but physician's. Guiding and irrevocable. She allows herself to be led, just as she did that night.

Her hands make nervous circumferences of his arm. These hands, so small and fickle, bespeaking deeper touches and hurried unfastenings, burrowing beneath layers of clothes. And she is almost undone, her back bared through the half-burst threads and eyelets of her dress. She glances at him, wide-eyed, the lush lineations of her mouth moist with sweat.

No matter, tamp this down. Such thoughts lead down avenues ending only in shame. And for what? Boyhood moon-eyed stupidity? Tamp it down, man. And what's more, your own fear. Fear that the boy will be lost, and with him . . . Tell her to go home, to wait. Take a dram and sleep. (Those perfect bedfellows: woman and opiate.) Let him worry about the boy and Mr. Woolsack.

"*Piss* on Mr. Woolsack." She shirks his arm, unraveling. "I want my son."

Suddenly he is himself of twenty years past: pleading, obsequious, wanting to help her if only she will let him. He offers her his handkerchief and she wets a corner with her tongue, begins furiously dabbing at her face.

He says, "You do no good running yourself out on the streets. No good for the boy. Let me take you home and I'll find him. My resources are—"

She flings the handkerchief away. "Oh yes! *Considerable* resources! Your uniform"—she tweaks his collar—"and your little hat! And all your friends, packed off for the war to run away again? What can you do?"

The doctor's hands are balled at his sides, one strangling the neck of his cane. "I can," he says, "do more than wander 'round like a veiled goddamn Arab keening and moaning, Madame. And more, I hope you understand that my means extend far beyond what I gain from my business with Mr. Woolsack, who will hear of this I can assure you."

Good Lord. To be roped into an argument, in the street no less, with a woman. Even with the city coming apart at its sordid seams this is too much to bear.

She laughs. "Go try and talk to him, and good luck to you!"

'Ti Vampire knows not half of what he's done for her; appreciates even less. Look at her: arms in winglike flap—a little of the childbearing weight unlost, the insignificant chin, the impudent puffs of flesh below her mouth. Genus Aetheopia, yes. Distraught, she is the very picture of her savage forebears; she sloughs her whiteness off, liberated into naked reckless animalism, raving and gesturing and saying that she, she will find her son and he may do as he damned well likes!

His coolness is a valve over an immense and seething sea of ire and—were he to allow himself the admission—resentment. He has already fallen prey to a foolish moment of bile, exacerbating her hysteria. Now he holds up his palms and lets her go. She, gibbering a litany of matronly woe, stomps off; catching herself on a corner lamppost, she thrashes through a group of the aimless infuriated and whirls around the corner.

The people at the corner wave the flag of the state, yowling in some unknown argument. And now the panoply of interruption continues as he nears a sooty old man sitting atop an overturned crate. The old man clucks his tongue and grins, saying, "Trouble with the little woman, eh?"

The old man's chuckle is unfinished when the doctor, striding past, lets fly with the weighted head of his cane and knocks him from his perch. The crowd at the corner turns his way, for the old man bawls now like a child—a noise that sends the doctor's stomach in uncharacteristic lurch. Heads cocked, the crowd hefts their clubs and flagstaffs as he approaches.

And without unsettling his stride the doctor shouts over his shoulder to the squalling old man: "'*God bless Abe Lincoln,*' you say? We'll have none of that you traitorous wretch!"

The banner-wavers cheer this hero of the cause, and he heads on, with every stride accepting of this new and wild world.

Elise

Eight

The Vulning Bird

Churchbells sound the hour. Eight o'clock. She pauses for the strangeness of the ensuing silence, when from the Square should be heard a round of cannonfire—a trio of belches from the ancient squat black cannon, calling curfew for the slaves.

She has come onto Royal from the boundary at Canal, where the self-satisfied gaze of the statue of Henry Clay oversees the demarcation between the First District and the Second, between the old town and the westerly sprawl. The clock at Faucheax's shirts makes clear what she knows by instinct—no one will call the blacks home tonight. And they are everywhere: pairs of old women parallel men engaged in fierce bouts of argument or storytelling. Eyes divert and take her briefly in, then roll back to their original locus and resume their declamation, loud, as a peeved person will speak loudly in one room so others in the next may hear him. On any other day you could see curfew nearing in their faces, a tenseness growing as they hustled to complete errand or task or snatched social encounter. Now their tension unravels into excitement, even joy.

She wishes she held her little cowhide martinet. Just to fritter and flick, like a horse's tail at flies. Show them that even if the order of the city is unmoored, the order of the world remains firm.

Look at them. On any normal day they'd be afraid.

If the police hadn't run, the blacks would be taken to the parish prison, whipped twenty-five times in the morning, their masters charged a fee of three dollars for their discharge; or if they made their way tardily home the master could have them sent to the calaboose himself, where the authorities, amenable to such matters, would happily absolve the master of appearing cruel by performing his duties for him. A bargain for the sensitive soul at one cent per lash.

She considers the methods of her friends: Mme Decorde not three months ago had turned one of her younger girls over to the police for lashes; Mrs. Schmidt has sent her old woman Genie for weeks to the workhouse at the lamentable cost of twenty-five cents per day. These methods and more are employed by Mme Frick, the oldest of them all, who reserves finer abuses for her (unspoken) half sister, Inés Pichon. Inés herself, household so rudely burdened by that strange little girl, runs things loosely. No whip or workhouse threats for her. Of course, Inés has her own reasons to avoid the dispensation of physical punishment.

Elise herself has little use for material applications of authority, though she will on occasion toy with the martinet. And God knows Angel would sell them by the pound without a thought, but never lay a finger on them regardless of slights or moronic mistakes. Rather she employs fear, the usefulness of the tales she has known all her life, and they theirs: the albino ghoul who drinks only African blood, an eleven-headed snake whose viciously patient ends reach all throughout the Quarter and only wakes after dusk, roiling out of the shadowy rubbish drifts where he conceals himself; a Congo panther known for its taste in dark flesh, imported and loosed by accident from a visiting circus. The bestiary does its work, silly though it is. Or maybe, as she sometimes believes, they are naturally loyal. Or maybe they don't believe the tales at all, and simply wish us to believe they do. The Sisters taught her Pascal's wager, and it might be the blacks have their own version. Still, in times of frustration, she will sit in her parlor, fingering the short tasseled ends of the martinet; a flicker of leather, the feel of plaiting against her palm, and her arm would be possessed of an age-old tensile vigor, a sense of purpose and command. Then again, there are beasts she knows they believe in for a fact; she has heard many times Ligeia and Bernice whispering about Dr. Sabatier.

Gutless Emile. To hell with him and all the mewling men who have refused to help her. She damns herself for a fool, forever believing in them only to learn new variations of their failings. She has seen their many weaknesses, numbered them like frayed threads. Without the proper attention, and often even in spite of it, there comes the inevitable unraveling and we are left suddenly bare, exposed and flushing.

She waits at Iberville, amazed at the unflagging energy of the crowds. This delegation of the implacable enraged goes rushing towards the river, faceless and dissembled, a reordered version of every crowd it has been her misfortune to encounter this sorry day. And she has read that during our most glorious recent battles the amputated limbs will form mounds outside the surgeons' tents. So the citizens are likewise jumbled, stirred, resewn.

But by what surgeons? What cutter of flesh oversees the butchery, the secession of soul from body? How the sickly boy from that night became one of them is fit to ponder. The next time they saw each other he was not the shadow of his boyhood self but shadow itself, the day she stepped with her mother into his office to be appraised for the match to Woolsack. She didn't even know his name, but there he was, as if ordained to be the one who would bind her to Angel and thus himself.

And she cannot bear to even think of her husband, that near-corpse animated by only madness. Of all the blame to be dealt today, he deserves it most of all. So go on, head for home, but never stop looking.

A dotard *négresse* crosses herself when Elise goes by. Beatific in her exhaustion, Elise holds up a hand in sullen and dismissive benediction. From one window to the next she sees herself, the Virgin wandered from a pietà, faintly bloody, grief bedraggled, but without even the corpse of a son to hold.

Her reflection muddles the pane of DeLouche's Jewelers, her heart shot through by the ruby eyes of the jeweled pelican therein. The shop is famous for its bedizened version of Louisiana's emblem. The Pelican in Her Piety: mother bird enfolds a clutch of gawping mouths, pricks at her breast for blood to feed her starving young. Its significance, so drilled the nuns, is that of Christ shedding his blood for the sake of a world starved of goodness.

And Elise has seen little recent evidence of Christ's or the state's compassion. (Though what can such a citizenry deserve?) Yet she loves the image still, for what mother in the world would not tear at herself to feed her children? Of course, her son has never known hunger, never suffered want; her breast is unmarred, but she would gladly open every vein to have him back.

Plumage of pearl and hammered gold, the pelican is caught in a writhe of maternal agony, her resolute red eyes say the bird knows the purpose of her pain, endlessly fulfilling her obligations by self-slaughter. What else can she do? The mouths of her babies are so eager, so bowed with need.

Elise turns from the coral blood-drips, the silver-downed infants, and starts on again, battening down tears with her footsteps. Another block, another squalling crowd.

A birdlike cry, a screech from up the street that sends her chest burning and she turns to see.

Wayworn and reeling: Joseph.

Her shoulder blades burst the last of her bindings as she runs for him, and she has wings, white and beautiful, feels them flung back across the sidewalk, and with them comes a joyous fear that she will take to the air before she reaches him, have to glide for a moment before she can descend and take him in her arms, which she does without flight or stumble, without missing a step. She has him caught and feels in her tear-shut eyes her wings enclose them both, exploding in the brightness of his hair. Strands catch in her teeth she kisses him so fiercely. He struggles, speaks, jabbers, and sobs, unbecoming of a boy his age but she is crying now as well and he must be sunstruck or mad with his talk of signs and ships that go underwater. She muffles him, hums so that he can hear her voice through her chest.

Something falls from him and clatters to the ground. She yanks her son aside, careful to hold him by one arm when she reaches for the damned pistol. But he is quick and has it scooped and huddled to his side. He will no more let go the pistol than she will him.

He glares so like his father.

She will swat him raw and have the thing melted down; pay the foundryman for use of tools so she can smash it herself. But for now she drags him, pillow-light alongside, through the fearful migrations of crowds, thinking, she will have this thing from him if she has to knock his head sideways, leave him in the parlor to be justly berated by the girls, then upstairs to Angel's room where she will slam the hateful thing on top of his precious papers and tell him . . .

A boy, Joseph's age, dances at their corner. A sideways, nervous step. He holds a scrap of paper in both hands, thrusts it towards her. A runner from the Jackson station, he claims, and is there, ma'am, a lady by the name of Pichon hereabouts? He has a message but the number's wrong, the last three places he has tried all answered with guns.

She points to Inés's house, not caring what news this might bring. Joseph's squirms grow stronger, boys' serpentine strength, and when she has him at their door she sees he isn't trying to get away but to look up.

There at the window of Inés's stands the little girl. Elise considers giving his ass a whack, to make the embarrassment total. No, let him look. She hums; her free hand strokes his head, his shoulders, and over the down of his arms to his hands and the hum snaps into a curse as she snatches the pistol away. Triumphant, kicking at the door and hollering for the girls to open up, she is greeted with overwrought concern of her household slaves, past whom she bowls, leaving flailing Joseph in their hands and, clutching the pistol in hers, starts up the stairs for her husband's room.

Nine

The Bells

For all his varied talents, General Butler is without music. And though the streets are thronged—a wall of hissing, spitting faces between which he passes with his troops at the drummers' beat—he is focused on his feet, keeping time by sight. He has no nerves in courtroom, chamber, Senate rotunda, or factory floor, but set him in a ballroom struck with waltzing tune or on the march at martial rhythm and he is lost. Despite all the dreaded practice drilling, all the stiff parading through the streets of Lowell, Boston, Baltimore, and the Capitol (where they passed under the review of the president whose regard is that of a rheumatic bumpkin glaring across the counter at a clerk in implacable penny ante haggle), his ungainly step remains unchanged.

He is flanked by his adjutant, George Strong, of the proud even stride and supreme indifference of a granite cliff beset by piffling waves, and Tibbets, who jitters beside at dogsbody trot and attempts to snare his general in some comment, perhaps for the relief of fear.

Even with eyes toewise General Butler spies peripheral mockeries: a child stutter-steps alongside, and with cruel dexterity tugs her eyelids down and draws her mouth into a froggish flap. The universal childish reaction to his appearance. The mercy of the dark and a low-tucked cap saves Tibbets from the jibes and mummery his eyebrowless condition would surely warrant. Others sing mocking tunes, address him with jeers the origins of which are known only to them. He takes his pace from their damns like drill-cadence, marches at the rhythm of their hatred. They shout the name of their native-son general, now surely scourging the Yankees in Corinth after dealing the bloodiest blows at Shiloh: Beauregard! Beauregard! Beauregard! More worrisome are the silent ones. They stare at him, and in their looks are repeated the glares his vindictive schoolmates would give whenever he prolonged a class-day with untoward observation or provoked a long and torturous lecture by questioning the parentage of Cain's wife or stood up and gave a speech demanding an end to fines for missing chapel. But now as then there are peeps of encouragement, the balled fists of like-minded fellows. *Good on you, Ben. Go get 'em.* (And he always does: twenty years after the fact, he has managed to install on the board of supervisors of the miserable Baptist college a cousin whose first act was to squelch mandatory chapel.) He holds fast to the snippets of encouragement as they wheel from Canal to St. Charles, disregards his boots for a moment to see the few who cheer him quickly battered into silence by others in the crowd.

His men tense and some make to break ranks and relieve the beleaguered loyalists. Butler calls them back. It's not worth a riot, and there will be time enough for correction.

Funneling through a sharp bend in the street before the monumental rise of the St. Charles Hotel hoves into view. No time to admire this the largest hotel on the continent, though like a tourist he has read the brochures detailing its gold leaf service (made in New York) and satin footboards (plushed in Paris). The St. Charles, he thinks, with its grandly theatrical air, would do well for Sarah. But tonight his quarters must be more defensible, and his wife left aboard the *Saxon*.

He wonders how she will pass the night. Sarah has lately been prey to nightmares. Last week, having returned of a morning from a reconnoiter with the ships at the Pass, he'd found Sarah shaking in her tent, bag-eyed from lack of sleep. Terrible, terrible, she said, and what she told slipped seamlessly from the waking world to dream. There had been a storm last night—yes, he'd seen. And the tent was shuddering, straining so at the stakes that Molly—her girl—had to go outside with a mallet, and just when the storm had abated and we laid our heads to our pillows there was a great crash of thunder that sent her bolting up in bed, the lightning-flash revealing outside her tent a figure. A man. Clawing, scraping, trying to get in. Then, somehow, she knew who it was so desperately trying to get in. Lorenzo, the Negro. A sutler's boy who tended jobs around the camp. She could see him clearly now, in silhouette they're so different, you know. He was hunched and horrible and thrashing at the flaps until he came shambling in and she reached to pull up a floorboard and she was battering Lorenzo as best she could but suddenly she had no strength and she was thrown back on her bed beneath *that debased visage* and then, of course, woke up.

She couldn't, simply couldn't, bear to see Lorenzo after that. So at her urging General Butler has left Lorenzo on the island with the remaining garrison, though with the admonishment to Sarah that she'd better lose her fear of Negroes soon; he couldn't very well banish all the blacks from New Orleans, now could he?

Ben, Ben, Ben—she'd shook her head—*you simply do not understand a woman's fears.*

Ah, he understands them well enough, though the women here seem to show little sign of any terror of his marching horde. They spit farther arcs of tobacco juice, cry louder, more inventive insults,

her revulsion at his touch these many years. She curses the spirit of her mother, curses the phantom thing before her.

He speaks to nether-reaches: "Woman, you don't know the half of it."

A shifting of bones, he turns to her, assumes a basking attitude. His socket accosts her; he holds to the stump of his right arm. The arm taken by his first wife. Her antecedent in the office of monster's bride. Angel opens his mouth, an arid cluck of a tongue once burned with coals.

"You think you've done some good," he says. "But out there, on his own, he might've had a chance."

"A chance for what? To be killed? Is that what you want?"

"No. To be different." He coughs. "Out there he had a chance to outpace fate."

"What do you mean, *fate*?"

"A dark one. That I'll say. And you, woman, will play the handmaid to it."

Drunk, demented thing. Old man shorn of sanity and all but the barest trace of humanness. To speak that way about the child she's saved. Elise kicks at the leg of his chair, screams for him to get up. She waves the pistol, damascening slickened with her palm-sweat.

Her husband doesn't stir. His face is turned away. Remains enthroned before the desk spread with the haphazard manuscript, the recollections of his sordid life. She has never read a page of his pointless jeremiad, his madman's decalogue. If she had the chance she would burn it and throw the ashes in his face.

Shadows of her years with him rise up, rage incanted, in her mind.

Her first night with him: the damp bed of their inaugural gropage, a painful and soggy-hot occurrence scored with the charivari of her sobbed disgust, itself worn down to shabby acquiescence.

She sees herself, big bellied, subject to the lone leathern arm, the chawed fingernails prodding her flesh, feeling for the quickened.

Cigar-holes in her dresses; tables swept of their contents with a roar; a wailing child. A pisspot full of blood.

She grips the pistol, harder now, kicks once more at his chair. Her husband doesn't turn. But she will keep trying, and in this great unburdening assault on what part of him remains unwounded by age and life and the violence of his days she will find a spot that still can hurt.

Eleven

A Gift from the Enemy

In bedside kneel she endures the sacred silence of her prayers disturbed by the snuffle and hiccough of Uncle Willie's zamba in the next room. She is used to other sounds; she has learned, when Uncle is about, to stop her ears with pillow to mute their squeaking, oinking loveplay. But she will not stop her ears while praying, lest some divine reply be muffled.

The women here are so cruel, she thinks, it's a wonder this one can weep. She recalls the jerking arms of the next-door woman as she tried to harry her boy inside and glared up at Marina with the red eyeshine of a bird at night.

She dismisses this woman and all others from her mind, for she is not yet to the point in her devotions of praying for anyone else. Now is the time to turn inward, ask for light by which to see her own sins. She has memorized the lines from the prayer book given by her mother, in whose voice the words now sound:

Consider your conscience, and consider where and in what company you have been this day. Call to mind the sins committed against God, your neighbor, yourself.

She scours her soul for sins but there's been so little chance of late, locked up in this room save for the reprieve of a silent, cold dinner that her contrition is brief. The sobs grow louder and she squeezes her eyes tight, moving on to her resolutions.

May she live a pious life in this world and be rewarded in the one to come. May she keep a closer watch over herself (though she can't keep a much closer watch than alone). May she attend more diligently to her duties (which are, it seems, to eat, sleep, and be silent). May she correct her evil habits (a withering memory of misused fingers). Accept O Lord, this her evening sacrifice and may it rise up as incense in thine sight.

She beseeches the protection of her guardian angel, who appears as Major Strong in shining silver breastplate and arching wings. He reaches out to her with a shimmering gauntlet, and the hair on his arms glows in holy light; his face shows none of the sadness with which he'd left her at the stinking Biloxi docks, when he'd dabbed a handkerchief to her eyes and even as the Mississippians jeered he'd kissed her cheek, the scratch of moustache suddenly recalling her father, but somehow also destroying him.

Now her prayers are entirely her own possessions. She has finished the acts of invocation and may communicate directly her desires: to go away, even if she can't leave this city and return to Cuba, to live perhaps with Major Strong (the idea itself so sweet she mustn't linger on it long, for that path is serpentine and lined with snares of scrofulous thought) or Mrs. Butler, for whose gift, her book of Shakespeare, she gives thanks.

In so doing Marina drifts in time, retreats to the days after she was plucked from the sands and her body kept covered in rags soaked from pitchers poured by nurses whose English sounded like someone plucking untuned strings of German; days thereafter sloughing off great sheets of skin, her back a pained constellation of boils; so ashamed of her stench that she at first refused the invitation to the tent of the commanding general's wife.

Our own little Miranda, the lady called her, and before Marina could correct her mistake Mrs. Butler was enumerating her own children—Paul, who is passed God-rest-his-soul, and dear Blanche who is about your age, and the second Paul, who is alive—circling back again to Marina who now found the chance to say that her name was not Miranda, missus. Yes, yes, the lady knew that, but didn't she, dear girl, know Shakespeare's Miranda? Her story had jogged the character from the lady's memory, and of course Mrs. Butler had played the part of Miranda herself, on the stage of course, and oh she simply must read it. She had it here somewhere . . .

So she'd taken the gift down to the beach, reading, awestruck, inventing her own meanings for the archaisms until one of the nurses dragged her back to the tent for fear of worsening her boils. And in the weeks that followed she would recruit officers for players (not needing to recruit Mrs. Butler who assumed what role she chose and seconded as stage director), passing the book each to each and inflecting their best, selecting from the bunch Major Strong for the part of Francisco, Miranda's savior. The happy diversion went so far and eventually drew such a crowd that when, one day, General Butler stumbled on the proceedings, rather than dismiss the troupe he sent away only the lieutenant who was playing Prospero and took the part for himself. There on the beach at Ship Island they enacted the scenes as duty and weather would permit, these sunburnt Northern men become Milanese, draped in scraps and quilts for costume, bending so naturally and gallantly to address their diminutive Miranda that she forgot their difference in size as high-voiced Mrs. Butler declaimed and directed and her husband lurched and smoldered, relishing the role of master conjuror.

She is praying for their souls when a glass shatters against the wall in the next room. Marina, eyes now open, brushes out the folds in her nightclothes on her way to throw open the door, steps out into the half light, and is swept up by a slave who has come to see what ails the mistress.

Mlle Pichon sits at her dressing table, arms folded at the foot of a mostly empty carafe. Marina tries not to look at her, favoring other sights. A stained patch of wallpaper, twists of glass scattered on the floor.

The slave is brushing up the glass when Mademoiselle calls Marina close. The smell of brandy hangs between them; the zamba's mouth fights to stay stern when it would obviously rather bow into a downcast curl and tremble.

"When I was a girl," says Mlle Pichon to her dressing table, "my mother would talk to me through the wall. If she heard me crying she would say, just as if she were in the room with me, 'Inés, you stop that squalling. A girl of seven years doesn't *cry*.'" She laughs, the strange smile-spread of her lips contrasts the look of pain in her eyes. "I half expected to hear her when"—she indicates the stain, the glass shards—"instead, what I get is you."

Marina, closer, asks, "Why were you crying?"

Mademoiselle misunderstands the question, directed not at now but her past, shudders as she produces from some hidden place on her person a slip of paper, which she begins to hand to Marina only to snatch it back, hold it to her eyes, and begin to read aloud as though to prove she can.

It is a message from Uncle Willie, who has, my dearest love, made the decision to stake his life for the honor and glory of his adopted country; he has taken the train, departing with the troops in continuance of this great cause of right; he hopes that she will understand, and she may contact his factor for the remittance of her monthly needs with the additional sum directed, and he begs her patience, for the care of his dear niece, who he hopes will be a comfort in his absence— here a mumbled loveprattle—Wilhelm.

She considers putting a hand to Mademoiselle's shoulder, but the woman's glare banishes the thought.

"So," says Mlle Pichon. "We are forced on one another. How perfect."

"I—I'm sorry."

"I'll bet you are. Trapped here with wicked me? And what does your uncle think we will do with this fairy-tale arrangement? Light votives and send him packages?" She gives her teeth a vicious suck. "Bastard useless man."

Marina feels no need to mount a false familial defense. Uncle Willie has been little more than a bouncing knee when he would visit Cuba and afternoon appearances here when he was not bringing over his gray cohorts to prod her for information. If it didn't mean that she was trapped in the care of this creature who now takes up the carafe and begins to fill a glass that isn't there, she would be almost glad. And she is glad that she is relieved of the ungainly responsibility to reply when Mademoiselle slams down the carafe and waves her off:

"Back to your room and your book. Ah!"—a crooked smile—"now that your friends are here perhaps they'll give you another!"

In the room she must now admit is hers, Marina resumes her prayers to the tune of the woman's unabated sorrow. She has prayed for her friends, for the souls of her parents, for her uncle even, and (in a moment of what she feels must be saintly beneficence) Mlle Inés Pichon. Next is the Angelus Domini, but the boy, Joseph, comes climbing up the rungs of entreaty she is sending to Heaven. She prays for him.

With this accomplished she begins the Domini, a prayer said in memory of the moment in which the Savior became a man. And God is only partially fleshed; sacrificial blood does not yet flow in the veins of the Lamb, when she hears the gunshot.

Twelve

The End of One World, the
Beginning of Another

The doom-crack shatters through the boards of the house, through Ligeia's lap where he rests his head in the hoopless softness of her housedress and the living comfort of the flesh beneath, and into his skull, where it stays, trapped even as the sound itself is instantaneously choked and in its brief absence the gunshot's power is assumed by cries. Ligeia holds him down against her tensing legs but the cries send her up and him in rag-doll tumble as she runs for the stairs. Following, he avoids the snatching hand of Bernice and stumbles on, slipping, drawn along by the progress of their terror to the hallway and the door of his father's room.

The Negroes flutter in the gap and his mother screams *no no no no no* to *keep him out, keep him out,* and he fights to get in against their dresses, against the hands that bathe and clothe and feed him and are now thrown over their eyes and mouths in attitudes of horror and disgust. A retch from above; a warm splash down his neck and he claws at the jamb, forces his head between their jostling hips and for an instant breaches.

This is not his mother, hunched beside the chair and holding out her hands in outspread rictus, a hesitant inch from what sits there. Her mouth is full of words and his is full of something like calf's liver, wet-glistering and dark. This is not his father, head lolling at the back of the chair. His father has one eye and it is bright and blue as Joseph's own and this thing has none but pits of outblown blackness. Smoke whorls from his head.

Joseph is drowning, his lungs filled by dark waters; what he sees tamps him full of screams but none can be drawn out.

This is not his father come alive and jerking in place, galvanic horror, tremor-wracked and tossing his head about, all smoke and ruined sockets, nose running blood with renewed life, who forces from somewhere in his glutted mouth a gurgle mounting to a roar that, were it not for others' shrieks, might be mistaken—no matter how tightly you shut your eyes or jam hands now to your ears—for words.

She stumbles backward and his father pitches to the floor, jitters the birthday pistol across the boards and she, hands upheld in disbelief, inches backward towards the darkness and the bed as though she were trying to escape the lamplight and its revelation of her palms caught with bloody snatches of hair.

Only when he is at last pried from the doorway and borne kicking down the hall does Joseph find the strength to scream.

PART 2

Burial Rites

One
Women's Work

"Did you wash him?"

Yellowed eyes wormed with shattered veins stare back at him; the girl, Ligeia, answers:

"When he quit moving we did."

"You and . . .?"

"Bernice."

"And your mistress?"

The girl shakes her head. She is shorn of obsequies, likely by the labors of her night, which, even to one who should be addressed at all times by a Negro as M. le Docteur and has seen much worse, were undoubtedly considerable. He will not correct her, claims more of the space between them, attempts to look determined rather than unshaved and tired—from the ride here, from the hurried dressing and gathering of his things, from Lydia's frantic appearance at his door this morning to tell him that one of Mr. Woolsack's servants was downstairs and something terrible has happened.

"So, you washed him."

She hums affirmative. "When he quit—"

"And when was that?"

Her voice is the emptying of an ashcan. "About an hour ago."

He does not allow this horror to take hold; in point of fact horror hasn't even the agency in Dr. Sabatier's mind to require parrying or containment; a true physician is possessed of an additional organ, ancillary but of imminent necessity, for the purposes of processing disgust and horror, all the misery of human carnage. Like the gallbladder would, if we so chose, process the harsh grasses of the veldt for nutrient use, so this organ long abandoned by the romantic and pathetic wallowing in their sympathies will for the doctor draw in horror—the image of an old man shot through the head, blinded and writhing out his final eight hours in immense agony, for instance—and render it into usable rational detachment. Far superior, as organic constructions always are, to the crude trap-rooms and mental oubliettes (whose hinges inevitably rust and masonry crumbles with time, releasing horror all the stronger for its long and solitary incarceration) into which the selfsame romantics and sympathetics shunt their moments of horror and lock them away with little keys not unlike the ones dangling at Ligeia's clavicle.

The doctor looks from keys to slave. In her eyes there is not a flicker of guilt for what she's done. He was there not five minutes ago, after ascertaining that the mistress was in opiate insensibility and the boy had been carted off next door and similarly drugged, in the room where Woolsack lay swaddled on his desk. He'd lifted the sheet to see the entrance of the ball, where—despite being scrubbed and scented—burnt ends of hair and faint black graining remained in the neighborhood of the wound. A starring where the barrel had pressed and air was forced beneath the flesh in the instant before the skull-plates shattered. But most of the powderburn had been scrubbed away, nor was there any trace of gunpowder on the offending hand, where a suicide's final act more often leaves its blackest residue. Still, a gunshot suicide's hands aren't always darkened; and though the wound was on the appropriate side of the skull, he'd had no time to gauge the angle of its entrance, for when he was examining Woolsack's hand he saw that the fingernails were broken and packed to the cuticle with clawings of wood and plaster. Before he allowed himself to look to the walls, the door, he went out to find the slaves.

There is something familiar in the slave's expression. The way the tip of her tongue presses below her bottom lip; she has the impertinence to look away, as though she wants this to be over. Of course he knows her face, has seen it wearing this same look in the course of thirteen years of visits paid to this house Woolsack insisted keeping though it was far below his means.

"We weren't going in," she says, bringing her eyes back to him. "Not until he quit."

"Am I to understand that in your fear and stupidity you left Mr. Woolsack there for *eight hours* and never in your tiny brain did you think I should be called? Do you mean to tell me that you allowed him to suffer for that long without so much as shouting down the street for a damned doctor?"

Corded tendon leaps behind her cheeks; she doesn't break his stare.

"Monsieur," she says. "We were worried for neighbors to show, keeping watch outside, and by the time we had him locked and Madame and the boy put down, I can tell you wasn't neither of us right in our own heads either."

"That is no excuse. And there is no excuse for moving him and washing him and cleaning the room." He interrupts himself. "Do you know what an inquest means?"

"No, Monsieur."

"An inquest is when another man, a man very much like me but from the city court, comes to your house and takes a look at a dead man who is shot through the head at a strange angle, the scene of his death scoured, his body cleansed of any traces that might indicate whether he met his demise by his own hand . . . or by the hand of his wife, the only living witness—"

She narrows her eyes.

"Who some career-minded coroner's man or court recorder will find highly suspicious, just as he will find *your* actions, my dear. And do you know what he will do? He will have you carted off in the Black Mariah to parish prison, where they will drop you, your friend Bernice, and even your mistress, from the gibbet. If you make it there, that is. I can't speak for your safety in such a time of civic unrest. Mobs everywhere. And who's to control their reactions to such a flagrant assault?"

He is spiraling into a place of his own darkness; somewhere, nudging near the organ that processes horror, there is another that secretes pleasure from the act of stabbing in the skewers. He cannot help himself and she, damnably, will not change her expression. Her eyes only grow deader. Oh, but he will make them light.

"And even the Northerners will not want to save you. And do you know why? Because they hate you. I use 'you' very broadly, comprehend? They hate you and they don't even know it yet because they have never been surrounded by you; they have never had the peace of every room in their houses undone by your chatter and your noise and carelessness or their streets littered with you, or had their lives disturbed by your bovine stupidities, hating every moment of their dependence upon you." He must catch his breath. "Ah, but very soon they will, my dear, and they will hate you and clap you in the cage at the back of the Black Mariah and cart you off for the noose."

Her lips bow and the burst veins of her eyes seem to have knit together in a field of red encircling the black irises where he, leaning closer, can almost make out his reflection.

"You spent?" she says.

Were it not for his detachment, he would have his hands around her throat. And here again is the nagging familiarity of her expression, her face, all the more bizarre for the fact that he of course remembers her, has seen her many times, and yet some lingering recollection eludes him, barely out of reach.

"We don't call," she says, "because we got him gargling howls like you never heard and Madame tearing out her hair and she in a shrivel ball and the boy so gone he won't be quiet. You go right now and take a look at his face; he cried so hard all the blood's come up from his heart and popped all over his face. And there's only two of us, Monsieur, and like I said by that time we weren't right ourselves. So, yes, we washed him. We did what women do and that is make their dead clean and presentable. That's our work. And we do our work, Monsieur."

He snorts. "That's all very fine, but none of it will matter—"

"If they inquest us."

"Exactly," he says, almost thrilled to be having such a conversation, so quick, with a slave. His temper has shifted, were it any other situation he might examine her, take notes, were it not for the burden awaiting him the next room. "And there will be an inquest."

"Unless?"

The city is in disarray; the police have fled; the courts are suspended; the jail—from what he's heard—has been emptied to make things harder for the Yankees. An inquest into a troubling little incident is the last thing anyone will be doing, but not so as this girl knows.

"Unless," he says, assuming the mantle of responsibility, "I take personal care of this matter, and for that I will need, Ligeia, a favor. But, mind you, I know the truth and should you speak of it ever I'll deny everything. And, barring a vast change in the law, you cannot testify against me but I can testify against you. And against Madame."

"She didn't shoot him."

"*That* is irrelevant."

She blinks, her exhaustion showing more now. And still she wears the look he cannot place.

"Well, Monsieur, what's it you need?"

In the third floor of the Woolsack house the bedrooms face streetward and open onto a balcony considered beautiful during the Spanish dominion but looms in grandmotherly baroque reproach to our modern lines of neoclassical design, the retaining wall featured with a single door providing entrance from the slave quarters that dangle in hidden clapboard precariousness with the privies in the back. The doctor has never come this far into the upper reaches of the house, and with voyeuristic excitement he opens the door to what must be the boy's bedroom. Empty. He steps to the next door fingering the ring of keys he's gained from the girl whose face still galls him with unpinned recognition. Finding the right key, he opens the door. The curtains of this room are drawn and its occupant remains. In a drugged crumple at the foot of the bed—Elise.

His horror-rendered rationality believes she did not do the deed, but how fabulous to think she might've. A graduation from biting off the earlobes of unwanted suitors.

She pendles in anodyne stupor, twisted in the half-torn shreds of mosquito netting as though she were suspended from the bedposts. He is not, of course, convinced of her innocence; he will pursue that point further when he is back in Woolsack's office-crypt. But, as he told the slave, whether she or the old man pulled the trigger is irrelevant to his needs. He wishes for her to believe that he suspects her of the deed. That will be seen to by the Negro girl whose expression still troubles him even as he watches her sleeping mistress.

He steps to the bedside, parts the tangled netting, and reaches for her.

Elise. They have unplaited her hair; they have sopped her with rags and let her scream herself out. And at the instant he touches her barely parted lips, this man who has traded in flesh at operating table and auctioneer's block, who has kept a wife for more than a decade, experiences for the first time in his life the sensation of truly having a person come into his possession.

He strokes her face and still she doesn't wake. He must go, down to the office where waits his subject and his bag, in which are the components of a still-experimental procedure, not yet popular on our side of the Atlantic, for the chemical preservation of the dead. He'd been one of the lucky witnesses to its early stages at the Académie française. He must go, but can't bring himself to take his hand away.

He remembers being rousted from his cold student's garret, shaking off the bleariness of wine in the chill of a Paris autumn night as he is led by a fellow-student to see the culmination of Professor Theophile Mercier's work. *Come and see.* Into the old barracks behind the largest lecture hall. The bolt shot, the door thrown open, his fellow-student rushing in with his lamp to show young Emile the body of a woman wrapped in an enormous spider's web of silken netting, hammocked, alone in the darkness. *Come, Sabatier, and get a load of our Jeanne. How long would you say she has been dead? Eight hours? No, my little fool, she's been dead since last February.*

As a result of Mercier's injections, the skin of the spider-webbed woman had taken on a bronzy, golden tone in the months of her suspension. And with her dark hair bunched and eyes sewn dreamily shut Jeanne had at that time called to his drunken mind the face of Elise.

Boy and man, the same woman dangles in your mind. You might forget her, put her away, or even see her once a week for a decade swinging there until you take no more note of her than a piece of furniture. Still, she is preserved. And now you have her.

With reluctance, and a final tracing of her mouth, the doctor quits her room.

Down a flight. Now he occupies Woolsack's chair, holding in his left hand the revolver. He marvels for a moment at the daintiness of the gun, the caliber sufficient to breach but not escape the skull, and thus the ball had raged heedless of brain-matter throughout the cranial vault like a blasphemer burst into a vespers-crowded church, harrowing the penitents and causing havoc from sconce to station, defaming idolatrous memory. He raises the revolver to the determined quadrant of temple, presses the barrel to his skull. From his desk-bier, Woolsack maintains an eyeless vigil over the re-creation of his demise as the doctor tries outflung elbow, affects an old man's palsied grip, feels for the appropriate angle. Unsatisfied, he considers Elise's height and that of the seated man, how she would have to cock her arm uncomfortably low, or perhaps if she had his head tilted back in an embrace. He considers calling for one of the slaves to stand beside him and hold the pistol at his head; but this bout of amateur detection is a waste, the corpse sours apace, and it will likely be days before he can secure even the meanest crypt in the cemetery. Standing, he lets the revolver lead him like a dowsing rod to the desk, where his instruments and chemicals rest alongside the deceased. Unpeeled of his shrouding, in Woolsack's flesh mutilations suffered long ago mingle with the fresher maulings of his ultimate act.

Dr. Sabatier regards him, the man for whom he worked at first out of courtesy to the departed father-in-law, then out of fascination for his age and maddening experience, and, it cannot be denied, the presence of Elise. He takes up his trocar by its bulbous end, bends close to the stubbled neck, locates the carotid, and begins.

At close range wounds become a haze; hatchworked cicatrixes meld. Only artists and those of romantic and sympathetic disposition dwell grandiosely upon viscera and relish the metaphorical prospects of wound and arterial effluence. The simple fact: death by contusion of the brain and suffocation due to the aspiration of blood from the lacerated arteries, the shredding of Willis' Loop. The doctor's eyes reduce all to Cartesian domains of body, an overleaf of corporeal coordinate by means of which our subject is mentally dissembled, chemically altered to withstand a corpse's desire to rot and return to mired beginnings.

Now Woolsack's blood is running down the trocar's tip and into the India rubber tube to the bucket at the doctor's feet.

Bodies in our New Orleans cemeteries are liquefied within three months, a consequence of climate. No longer. This technique of embalming, of preparations for the dead, is far beyond the scope of pitiful and antiquated womanly dabbings and soaks. Here, in chromide and alum, is the future. For soon, with all the bodies coming home from battlefields, the appearance of life will be as important as foreshorn life itself. No one in New Orleans has yet attempted what he is about to do. A shame he can call no colleagues in the coming days. His handiwork will be seen only by a child, a woman of dubious capacity, two slaves, sextant's men, and the darkness.

The retraction of the trocar's tip from the drained carotid comes with a puff. Flesh purses where the point has been. And as though he were himself injected, but with recognition rather than the solution of chromide of alum he now applies, the doctor places the source of his memory of Ligeia's look. He fights laughter, at his dodgy mind, at the strangeness of circumstance. His shoulders shake and he must slam aside his instruments and let out a wild peal or two, over-loud. The world changes in the span of a day, infections arouse unforeseen symptoms, and yet we still bump blindly against figures of the past, specimens preserved in the haphazard admixtures of memory so that their parts slough off and swirl together.

He sees the slave's face. Five—six years ago, he'd brokered the sale of her child.

The corpse before him had wanted the little boy out, and the doctor had dutifully complied. A two-hundred-dollar chap.

The doctor looks to the shell that will be beneficiary of his arts. And though the old man had despised the Confederate cause, pledged not a dime of his considerable fortune to the defense of the city and the outfitting of troops as did so many others, he is emblematic. Here is the wretched South; here lies the avatar of Secessia in ravaged mortem. That dreamstate encompassing seven hundred and fifty thousand square miles and nine million souls. And we are all, he thinks, in a constant state of secessia: soul from body, youth from life, husband from wife. We die but secessia lives on. Even now preservation flows through its veins, and the corpse will keep its flesh for years to come.

Two

"A Thousand Paths, Where Every Clue Was Lost"

The crowd outside the St. Charles Hotel, grown from a trickle of weary drunks upon his relocation in late morning to full-throated mob by one o'clock, cries that General Butler is asleep. Asleep as he legendarily was while the guns rained hell and his troop-line buckled into ignoble retreat at Big Bethel, the only action he has seen in his time as major general.

The long hat-and-cloak table of the ladies' parlor has been dragged across the room to make the desk at which he sits, unmoving, these past minutes. Military matter, neatly stacked, occupies a single rosewood corner, its ranks threatened by a steady invasion of letters, dispatch scraps, scribbled invective from the populace; the remaining expanse awaits filling by the figures of the city. He has sent emissaries to the banks, to the storehouses and newspapers and foreign consulates—to City Hall. They will return with falsified pages and hopefully some recalcitrant city elders, ready for capitulation. Brother Jackson, named for the general under whom their father served at this very site, has taken the initiative to begin a survey of the saloons and taverns and coffeehouses, certain venues perhaps frequented nearly half a century ago by the father neither of them can remember.

Outside, the rioters call him a drowser, make sawblade snores at the window. General Butler does not move.

He is, in fact, reading—an open and well-thumbed copy of *Gardener's New Orleans Directory of 1861*, wherein are listed not only the names of citizens and their businesses from patent clerk to prostitute, but the offices and officers of the city government in all their varicose and labyrinthine forms. Pity the poor devil who had the task of hacking any semblance of order from the tangled knots these people call a municipal government, which appears to him as a colossal obfuscation. Boards and committees that would have five members in Boston have fifteen here. The needless gothic embellishments of sub-subcommittees for waste and streetlights and levees and gasworks and draught-animals. City government arranged on Chinese puzzle-box lines, with no compartment containing a plurality or avenue to the offices above. A quorum of counterproduction, at first maddening and perverse until you consider that the arrangement is innate to the character of the place.

When he reads, Butler's eyelids droop lower even than usual, and with head inclined he is often mistaken for dozing. General Grant, so he hears, napped while the corpses piled high at Shiloh.

Tibbets's voice: "Should I draw the curtains, General?"

"I've had about enough of them myself," adds George Strong.

Butler listens. Outside the people drone like an enraged apiary. He does not move, nor give orderly or adjutant an answer, but lets his head tip farther forward. The panes rattle with the laughter of the crowd.

"Should I . . . ?"

"General, sir?"

Still downward slumps his head; he exhales, fluttering his lips so that the ends of his moustaches whistle. He struggles not to betray himself with a smile, fights the concussion of withheld chuckle threatening his broad shoulders to quake now that even his men have taken the bait. When he feels the pages of the directory at the tip of his nose, in a single motion Butler snaps himself straight and with eyes bright and open as he can manage grins at the crowd and gives them a wink.

The windows may come apart with their surprise—Tibbets and George stepping back from the thunderous yawps—as even rebellious hearts cannot help but cheer and dance for a moment at his jest. All, he sees, save one who stands at their forefront. Dark of hair and whisker, a man of maybe forty—too old for rabble-rousing but given some primacy by his fellows—he wears in his collar button a large tuft of the flag of the United States. He exhorts, baring tobacco-stained teeth, pounds the shreds of stars and stripe at his breast, shakes his fist at the general, and meets his eyes. Vitriol subsumes the whoops and George Strong, brushing past Tibbets, takes the tasseled cord and yanks the curtains of the nearest window closed. Moving about the room, Strong hauls curtains shut, calling for Tibbets to do the same until they are left in darkness.

Butler sighs, waits while lamps are lit and in orange-glowing succession the room is illuminated corner by corner, unscrews the bell of his desklamp, and lights the wick.

In the glow and flicker he espies his adjutant's frustration. Butler looks to this strapping Vermonter, a major though barely twenty-three. "George," he says, "the essence of humor is not to make the other man laugh, though it naturally occurs, but to make him realize that he is the joke."

"I'm not sure I follow."

Of course you don't. Square-jawed George, tall trim George whose bedside is stacked with letters from a lovely young wife and the admiring girls of home, able to shut your eyes and remember the swoons of the milkmaids of Vermont, and of whom the little girl they'd rescued was troublingly fond. See, George, when you've been joked about all your life you must learn to turn it back. There are few better things than wrenching the giggle from some dullard's throat so that only a smile, a front maintained against the sting of rebuke, remains. Or take an angry man, hammering his fist on your desk over some courtroom sleight of hand, some unexpected brief—all he's angry about is being outwitted, being beaten. Do not gloat, do not meet his rage, but find some humor in the situation, even yourself, and twist it into a laurel he may wear upon his loser's head.

"And if all else fails," Butler says, "simply remain composed and give him time to cool. But if this is unsuccessful, if he maintains his rage and threat—crush him." Stamp out his pitiful flame like you would a fleck of ember escaped from fireplace grate. Put your boot to it before the carpet catches fire.

He considers the man with the flag-scrap boutonniere as the crowd strikes up the "Bonnie Blue" ditty, answered in chorus by the guards barking for them to keep back.

"I'm afraid," says George Strong, "we have more than a little crushing to do."

Butler trudges through waterworks and drainage-sectors divided up like fiefdoms, the commissions spread among four competing municipal districts and the two incorporated cities. Boston, the torch by which he makes his way through New Orleans's interminable turns and catacombs, is a poor light. And he knows that there is no lone Minotaur lurking in the umbral reaches of the city's obfuscations, but a beast in gestalt.

The hotel steward appears at the door, asks timidly from the bright outer world of the monstrous St. Charles if the general will be requiring anything.

"We're fine, thank you," says George Strong. "You'll find New England men prefer to serve themselves."

Muttering, the boy retreats into recesses unimaginable for those without the concierge's brochure, and even thus equipped you may find it difficult to navigate the hotel's three hundred and fifty-nine rooms, bifurcated along lines of gender—ladies to the westward side, gents to the east—themselves containing twelve private parlors, a half dozen stairway sitting rooms, connected in intricate lacing of guest-stairway and deeper recesses wherein servants may climb unseen from the backside kitchens, over which are flung their own quarters, down into the cavernous dining rooms (similarly separate) that hold eaters in the hundreds and are fronted by their respective saloons (where Jefferson Davis held court before the convention in '60) and drawing room (wherefrom Butler now contemplates the expanse), then into the basement barroom—an uncommon thing in this city to have any space underground, but dryness is afforded by limestone walls and flooring three feet thick—the octagonal den lined with Corinthian columns themselves festooned with playbills and slave-auction notices his men have taken to ripping down—and terminating in the cave-reeking bathhouse, where a hundred men may steam away the city's grime.

We consider only in passing the portico fronting the hotel, one hundred and forty-five feet long, the titanic granite breaker at which the rabble of the city now flings itself, and the crowning dome, among whose turrets once stood a fifty-foot-high statue of George Washington that was felled by a fire and collapse eleven years ago.

Though Sarah would adore it all, for prudence's sake he keeps Mrs. Butler aboard the *Saxon*. He is not yet willing to test the limits of Southern chivalry, but he will have his wife on land before nightfall.

He will have to do something about the attitude of his men. Not just George, but much of his staff have taken to berating the hotel workers, Negro and white, about the self-reliance of Northern men. Useless when someone's trying to give you a glass of lemonade, a silly pose that breeds discontent and only furthers the people's belief that we are a nation of Ichabods, lecturing away. As though we all stoke fires, cook meals, beat rugs and children ourselves. Butler has no such illusions, nor need of them. He understands himself as an aristocrat of lifestyle and a democrat of politics. Where others might see contradiction, the general finds only harmony.

"George," he says. "Do you recall the man outside wearing a piece of the flag of the United States?"

"No, sir."

"I see the rascal," chimes Tibbets. "They got him on their shoulders."

"Check the window and see. You'll find he's of middle age, dark, face a bit bleary from drink, and vociferous."

Strong complies, shoulders alongside the orderly and peers out. "You described the villain to perfection."

"The general never forgets a face," says Tibbets.

Without looking up from the directory, Butler says, "Let's find out that man's name, shall we?"

"Do you want him detained?"

Tibbets is tapping at the window, pointing, presumably, at the man and mouthing *you*.

"Just his name, thank you."

Strong goes to pass the order on. The man's name is a formality; give George something to do besides unsettle the help. Butler already has the man's face; and were there an artist nearby he could go into more meticulous detail: the snarl of a scar at his right upper lip, the bushy blue-black brows. He could pick the man out of any crowd, as he's done in courtrooms and bustling commons, hailed a man he'd seen months back in an actuary's office; he can recall the face of all who've stood beside him at the bar in twenty-five years, call to mind individuals out of the multitudes of the accused and the aggrieved. In his mill he is a hero for addressing each smudge-faced girl on the line by name; when he was in Congress he could claim to know the greater portion of his district by heart. And one might think his mind overburdened by the cast of a lifetime, but just as people tend to take undue notice of his face, so he commits theirs to memory.

Tibbets lets the curtain slack, comes to pour him more coffee, as his emissaries trickle in bearing the various refusals. The owner of the newspaper *True Delta* refuses to print his proclamation; at City Hall the mayor and his people refuse to come to the St. Charles and meet him; the banks refuse to surrender accounts of their specie; the consulates refuse to detail the sheltered holdings of foreign nationals; and on and on so that he is glad when the litany is interrupted by Strong with the name of the errant spark: William Mumford, who openly admits he is the man who tore the flag of the United States from its staff at the Mint.

He will deal with this Mumford in time, just as he will roust city elders and impertinent printers and bend all refusals into pleading acquiescence, but for now his eyes return to the directory, the catacombs yawn and contract between walls illumined only by nitre; deep in the dankness of Southern calumny and disregard, he hears the crowd sing. A chorus of sparks building to an inferno.

Marina

Three
Discovery

She rarely parts her eyes from him. Like those of a new pet, even Joseph's minor stirrings are novel. She studies him as she would the fantastical birds in the Bishop of Havana's garden—emerald parrots, macaws, and parroquets in their enormous lodge, flighty and loud or hunched in sullen molt. And there was always the temptation to stick a finger past the bars and give some relief, so she imagined, to their confinement: you might be nipped or you might make a friend.

Marina shifts for inland seas of sweat imparted in the sheets, measures the distance from her bed to where he lays on the chaise, dulled to the world by what he has witnessed and whatever Mlle Pichon had tippled from a tiny blue bottle into a cup of wine he'd taken with mute and insensible acquiescence when he was brought to her room last night. Marina hadn't had time to say a word to him before he collapsed to the cushions he now fitfully occupies.

She has never known a suicide, much less the son of one. See here the weight of the father's sin at work upon the visage of the son; these jerking limbs, charged by what must be nightmare—which preys upon sleepers regardless of time. His moans are not moans at all but words shuttered by grit teeth, the conversation occurring at the back of his throat told by hitching windpipe not yet distended by Adam's apple. It may be that he talks to his father, as she did in the sunblasted days before her rescue, and long thereafter.

It may be that he sees his father in Hell.

She summons to mind the gaunt, white-shocked fearsome man she'd seen depart the house next door most days, toting a long cane that doubtless concealed a wicked sword whose blood-gutter had performed its office many times. How he would stop at the last step before the street, taking a long breath as he aimed his patched eye at pedestrians who doubled their steps to be out from under his gaze. To watch this scene played out, as she had many times even in the brief course of her stay, was something like living in the neighborhood of an ogre. As though you were the nearest house, never mentioned, to the villain in the story.

She knows that in Heaven the maimed are reunited with their missing parts, replenished after long purgatorial remittance, just as we are to meet again lost loved ones in that Blessed Kingdom; and so the damned may be eternally dismembered for their transgressions.

And in his dream, does Joseph hold speech with his father's severed head? With his eyeball rolling down the scream-wracked halls of perdition? With limbless trunk while devils use the sinner's joints to pound their toms?

She can only know his dream through intermediary flesh, though she knows that the nightmare will never leave him, just as whenever she shuts her eyes she sees the storm. Mother and father have long bobbed in the waters of her dreams, swept farther and farther from her reach—for she is always reaching out—until they are tiny blots on a darker sea and she is awake. She contents herself with the knowledge that her parents are better off; her prayers shorten their time in the anteroom of souls and speed their way to paradise. Joseph will have no such chance. His father's damnation is irrevocable. And it may be pity at this fact that sends her slipping now from the bed to crouch beside him at the chaise.

She holds the back of her hand before his nose, feels his breath. He draws inward and she expects he will awake. When he does not, her touches are emboldened: an ear is traversed; lips are rimmed; she presses her palm to the confines of chest from which his heart seeks to escape. And all the liberties she takes with his body are reckoned with her own—a prodding investigation, for similarities abound. His moans come louder, lips puff apart, and she allows herself to pet his head. Hair not unlike her own, perhaps finer. She brushes tensing cheek, her fingertips disturb flossy ends of down. Now she seeks confirmation in her own face, in the similarly flossy growth her thirteenth year has given dominion over her features. Neither have breasts, though she plans to one day, and it seems their likelihood of endowment is at the moment equal. On she goes, and inevitably these discoveries draw her eyes to his legs, crossed as though to deny her immodest thoughts.

She has seen boys, older than he, pants around their ankles, watering the lemon trees of Don Francisco's cafetal; thin brown legs and between them bits of little novelty, save for what must be an element of convenience. Particularly in the open country, it must be preferable to be afoot rather than rocking back and forth on splashed heels. For all she knows this boy of the close-grown city has never pissed anywhere but WC or pot.

His eyelids flutter—Marina frittering his lashes—but still he does not wake. She feels invested with empire over a small and troubled mirrorland. Flicks become plucks and pokes; she pinches his arm, his hips, like her mother would a chicken's breastbone on marketing day. She tugs tufts of his hair but he only nuzzles deeper into the cushion. She has begun to play the chords of his ribs when his arms come alive, swiftly weave hers, and pull them close.

Now not a moan but something of a coo, a low hum of comfort as his twitching ceases and he hugs tighter to her arm. Suddenly bound in awkward bedside vigil, she fights the urge to tear away and the fear of being caught, trapped, shorn from her own life and grafted to another's dream.

Elise

Four

Obsidian

Time moves like a cripple, jolts with curious speed and then in awkward shamble stalls to catch its breath. Spans filled with images she wishes weren't from life. Black-veined gobs of gray, like the belly meat of a trout. Blood in a mysterious cloud passing through a candleflame to pop and hiss.

She regains the world by means of shattered senses. She knows this is her bed only by the smell, that this is her room only by the appearance of a lone orange patch of sunlight standing vagrant in the corner, harried off in the middle of her stare by watchman dark. She clings to the bed as though it would be rid of her, as though it were mounted on the ceiling of a cave and her grip is all that saves her from the floor far below

False night. See how the light appears on the floor in its accustomed corner, creeps now slowly up the wall. Only a passing cloud.

Her wardrobes show in shadowy eminence, one drawer containing in oilpaper shroud her single suit of heavy-mourning black.

Concentrate on this, death's habiliments and procedures. Not on Angel's voice. Not on the sound of him thrashing like a bucketed crab. She will need much more than a single suit, for now she hasn't lost something as simple as a mother or a friend. Husbands, legal or not, warrant time and sacrifice of us, even in death. They beg for us; even when their eyes are exploded they look for us, even when their voices are croaking shouts like someone drowning at the bottom of a deep, deep well. She clings to her bed, envisions her clothes pitched into great vats to soak up blackness, unseamed taffeta scraps sewn into the ornaments of the absurd proscriptions of marital grief. And if she speaks the numbers, the rules of mourning, she might descend from the cave wall safely and his voice will not resound so loudly in her mind. More than two years, somewhere between the English and the French custom. Nine hundred and fifty days before she will bear brightness again. A year and a half before she may trim collar or cuff in white; two years before the allowance of gray; an interminable afterward while color is slowly reintroduced. She has seen girls married off at seventeen and within months were made gloom-shrouded avatars for husbands who'd done not much more than bloody a good set of sheets. And there were those girls, low or high, who themselves died, and for whom husbands dutifully adhered to the widower's tradition: a black armband on their usual suits. Worn for how long, she cannot say. There are far fewer rules for men.

Men whose heads smoke as if Hell were something they kept inside.

There is a moist glisten to the blackness of the room, like the sheen of the black mirror Mme Frick's late husband brought back from our national adventure in Mexico. Four-foot face and foliated frame hewed all from a stone called obsidian, an opaque glass naturally occurring in those parts, the black mirror gives back less a reflection than an image trapped in inky waters, trying to escape. Whenever she is in Frick's house, Elise always seeks out the mirror; she feels a kinship to the stone and its absolute darkness, silkily smooth in feel until you reach its points of razored leaf. Blades are made of it. Axe and arrowhead, points of spears. The Aztecs used obsidian for their sacrificial knives.

From her holdfast in the roof of the cave, Elise sees squirming virgins stabbed by befeathered priests. Stabbed with the black stone she is to become. Yes, if she makes herself into the stone she can descend from this height, she can reflect the screams and what she's seen.

She will bind herself in black, revealing only her face of unquestionable and startling whiteness. She, mirror and reflection both.

She does not want her son, as might some mothers at this moment, to hold and rock and share a trembling recollection of what he'd seen. What she'd made him see, dear God. Her features bunch, her eyes squeeze shut, she feels the sob boiling in her throat and flecks of snot trembling at her nose. She hopes her son is not in a cave of his own; she hopes he is asleep. She cannot see him. Not yet. Not until someone comes to help her down. If he were brought to her at this moment, there would be his father's face.

She presses herself deeper into the bed, and the sheets against her face are cool and slick as the obsidian mirror.

Time and fire form the stone, and savage talents hew it to a dangerous edge. She has passed through the flames and the quarrymen have come. And in such hands what shape will she take?

Five

Islands

Disentangled, they sit on the carpet of her room, separated only by plates of warmed-over fish and rice. When one of Mlle Pichon's girls brought their dinner, Joseph's head was clear enough to ask her what was the time. Six o'clock. A late dinner so you'd better eat now and quick. He'd nodded, the foggy slowness that has oppressed his mind since he woke knotted with the girl returning, overwhelming him so that even now as he watches her idly fork flesh from bone he cannot bring himself to make his hands move from his knees, where they serve to prop him up. This must be how drunkenness feels. But the drunkards he has seen are happy (when they are not fighting) and he is not. He is not sure what he feels. An absence. Numbing shock coupled with the strangeness of waking with his hands on the ship-wrecked girl. Her eyes so close to his that in the moment of their waking his first sight was the twin black irises widening, eyebrows jumping in shock as they both sprung away from the other.

He can't keep his eyes on her; Marina doubles and smudges in the lamplight.

She sets down her fork, leans across their meal until her face is unavoidable, and says, "My parents both are dead."

Her English is strange, of indeterminate accent. He tells himself she comes from Cuba, but she might be from the moon. He blinks, and her face grows indistinct as though he were alone and trying to recollect her. He marshals what reply makes sense, thanks her.

And though his own words and their reason for being spoken sink into the muddle of Joseph's mind, Marina seems to understand that he is thanking her not for her parents' death but for the admission, for joining him. She smiles.

"You were on an island. . . ." he says, tilting towards his dinner. Flies have settled in the gray meat along the fish's ribs. A small spotted trout, baked whole. Joseph's stomach climbs up his throat. The fish's eye is hollow, burst by the heat.

"It was mine," he says to the fish.

The flies dart and scurry, preening their faces as they dance on fishmeat.

"What was yours?" Marina's voice is soft, far-off and fading. They exist as identifiable words for an instant, then dissemble into jumbled vowel and consonant.

"What was yours?" she asks again.

A moment of awful clarity as the image of the birthday pistol sharpens in his mind.

He looks up at her through burning, wet eyes. "It was my gun."

"The one your mother took from you outside," she says.

Joseph feels himself shrinking, in layers like paper wadded in a fist. An uncontrollable thrash, fighting tears, sends his plate skidding across the rug, but Marina has swept up his small glass of wine, wine that tastes of wormwood. She holds it close, the way he held the pistol to keep it from his mother.

There is no stopping what follows. Between gasps and stammers he gives out what he has seen, what he knows, what he wonders, what he fears knowing. It was his gun but she brought it upstairs—mother stomping up the risers, the slam of the door to his father's office and a single protestant bark of the old man's voice, subsumed by hers, the tirade following for almost an hour, muffled only when Ligeia drew him into her lap, cupped her palm over his free ear. But no matter how he burrowed or hummed, there was his mother's voice rising shriller and angrier until . . .

As though she called the shot into existence.

And hadn't she?

And what he curses, moans out at last is that he doesn't know which one of them it was. What is he supposed to hope?

When Joseph opens his eyes Marina is there, knees drawn to her chest. The roaring in his head abates. She speaks.

"Now, I'll tell you about my island," she says. "And then you can tell me about yours."

Six

The Season of Masks

When by speech the gates to the afterlife are opened, it seems every skeleton will have his rattle on the tongues of the living. In this way the conversation of the gentlemen gathered at the Gem Saloon has shifted from Angel Woolsack to William Walker. Tragically taken from us, both. The latter by Honduran bastards on some godforsaken beachhead fort, the former—Dr. Sabatier has assured them—by terrible accident.

"Like Walker," he says, returning the focus. "My friend wouldn't wish to meet his end in any way but combat. I firmly believe he was preparing to go out and meet the enemy."

Pierre Soulé, former senator, of operatic features and the bearing of one who has shot noblemen in duels, begins in the crisp Parisian accent he has retained despite having come to New Orleans some twenty-five years ago as an exiled revolutionary, pronounces the greatness of both men, who despite the fact that they were never members of this association were held rightly in high esteem: "May we all profit by their example in the coming days."

Tableware rattles with affirmative fists. The air of the private dining room is filled with glass-chimed dolorosa as Dr. Sabatier fights back a scowl at Soulé's usurpation of his point. The gentlemen foregathered on this the evening of the second day of the occupation drink deeper than usual, as though to make up for absent throats. Twenty-four of the thirty chairs surrounding the table inlaid with the arms of the Mystik Krewe of Orcus are vacant. Some have gone with General Lovell to raise sabres and shout orders and meet the product of Northern foundries; others retreated to the interior like disfavored Roman senators with what riches they could carry. These remain: Pierre Soulé, René Armand, H. P. Arthur, Albert Deschamps.

The untenanted sockets of Venetian masks hung about the walls bear indifferent witness to the irregular flows of brandy and conversation. Masks of startling colors, feathered and beaded, studded with jewels, expressions inscrutable or of archetypal emotional contortion. These are the adornments of the Krewe, who in this same room not five years past came to the grand and fantastical design to commission immense floats on which they might be drawn through the carnival streets. A striking concept now aped by lesser outfits, but such is the fate of those who set the trend.

At the head of their table is Soulé—author of the Olsted Manifesto rightly staking the United States' claim to Cuba, the tantalizingly close jewel in the Caribbean; voice of Southern empire; the masterful litigator who, next door beneath the dome of the District Court, four years ago secured the acquittal of the filibuster Walker.

Dr. Sabatier matches mask to man—his own monstrous white visage hangs below Soulé's exquisite purple aquiline frowner—studies what constitutes the somewhat wilted flower of New Orleans gentry (comprising an association that ostensibly plans pre-Lenten revels, but like anything else in this city serves far more than its stated purpose) for betraying signs of cyanotic infection: fear, suspicion, signs of doubt. He has done so from the moment he told them of Woolsack's demise. They are, he must admit, his friends; he enjoys them with the same appreciation for absurd spectacle as he does riding masked atop a papier-mâché dragon with the face of Charles Sumner, drawn through the streets by a horse-team decked as unicorns.

He looks to the hands that were this morning on Woolsack's corpse. This momentary strangeness goes without comment from his fellows, and he adopts an increasingly bemused and grief-stricken expression not unlike that of René Armand's red mask. There are nods, hands firmly pressed to his shoulder, eyes he imagines cutting suspiciously across the table. They pity him, for having done what the friend of any suicide would do—play the death off as accidental. They suspect him of a gentlemanly untruth, and that is precisely what he wants. Emile the stricken friend, the dutiful fool willing to proffer a little falsehood and perhaps a bit thickheaded in the matter as a result of his grief. After all, he'd accepted nigger women at their word, and hadn't he said that Woolsack's woman had been in the room when it occurred, but he hadn't spoken to her because she was "insensible"?

He lets himself play the fool in order to sow in their minds other doubts, other theories. Idle whispers will turn into suspicion as the story is passed and like syphilis grows more virulent in their gossipy wives and even looser-tongued mistresses—who may in fact recall the girl who bit off a boy's ear.

Whether she ever needs know it, he holds Elise's fate by a cord. Should she prove difficult he may snap it at a moment of his choosing. He must remind himself that this little intrigue is a pastime, a way to stave off boredom while pipes and Cubanos throw up a roof of smoke and the fellows gabble. The doctor watches Soulé, who remains silent as the others' conversation reels and whirls.

"I'll speak no ill of the dead," says H. P. Arthur. "But the man always unsettled me."

René Armand, small and florid, addresses his snifter: "The Yanks won't allow for carnival, I'm sure. This Butler's already throwing men in prison. Frank Long of the *Bee*, this morning."

"My father," says Albert Deschamps, "told me once that Woolsack had killed more men than yellow jack and Savannah Frank both."

"Women, too." Armand leans closer to the table. "I hear he's locked up old Twiggs's wife in the calaboose herself."

Soulé signals with a hand, a gesture the doctor is quite glad to not obey and so finds something in the far corner to distract his gaze while Pierre declares: "Gentlemen, New Orleans will be rid of Benjamin Butler and Louisiana of the invaders before All Saints'."

Bleary-eyed and brandied as an Ortolan, René Armand casts back against his chair. "It's not damned All Saints' I'm worried about, Pierre, but Mardi Gras."

Amid the laughter and the slosh of snifters replenished, the doctor says, "Let's hope you're right, Pierre."

Soulé gives him a jurist's jaundiced eye, then encompasses the rest.

"We have won by far the lion's share of victories in the field, fought solely in defense of a newborn nation. The powers of Europe are poised to come to our aid." Pierre cups his glass. "New Orleans's present situation is unfortunate, but it was not a battle lost. Not here or in the eyes of our European friends. The forts were abandoned, the defense mismanaged, that damned Lovell . . ."

Ayes and toasts to the orator's health. The doctor slumps in his chair, bored. There is no more talk of Woolsack or Walker to be had. Pierre rings the bell for the Negro waiters to come and bring another round of bottles. We must, according to Soulé, bide our time and hold out against the invader. Stymie his efforts; belabor his cause. Make him take four steps to cover a single foot. We will begin tomorrow, at the meeting of the mayor and council—and whatever prominent man wishes to be present—with General Butler and his staff.

"Well," wags Arthur. "If there's anything we know in New Orleans it's making things take triple the time."

Forced chuckles, the avatar of the city's bottomless self-deception and complicity in its own national ignobility.

Now some of the gentlemen are asking what sort of man is General Butler. After all, Pierre has met him on more than one occasion in his capacity as Democratic statesman.

"He is a good attorney. Agile mind. Avaricious"—laughter from the men—"as any Northerner. He is the sort of man who stood by the South's side until the question of secession came to be. Of course, I believe it was only to keep the cotton flowing to his mills. He is the sort of man who voted forty-seven times for Davis on fifty ballots. Then for Mr.—now General—Breckinridge . . ."

The doctor raises a finger, interrupts. The brandy has struck him deep enough. He is tired of the oratory. "Come now, Pierre. We can read all of that in the papers."

"Not for too damn long, it seems," says Armand.

What Pierre has to say requires throat clearing, the fist at his lips opens with a flourish as though to reveal Butler's character within.

"Butler," he says, "is a difficult man. He not only sees greatness in himself, but he looks for the means to attain greatness. He will serve his own interest unerringly, which for the moment is allied with that of the Northern states. And he is of their breed, a lecturer, prudish yet mannerless—but he is not self-righteous as his fellows. That Northern trait he does not possess.

"Of all the time we spent together, in the heady days of fifty-nine and sixty, the moment I recall the most is this: We were taking a drink on the veranda of the Mills House, in Charleston for the convention. He was a congressman then. Fresh from taking Secretary of War Davis on a tour of Massachusetts. Imagine them together! Stopping at inns, picking apples! Butler leaned against the railing—it had been a hard day at the committees—and looked out on the street. He seemed to forget I was there for some time. Then he said, 'Pierre, did I ever tell you that my father took letters of the marque from Bolívar?' I told him he hadn't, though I did know that his father had served with distinction with Jackson at New Orleans. 'Yes, indeed,' he said. 'I have his sword in a glass case in my parlor. And his father's sword from the Revolution. And his father's before him, from the French—pardon—and Indian wars.' 'Strange then,' I said to him, 'that you didn't go out for the army.' Butler smiled. 'My mother wouldn't allow it,' he said."

The others grunt amusedly; the doctor watches.

"The day's talk had been laden with threats from the majority, who saw our situation and decried the inevitability of secession. As you know, I was not among them. And Butler was quite exacerbated for his part. So there he stood, looking down Charleston's main street with an expression of almost wistful appreciation. I joked with him: 'Are you sizing up to buy the place, Mr. Butler?' 'Oh, no, sir,' he says. 'I was just wondering how these corners would look with gun emplacements. How the roofs would look on fire.' And here he stood, in every way enjoined with our cause save secession, which even I accepted as inevitable eventually, thinking of war. So I ask you, gentlemen, what do you make of a man like that?"

Seven

His Origins

"How's this for a second honeymoon?"

General Butler holds his wife's hand and they sway atop New Orleans. A glittering nightscape sung with the expectant gasp of gaslight; bats flutter, chirruping above the rooftops, and slash into arcs of light, snatching from clouds of insects and angle towards the river where sits the idling fleet whose riggings and moorings bear points of illumination in fear of sabotage. It is late, near ten, and Sarah has been only an hour off the *Saxon*, dinner put off to European hours so that he could tour her through the St. Charles to where it is capped like some confectioner's extravagance in Corinthian excess by the domed promenade.

"Well," she says. "It's not Paris. . . ."

"No, more like ancient Rome."

From his vantage, the city is decadent enough to stun Gibbon. The colossal edifices of crazyquilt construction, the putrid waterways, the coffers a million dollars in arrears. His wife nudges close, as she would on a November evening on the veranda of their house at Belvedere, at the peak of Lynde Hill, overlooking the smokestacks and tenements and redbrick stolidity of Lowell set orderly among the darkening canals and affixed in orderly perfection beneath the arrowhead bend of the Merrimack and Concord's confluence, rather than this Mediterranean gewgaw collection spattered in uneasy alignment and clinging to a temperamental and immense river.

The bun of her hair brushes his cheek. Sarah has put her maid to good use; Butler can see poor Molly pinning and preening in the cramped quarters of the *Saxon*, twiddling the wisps of brown hair that curl with unmatronly buoyance before Mrs. Butler's ears. No granite-faced New England lady, she. A bit of New York in her, thanks to a childhood of verse and acting, to her years on the stage made possible by a doting father and his money.

"You are the only one," she says, "who could make order out of this."

He folds Sarah's arm between both of his, strokes her to the glove, lost in admiration of the discrepancy in beauty between himself and his wife, a sensation, more often pleasant, he has experienced from the moment she inexplicably agreed to marriage. At such times he likes to smilingly question his fortune. What had he done? He had no money to his name. His prospects were the same as any junior associate in a Boston law firm. He was no bumbler, but neither was he charming. (Looks were out of the question.) He was dogged in pursuit of her, but he did not wear her down as some men attempt. If Sarah had refused his backstage flowers at the shows he could attend or the gifts sent to those he couldn't, he would have receded. But she—daughter of Hildreth wealth, allowed to while her time before the footlights—had accepted gift and giver hintless of condescension.

The smell of lavender. She kisses his cheek. And in his moment of reverie he must fight down the dark, invasive thoughts, swarming bat-like at the tail of his pride in her beauty—the distinct impression that she chose him so that she could be absolutely sure she was the finer of the pair. Why not a polished scion of wealth, tanned and aristocratically muscled from hunting weekends and yachting ventures, or some dashing actor permanently costumed? Because with you, Ben, she can always be certain she holds the upper hand.

When she kisses his cheeks he is aware of their enjowlment; when she looks into his eyes with inexplicable longing he knows the heaviness of his lids and the wild reel of his vision. When she, never letting go his hand, steps gracefully over the marble floor and curtsies, he is aware of his ungainliness. She makes a little minuet, waves for him to dance.

She is so happy, and he will perform. Furtively, grinning encouragement, Sarah begins to work him through the waltz. Despite her years, his wife retains the anxiously made-up bearing, the optimistic confidence, of an understudy who believes that with each passing show she will be called up suddenly to take the lead. But to which, if any, has she been suited? Past performances as Bernadette or Beatrice, young bride to ambitious attorney, as mother to three children—two of which are alive and not yet eighteen—have yet, it seems, to do her abilities justice. The domed promenade in which they twirl he has ordered lit for the occasion of her arrival. He has given her another stage, another role: wife of the conqueror.

At dinner he reads aloud from the choicest threatening letters he has received since arriving in New Orleans. He smiles, laughs with his officers, affects an indignant drawl. He has become correspondent with a hoard of furious oracles who foresee for him various deaths alike only in their specificity. *You will be blown next teusday morning through the back with a shot-gun. You will be stabbed in your (considerable) gut. You will be overwhelmed on the street and hanged from the statue of Gen Jaxson.*

Their authors are anonymous by rule, comprising a panoply of pseudonyms: Brutus; the Asp; Southern Steel; the Bloody Magnolia;

Memphis Jake; Three-Eyes-Watching. One is even addressed from the Devil himself, pleasantly relating the current condition of Hell (he expects a hot summer; the imps are in good health) and his excitement at the general's forthcoming descent. *We eagerly await the return of our most esteemed servant, Benjamin Butler. Yrs in sin, Beelzebub.* Beneath the signature, Butler shows his guests, is the ink-stamp of a cloven hoof.

A good diversion in this vast dining room of sixty tables woven between another array of the massive columns New Orleans believes to be the height of architectural elegance. His officers laugh louder with each flourish of accent and mannerism; Sarah adds her voice on occasion, delighted to be breaking the St. Charles's separation of the sexes for dining.

He neglected to bring the pile whose authors claim to be Union men, those warning of plots and capers and societies of murder. He has noted the names. And he has hidden well those that mention Sarah. Only these called up rage. His wife is to be subjected to various carnal brutalities. Sadeian torments described for the most part in feminine script, bolstering the general's growing impression that the women of this city are more twisted than the men.

He remembers Sarah's words: You can't know a woman's fears.

When he reads a letter "from a Southern Planter's Wife" his staff interrupts the boasts of burnt cotton and indomitability with tales of their own encounters with the fairer sex of the city. Colonel Phelps has been spit upon; George has been subject to lewd hand gestures; Lieutenant Kinsman has been unable to take two steps without the sidewalk clearing of ladies; all have been cursed, harangued, wagged at.

"By God," shouts brother Jackson, clapping at the table. "These women!"

The general feels his rage misplaced, but nonetheless gives it vent. "Sir," he says. "Will you kindly refrain from striking the table like it was a Chinaman's head?"

The space of silence, his wife's pursed lips, his brother's cheek bunched at one corner of a sneer, he fills with a choice bit of the letter.

When you reflect, does not your position fill you with wonder? In the early periods of your existence, a cunning, industrious, cute, little Yankee, running through the streets crying, "Here's the Low-ell Morning In-tel-li-gence!" And now, now! Oh Jove! Look down upon this miracle!

The death the planter's wife offers is inconsequential; she despises him not for invading her country, not for being a Yankee, but for having the gall to have risen above the station she imagines for him. The officers are delighted. Was he really a newsboy, perhaps a printer's devil?

"My husband was not 'born in a garret,'" says Sarah. "I can tell you that much."

Lieutenant Corchoran's band files through the dining room, through the tall French doors and onto the balcony. A few yawps issue from outside. To the blurted tuning of instruments the next course arrives, mushroom-studded doves in gleaming dark gravy.

"And what *do* you think, dear, of your present position?"

Glasses are filled, a sarcastic toast made to the health of his correspondents.

"He worked in a bookstore." Jackson Butler leans in to the nearest officer, a young captain named Rathbone. "Anything else would've bowled little Ben over. He'd have had ten kinds of pneumonia if he was out selling papers, but tucked away with all those books and a nice fire going in the grate—"

Before Jackson can finish, the band roars into the "Star Spangled Banner" and the general allows himself to receive the anthem's strains as an invalid might take the waters. Outside, the crowd warps the lyrics into some bawdy upbraid. His brother smirks at choicely ribald lyrics, loudly continues with his story. The general looks away from the table. They are small and afraid, and none of them seem to understand how much their lives depend on him.

Eight

The Odor of Sanctity

Saturday noon. Life unhinged creaks and gapes, admits those you do not want to see. Elise can hear them, cautious voices in the downstairs parlor, even as Ligeia rustles with her dresses, darning the seams of the suit of heavy mourning black last worn on the occasion of her mother's death. Tiny holes from the mouths of moths to be closed or covered in bunches of crinoline, pills of mouse shit to be dusted off.

It had been Ligeia who, in the early dawn-lit hours, pried her from the roof of the cave, from the face of the black mirror; who gave her water and held the basin and her hair while Elise shuddered through opiate aftermath, and now, as she fits Elise in blackness, gives a false smile and says how her mistress should be proud to have kept her figure all these years.

Since waking, her thoughts have slowly acquired shape, sharpening out of the nightmare haze of the past hours. She forces herself to accept Ligeia's compliment like the bitter tonic it is, saying, "It helped not having another child."

"Yes, Madame. They say the second is the one who makes the hips really spread." Ligeia's gaze returns to her work; she lips a brace of needles. "But I wouldn't know about that."

No, Elise thinks, you wouldn't. Clearer though her thoughts may be, Elise is not yet steady enough to direct them past what is doubtless an insubordinate reference to the difficulties of five years past. To the boy, Robert. Between the juts of starker considerations—her husband's body, her son's condition, her hip pricked just now with needle-tip—there lurks the question of where at this moment Ligeia's son is. Elise allows herself a vision of starched shirt and tails, a silver tray held in white gloves, but the whiteness of the gloves, of the boy's eyes, disperses into bright boles set among a field of brittle stems. No, he would still be too young for house or fieldwork. Sold north he might gather dross, or, if he was bought by a sugar planter, harry rats from green cane stalks. In the city, depending on his price, he could be anything from brewer's skimmer to gambler's runner. She is neither sad nor happy with these outcomes; the boy was sold at Angel's insistence, not hers. Downstairs, a voice rises in pitch for an instant and subsides. Her friends. She knows that the ladies must have thought, and may still, that she pressed to have the boy sold because he was her husband's issue—a shame plantation mistresses may put away for space, but unbearable in urban quarters.

"Almost ready now," Ligeia says.

She had never pressed. She never said a word to Angel on the subject of the boy whose first years were spent in such proximity to their own that they became far more than playmates but had by the age of six and five, respectively, taken on a brotherly aspect.

In many ways, she prefers not to know the boy's fate or her husband's reasons, just as presently she wishes she were not preparing to descend the stairs and see her friends. See his body.

With a breath Elise tests the give of her corset, feels the tensing of the eyelets and laces only she and Ligeia know are colored for mourning. Ligeia, on her knees, pins and threads, and Elise is reconstructed with each stitch, swelling at the girl's supplicant adornment of her, as though she were a statue of the Virgin decorated for a feast day.

"There we are, Madame."

No need to glance in the long mirror. Out the door now while Ligeia collects the scraps and dropped pins from the floor. Take the steps. One more turn. But wait—below, the collective murmur grows and contracts. Inés must be suffering down there, as she always does in the presence of Mme Frick, who by slights punishes the half sister she waggishly calls "adopted," punishes as she never could the father whose resemblance they share. There's her voice now, in bitter lilt:

". . . *really*, my dear, it's not right to complain about your difficulties when Elise has . . ."

She sees Inés buttoning her lip. The lip—so she's told Elise—that her half sister used to say stuck all the way out to the levee, and when little Inés would uncontrollably pout at the taunt, her tormenter would cry with glee, *See! See! It's going all the way to Algiers!* She thinks of their father, thinks of the man who had inflicted them on each other by taking in Inés's mother upon the death of the lady of the house. Elise, of course, had never known him—but how much can we ever really know of men and the fathers they become?

Halted on the second-floor landing, just below the door to Angel's office, Elise is overcome with fathers. Their buried reasons, their malicious love. Her husband often spoke of his—how he never knew the man's name, how he was tortured as a boy for the smallest transgression. Coals on his tongue, a rod across his back. Her own father resides in shadowed attic reaches, where she prefers him, occasionally making himself known in her stride, her voice when angry, the ease with which she dismisses things and people.

Turning back, she finds Ligeia coming down the stairs.

"Go on, Madame. The doctor has M. Angel looking well."

"The doctor? It wasn't you and Bernice?"

"He came yesterday morning when we'd done with the washing. Said there were things he wished to do, to take care of the Monsieur." Another sigh. "You see for yourself."

But Elise is not thinking of her husband's corpse, of the preparation she herself should have performed. "Did he say anything else?"

Ligeia wrenches her gaze from the ceiling, winces.

"No, Madame," she says. Then, thinking better of her answer, she adds, "He said he would be taking care of things. The funeral. That you shouldn't worry."

A tightness claws Elise from chest to temples. "He must've asked what happened. . . ."

The slave's mouth is pursed; she does not blink. "He seemed to have it figured out well enough on his own."

Elise hears her name, followed by a subtle tonal shift in the discussion. She lingers at the landing, hoping not to play so perfectly the role of the widow who walks in and interrupts the bagatelle of mourning-tattle, the parlaying of secrets and guesses, the stealthy hairpin jabs of intentional indiscretion when curiosity has outstripped caution and everyone pretends to be embarrassed for being overheard saying things meant precisely to be.

She is prepared for this, for the eyes turning in sympathetic falsity to her, for the ladies rising, for their sisterly embraces. When she has escaped their arms and their mouths, only then does Elise look to the body resting on a cloth-covered bier in the far corner.

Angel looks wrong among the flowers and scented waters, the plucked blossoms of her hibiscuses and requisite gloomy ratafias of rose and mint and lemon, among which burn small candles whose smoke thinly rises just as it had from his head. Like a dagger in a bassinet.

She breathes deeply, steadying.

From the nuns Elise learned that the bodies of certain saints, and even some laypersons of spotless character, after their deaths gave off a pleasing odor that signified the purity of their souls. And when she was a girl she attended vigils expecting roses, and found only rot. The sweetness heaped around the corpse would only serve to perk her senses, allowing purchase to the rank. But now, sitting in her parlor, instantly enwrapped by her friends' wake-talk politesse and the heat of the closed room, Elise is adding in her head the hours since her husband's death. He should by now be growing rank, but is scentless as a waxwork. She looks again to the bier.

Elise makes note of the ladies: Mme Frick is regally silent; Inés keeps close; Mrs. Schmidt wears an expression of doe-eyed beseeching and says that she has brought cakes; Mme Decorde has gone through the trouble assembling a mourning wreath, but she has waited to ask whether Elise would prefer it hung on the front door or inside, if—

"I wish to keep this more private," Elise finishes for her.

Inés must notice the tremble in her fingers, if not her voice, for she reaches from her wedge at the wing of the sofa nearest to Elise and takes her hand. What is meant for a bolstering squeeze only serves to remind her of the weakness.

Says Decorde, "Dr. Sabatier thought that might be for the best."

"A very *sensible* man," adds Mme Frick. "He was just here, but said he'd come only to make sure the carpenters had come to do their work. Passing through on his way to a meeting with the mayor."

The others' eyes are corner cast; Inés pumps her hand. She knows damn well that her house is not on Emile's way.

Mme Decorde leans forward. "He really did a fine, fine job."

"Oh, yes," says Mrs. Schmidt. "Amazing."

Inés rolls her eyes, and Elise half expects that next they will urge her to go and admire her husband's corpse, to nod appreciation for

117

whatever improvements Emile has made. But they do not ask. Elise, reconstructed in blackness, tries to cling to her small foothold in the newly reconfigured world. Mme Frick, in one of those friendly efforts to misdirect emotion or pain, initiates an unlearned conversation between the others about what the city elders will do today in their meeting with the Union general. Elise takes none of the bait when Frick adds that since the doctor will be attending the meeting, perhaps he will give her a firsthand account.

Inés, closer: "Joseph's fine," she says. "Better, really. Do you know, I found the girl laying at the foot of his bed, him sleeping like an—" She stops herself.

The girl. Some trouble there. She pats Inés's hand. "I'm glad to hear it. Thank you for keeping him." She forces out the words, struggling as she does to reconcile her gladness at hearing that her son is well with the lingering desire not to see him.

Frick is calling the mayor, the city council, and the generals all cowards of one kind or another and the pair, Decorde and Schmidt, more benignly agree. Like that Sunday—a week ago, is that all?—when they were dragging around the neighborhood with their petition, begging for the bombs and shells to rain down.

Inés continues, "You just tell me when you want him back. But for now I'm not minding having a man about the place."

Elise leaves this hooked morsel unbitten as well. It takes no great leap of her occupied faculties to discern that Inés's man, like so many, has trundled off to join the fighting from which New Orleans is now absolved. In their friendship, Inés has always been the one to bring her travails to the forefront, and whereas her friend's difficulties are normally welcome for their relief of Elise's responsibility to confront her own, their contemplation is at the moment an unappealing prospect.

Instead, she takes note of the rug, up the legs of the furniture occupied by her friends, the cups in their hands, Bernice, who, thanklessly and looking as exhausted as Ligeia, had refilled them, and all the sundry household trappings until her focus is the house itself, and conversely herself within it. Her body, which she now owns in a way she has not in her entire life.

The ladies' dialogue comes to an abrupt end as they each slowly bring their eyes to Elise, drawn by her untethered glancing. In searching both the faces of her guests, now pinched in unsettlingly tolerant scrutiny, and her own nagging fear, she finds the reason she cannot yet see her son, why she would rather have him ensconced until the funeral with the strange little girl doing God knows what than at her side. She couldn't stand for Joseph to look at her the way these women do—with suspicion. And, she knows, he will.

As though I'm the one—she thinks, and the words slam in her mind with the same sorry dull triumph as did the birthday pistol on her husband's papers; and her head is filled not with the roar of report that followed but the gunshot's tailing tinnitic whine that mounts to a shrieking spear of pain driven through her ears until, in vain hope to let free the noise, she strains her jaw wide.

No sound escapes her. And for an instant, opening her eyes, she sees Emile coming with the others who have risen from their chairs. Then he is gone and there is only the surge of black-clad female bodies. She crumples in the chair as they close in, makes herself small as though to save her softer parts from their mauling sympathy.

Nine

Meeting

Not so ugly as he's drawn, the general. A sound taxonomist might call him ursine, knowing that the closest relative of the bear is the pig. Yes, Butler embodies the indistinct space between: bearishly broad yet hog-jowled, powerful yet pitifully acquisitive, overturning massive logs to nose for the smallest grub.

Cyanosis's vector sits behind a massive table, his officers in apostolic flank, a uniformity of chestnut hair covering their heads and faces to varying extents. A stark contrast to what could be a troupe of actors—so varied are the persons and costumes of nativist mayor, justice of the peace, court recorders, councilmen, attorneys, and Creole functionaries and businessmen. The doctor has come with these emissaries of the city to the unexpected arena of the ladies' parlor of the St. Charles, arrayed in a crescent of chairs embroidered with Oriental blooms, occupying places where their wives would have sat in better days.

Dr. Sabatier is here as representative of the Board of Health and Sanitation. When the time is right, Pierre Soulé had said, when they were all gathered in the mayor's offices swimming in the smoke of anxiously puffed cigars, talk about yellow fever, give them a scare.

The seating arrangement must be some calculation on the general's part, a deliberate unmanning of the New Orleanians now they have at last come into the esteemed presence after days of delay. The general will not give them his eye, looks to his officers for the assent to begin.

And those eyes! See how they struggle even to move orderly side to side, much less hold focus. An easy diagnosis of strabism, present no doubt from childhood. Worse yet, puddled lids reduce his strabic orbs to slivers; he raises them only so much as he goes about the salutations and introductions, apologizes that General Williams could not be present as he is at *this moment* maintaining order over the *roaring mob* of *your* citizens massed outside these walls. The hooded gaze in which the general holds them could be mistaken for dolorous contempt. Dr. Sabatier knows better: blepharoptosis of the . . . ?

He has lost the name of the afflicted muscle, and outside the people are indeed roaring. On the emissaries' arrival at the St. Charles a leprous-white orange relieved Mayor Monroe—particularly injuring, one would think, to the esteem of a man elected on a populist wave— of his hat; jets of tobacco juice were spit at them by young men whose ballooning cheeks reminded the doctor of statues at a Roman fountain, staining the lapels of various dignitaries and even spoiling the philosophic tumble of Pierre's hair, now slick against his forehead.

The commanding general brings his peroration to an end with the word *cooperation*, and a strapping young officer with major's bars produces a sheaf of papers and, standing, reads an invocation of the United States, its laws, provender, and sanctity restored henceforth.

The doctor listens, semi-intent. On either side of him the emissaries twitch with every mention of the nation they have for the past year cursed from taproom to platform, and the general must be relishing their patellar-like jumps—see the creeping satisfaction at the corners of his drooping lids.

"*Levator palpabrae superiorus,*" the doctor whispers to himself. That's the muscle; and with proper tools in the right hands it would be so easily corrected. Pierre, from his place at the right hand of Mayor Monroe, fixes him with a sideways glare.

And it might be safe to assume that this General Butler knows his audience shoots, hangs, drowns, and draws him according to the justice of their minds. Doubtful, though, that Butler imagines one has him on a gurney brought into no ordinary sawbones' garret but the operating theatre of the doctor's dreams.

"Thrice before," reads the officer, "the city of New Orleans has been rescued from the hands of a foreign government and still more calamitous domestic insurrection by the money and arms of the United States. . . ."

The emissaries grumble, and the doctor watches the faces behind which the cogs of duller minds slowly mesh in effort to discern which three. The United States in their magnanimity liberating us from Napoleon's France and puppet-Spain; the United States in their unending graciousness saving us from one of their own, Aaron Burr; the United States in their caring husbandry sending Andrew Jackson to redeem New Orleans and sweep across the lowland south in bloody horror for the next two years. The doctor steps back from the door of the operating theatre for a moment, the Battle of New Orleans on his mind, where the commanding general's father fought, so Pierre had said. The father who died of yellow fever. So Butler considers himself descended of American liberators, his inheritance: the duty to save this troublesome city. The weight of a father he never knew. And what more do we inherit from our fathers than expectations? Save perhaps for a congenital defect of the eyelid.

The proclamation rumbles onward to its litany of edicts: protection of the flag of the United States; the oath of allegiance for those who wish it; the return of Federal property . . .

Nothing can be done for Butler's strabism, but the ptosis can be handled in a cinch. Through the anteroom of his dream theatre, where baths of boiling water fill the air with steam and taps of antiseptic await his hands, the instruments hang purified on hooks. His ablutions made, the doctor dons his sterilized smock and enters the glass dome of the theatre by a door sealed with India rubber. The door sucks shut and here is his patient, transferred to a zinc table, fixed by grips into a supine position, his head held in padded clamps.

"All assemblages of persons in the streets, either by day or night, tend to disaster and are forbidden."

In the dream theatre Dr. Sabatier is sealed off from the poisons of the world; the air he breathes passes through steel compartments in which gas flames burn away the smallest infections. If he wishes to address the students and colleagues seated round the dome, he may do so through a tube that runs out the glass into an immense tympanum.

"And, finally, it may be sufficient to add, without further enumeration that all the requirements of martial law will be imposed."

General Butler's fists are balled on the tabletop. He straightens himself, raises his chin, and nods thanks to the young officer, who resumes his seat. Without salutation the general begins: He wishes to leave the municipal authority alone. He is not here to collect taxes and try pickpockets. He wishes to confine himself to the duties of governing his department.

"The question is," he says, "whether you gentlemen are amenable."

Outside, the rioters have taken up a guttural chant, punctuated by handclaps. The councilmen look to their betters; Mayor Monroe investigates his boots; the chief of police seems bewildered by a problem not solvable by lash or baton. It is Pierre who leans forward from the pack.

"If it is the case that you want nothing more than to govern your military department, I would say the best place for you, General, to do so would be in Chalmette or Algiers. Not New Orleans."

The doctor is making his first incision—an ellipsis from the eyebrow fold across the lid. An orderly spirits the offending flap away.

"I am accustomed," Butler says, "to hearing threats from Southern gentlemen, but I must confess I did not expect to hear them on this occasion."

Pierre must know the ire to come; he presses heedless on as if to speed its arrival: "No threat intended, General Butler. I only hope to show you the spirit of your convictions. Your true nature. If you wish only to govern your department, you'll find it much easier to do outside the city limits." A catlike grin now. "I understand that General McClellan holds the same opinion."

An overstep. A brash mistake, Pierre.

The general glares, and the doctor presently gives him more orb to direct his rage. In his dream theatre the doctor pares lachrymal flesh from yellow rind, makes harp-string plucks of ligature. The steaming hands of his orderlies dab for effluence and he makes his three-point sutures of silver thread.

The walls of the ladies' parlor receive the crowd-roar like breakers. Pierre sits back, eyes the mayor for a rejoinder that will never come.

"Martial law will only make things worse," says Soulé. "And we are coming to the fever season. You must think of your men. . . ."

Here is his place. He is supposed to blunder into the same trap as Pierre. But this is not the same Pierre who could secure the acquittal of a Walker; Pierre Soulé would not be making these blundering moves. This is an exhausted man, a man whipped by his position, having climbed to uncertain elevations and found the air chokingly thin.

General Butler inhales, a look of recognition on his face. He says that he has made a study of yellow fever for some time, and when this foolishness is at an end he will apprise them of his plans and the parts the municipal government is to play. "Now, didn't General Lovell govern New Orleans under martial law?"

Before Pierre can answer, here is Mayor Monroe: "That was to protect the city from traitors!"

"You mean Union men."

Pierre is shaking his head, allows the mayor to take his place in this paltry Socratic.

"How many 'traitors' had General Lovell to contend with?"

"I couldn't say. Hundreds, maybe."

"Well," says General Butler. "If martial law was good enough to keep down a hundred traitors, then I suppose it will do for me to govern a hundred thousand.

"What you all have to accept," he says, "what I will make you accept is that New Orleans *is* a conquered city. And get this straight, gentlemen: it has been conquered for years. Have you looked at the figures? The population of your city is greater than Boston, just behind Philadelphia, and for a good run you exploded with growth; your commerce was gigantic. I salute you. New Orleans was—and some of you may think it is—to be the jewel of the West. Controlling the Mississippi and the commerce of her contiguous states, she would in time rival the cities of the East.

"And whether you realized it or not you were in combat with the central states and the East all along. You have been fighting a commercial war, and you have lost. The army hasn't conquered you; the Erie Canal *has*. A mid-country farmer can ship his goods east without exiting your little cloaca here. Are you following me, gentlemen? You plateaued. Even before the onset of hostilities your commerce was flagging, exports down by thirty percent.

"Yes, gentlemen, I'm afraid New Orleans fell long before I arrived. Of course, New Orleans will hang on. She will be prosperous enough, a slow death, and in the end will be the sum of her absurdities, of her failings. So do not presume to behave as though your city deserves any deference, as though you hold the key to anything more than a curiosity. Do not presume that I come here in awe or fear. I come here to govern my department, to see to it that through your foolishness you don't hasten the death of your city."

Pride rises like steam from his officers, and the emissaries stir in their flowered chairs in various attitudes of dejection and affront.

The glint of the doctor's needle is not unlike that which appears in the general's eyes as something thuds off the near window.

"George," says the general to the young officer who'd read the proclamation. "Go and tell General Williams to instruct the mob that if they do not desist he will turn the cannons on them."

"S-sir!" Mayor Monroe might fall from his chair and the others babble pleas as the officer exits on his errand. Hens in the yard, gabbling round the block. Other than himself, the doctor finds only Pierre is silent. The stare of a duelist.

When the officer returns, the crowd is in sustained howl. General Williams cannot hold them, he says.

"Well then, George, give General Williams the order to fire at will." And with calculating glance to the mayor's paling face, he adds, "That is unless Mr. Monroe would care to address them. Otherwise the grapeshot will do its work."

The doctor is drawn from his reverie now, sees himself hustling through a scoured crowd, the fallen with eyes aghast regarding their own entrails, the piecemeal scattering of human form, the ubiquity of blood. And perhaps Mayor Monroe sees the same, for he is presently urged to his feet, follows the officer out of the ladies' parlor to the near balcony with the dragging gait of a condemned man belaboring the trip to the scaffold.

All are silent, listening to the resounding yowls outside, soon subsiding, and the mayor's voice wavering above an undercurrent of growl. The men in the parlor fiddle with their cuffs, itch their moustaches, exchange glances and scowls until, to a sudden wave of applause and condemnation stoppered by the closing of the balcony doors, the mayor returns. Wiping his forehead, slinging sweat to the floor, Monroe throws himself to his chair. The people will disperse.

And now Mayor Monroe is the other sort of condemned man, the one who strides to the noose so swiftly he outpaces priest and hangman both.

"You talk about threats," says the mayor. "And that's what you've given us." He looks to the others. "A-and if that's what you want, then I hereby suspend the city government and all its functions. Do as you see fit."

Monroe dangles, feet kicking for ground. The emissaries will not speak. The doctor watches this butcherly incision fill with blood until he can no longer stand it. Staunch the flow, man.

"A point of order," says the doctor. "If I may." Heads turn; Monroe gives him a snort. "A matter this grave cannot be disposed until it has been considered and acted upon by the entire council, in session."

Pierre has the mayor by the shoulder, gives him a word. "Yes, yes," says Monroe the longshoreman, used very much to stirring crowds of workmen while the moneyed and scented whisper in his ear, for an instant seems thankful for this absolution before turning bilious to the doctor. "And when would the esteemed councilman prefer such a meeting to occur?"

Without pause the doctor says, "Tomorrow morning, ten o'clock?"

And in his dream theatre Dr. Sabatier steps to one of the antiseptic taps, rinses and dries, takes the speaking tube in hand, and addresses the onlookers, careful in his oration not to betray a note of triumph. The general lies sutured and sedate; what could be a smile parts his lips. Dr. Sabatier thumbs closed the tube as students and colleagues rise, and he cannot hear their applause, rather the hiss of the purifying flames. He, breathing pure perfection, bows.

When the mayor agrees, it is as though the air has been let out of the room; the emissaries swiftly seek exit and breath, orderlies appear with their hats and coats and the audience haphazardly dissolves. They will reconvene with General Butler after the council meeting tomorrow.

Risen, Dr. Sabatier takes his hat and cane from an eyebrowless young man, sees Soulé watching him darkly from the doorway where the emissaries crowd and confer. Poor Pierre, he has no idea how far the fall will be.

"One moment, sir."

The doctor turns to see General Butler coming from behind his table, breaking free of his milling staff. Quick for such a stumpy man. How quickly he bridges the gap, extends a hand.

"I hate a meeting where nothing is decided," Butler says. "Don't you, mister . . . ?"

He gives his title and name. "It happens too often. We end up back at the beginning."

"You are on the board of health, are you not?"

The doctor smiles. "I am. And I would like very much to speak with you about the city's present sanitary condition. That is, when you have the time."

The general sizes him up in the minute way of a man who prides himself on his observance. "Absolutely. Next week. Monday afternoon?"

He cannot withhold his excitement, so close to the infection he is supporting blue. "If you were to enact but a few of the measures—"

"Measures of yours," the general says.

"Suggestions. As yet ignored."

General Butler smiles. "Ignored by your fellows, eh?" He puts a hand to the doctor's back, leads him to the doorway. Pierre and Mayor Monroe are lingering at the steps leading down to the barroom. "I should say they owe you a debt, doctor. Though they'll be loath to show it."

"My only concern," he says, "is for the welfare of the city and her government."

"Well, come calling Monday, three o'clock," says General Butler. "Whether there's still a city government or not."

Ten
The Ovens

The cemetery sweats. Dew drips from angel wings and makes name-wormed obelisks illegible. Glossy vaults, facsimiles of mansions for occupants of child-height. The procession weaves the slickened monuments and statuary, and Joseph avoids the eyes of the stone people, dabs his face for they cannot. Sunday morning, the fourth of May, as Ligeia told him—*you'll want to remember the day*—when she helped dress him in the funeral suit he has about outgrown. Thin wrists jut from the cuffs of his frock coat, foreshortened trousers retreat from his ankles. He lets his chin sink into the piled cravat Ligeia cinched tight not thirty minutes ago, when he was brought for the first time in two days home, to be dressed and presented to his mother. She who reaches over and lifts his chin as they go, a few steps behind his father's coffin. He lags, rejects her pace—the same strides with which she took the stairs.

It is two years since he's had need of these clothes, since the passing of the grandmother who was his great instructor in the ministrations of death. Their outings were chiefly to the memorials, vigils, masses, and interments of those crossed over, hushed graveside conversation he knew by tone to be secret and thus marvelous, the crow-walk rustle of the ever-diminishing group of old women. From Mamere, aged and abandoned of husband and all her children save Joseph's mother, he learned that death is an ornate matter, and delicate. Handle it as carefully as a demitasse. Give the dead fitting monuments, care for them as you did in life. But there were harsher lessons too. How she showed him the place where those who do not matter go, those for whom none care enough to mourn. The ovens, she called them. And they do appear better suited for bread than bodies, these half-moon tombs piled four-high and in rows of a dozen, making up the walls that enclose the finer graves.

This is where his father will go, in the coffin borne by sextant's men whom Dr. Sabatier, at the head of their train like a priest, directs towards a black-sheeted trestle beneath an open half-moon. Here the coffin comes to rest; the procession halts.

Joseph tries not to look into the oven's mouth. He tries not to imagine its previous tenant.

The city owns them, Mamere would say. *You pay rent by the year, and if you miss, if your family doesn't pay, what do they do? Men come with shovels and they scrape you right out.*

His mother holds him tighter; Dr. Sabatier has begun to speak. Joseph cannot hear the voice of his father's friend, only the rake of shovel-blade over stone and the crackling of flames. *That's where you go once they've scraped you out. To the fire, to the pit where the fever-dead go in the bad days when there are too many bodies and not enough earth and stone and time.* Like much of the cemetery, he has seen this place too: a collier's mound, fed with embers and the disinterred. He was eight when the fever last raged, when he and his mother were packed off to the house at Berwick's Bay to wait until the air crisped and the dying was done. He remembers seeing the bodies on the way to the train station, laid out in rows along the street, filthy sheets and bedclothes piled in the yards of shacks. The flies. At least in the oven there would be no flies. *But the weather here is bad for a body, baby. If you don't have a good copper casket, or a lead one . . . if you're in the ovens . . . in a few months it's all they can do to shovel what's left of you.*

The doctor talks on and Joseph feels the sweat on his mother's palm. The ladies huddle close, distinguishable only by the patterns of their veils. Beside Mlle Pichon is Marina, borrowed shawl hanging overlong to her waist. She stretches past the swell of Mlle Pichon's chest and meets his look.

After two days shut away in Marina's room, he is not sure if he knows any more about her than he did when she was a window-bound specter. He knows that he feels better when she touches him; he knows that she misses her parents. She likes to ask questions—better still to be asked them, because she likes to tell. Of microscopes and the way island sand looks beneath them, of soldiers playing princes, their general a monster.

Past Marina, down the far end of the oven wall lean a pair of men. They have no shovels, rather a wheelbarrow piled with bricks and tools of masonry. They wait with the detached impertinence of workmen.

Joseph turns, tries to hold to the doctor's words. He calls his father a man of achievement, of honor. A man who was present at the laying of the foundations of this state. Mamere would call his father a fright. She would cross herself whenever she spoke of him. *You are not like him, my dear.*

A gurgle in his mother's throat as at some signal the coffin is borne upward and driven home. Now the ladies flutter about, encircle them, and he is pared from his mother's grip, his head stroked, his cheeks though dry are attacked with embroidered monograms. He thinks this is how a man must feel when he is mortally shot or stabbed and the people rush out to dab their handkerchiefs in his infamous blood. He is pressed from one breast to the next, bandied between hoops of skirt, fingernails behind his ear guide his cheek to the mysterious give of flesh beneath fabric. With each soft depression his stomach grows upset; he sees in the corner of his eye the doctor and his mother off alone, talking. In somber fury the ladies crouch around him, cooing, dabbing, embracing, trying to wring out tears, and at their periphery moves Marina.

They let him loose at last and form a little circle to coo more at what they imagine will be a precious sight of the little girl comforting the little boy; Marina shakes her head and tries to break from their cordon but she is pushed, urged now to go and give him a sisterly embrace, a kiss on each cheek. Marina performs, her lips curled inward so that he feels her teeth, and they are separated but set free, she disappearing within the drove of ladies, he urged towards the gate and the carriages without by the cupping hand of Dr. Sabatier. The hand that, when he was small, had pressed down on his chest while its fellow applied stitches to the lip he'd split on fireplace bricks. He remembers struggling under the man, cursing; he remembers his father in the doorway listening while Joseph fought the needle and screamed that his father would kill this goddamned bastarding man. *My daddy will kill you, you sonofabitch I swear.*

His father's son, the doctor had said when he finished. And Joseph, hissing blood, had seen his father's shoulders shaking in the doorway, laughing.

He must find out the tomb's rent, make sure that his father is never scraped out. Climbing after her into the carriage, he tries to ask his mother but the doctor shuts the door loudly behind him and the horses trundle off. So he presses to the window and watches the mourners recede until they turn onto Toulouse.

His mother is a shadowy presence beside him. The carriage bucks, its springs squeal, and all the while she looks only at him.

After a time she says, "You know what happened."

They have come to a stretch of uneven brick and Joseph is shaken to his bones. His voice quakes as he answers her. Yes, he knows.

The shadow shivers differently than him; she rustles in her blackness and nods to herself.

"Will I stay at home with you tonight?" he says.

Shadow-mother hunches over, hands at her face. This is the second time in days that he has made his mother cry. She peels back her veil and studies him with squinting eyes.

"Of course you will," she says. "You're mine, aren't you?"

PART 3

Uterine Fury

One

Vannuchi's Museum

Admission: fifty cents for adults, twenty-five for children and slaves. Marina stands before the doorway of the house of wonders, unsure whether she likes the leveling of price, whether she is worth more or less than a slave. She would ask Joseph but he dawdles a ways off, nearer to the street where cabs and gigs roll by. In the two weeks since his father's funeral he has been intermittently in Mlle Pichon's charge—and so in hers as well—for day-trips to parks and shows and galleries. He watches the human tide of a Tuesday forenoon, so small he disappears for a time in the surge of Canal Street. And she is glad for these chances to escape her room, glad for the chance to be near him, glad to escape Mme Frick's interminable sewing bees, where Pichon and the others work at an enormous gilt-fringed flag for a rebel regiment while Marina, pressed into service for her size, fetches dropped thimbles and needles and spools of thread.

When Mademoiselle calls for them to take their tickets and go in, Joseph hustles over to hold the door. Mademoiselle, passing through, gives no regard to his kindness, the way those who know they are women and beautiful do. Marina follows her in, suddenly aware of the awkwardness of her limbs, the outsized gangle of her gait. Lately she has practiced walking in the mirror of her room, approximating what she remembers of her mother's step, but she feels herself go into the museum with neither the unthinking nimbleness of a child nor the hip-led grace of a woman. She is the link strained by both ends of its chain. The door shuts and Joseph follows after her.

Darkness infused with carpet musk and trapped breath. Music and the hushed voices of other visitors pipe from deeper reaches, all bound in an increasing drone. The corridor grows lighter; at its end stand six figures in the wigs and full footmen livery of another century. She is not bothered by their glossy, frozen features; she has seen wax-works before. But she has never seen wax men whir to life and execute in concert a courtly bow.

Marina skitters through, almost running into Mademoiselle, who gives the footmen a giggling curtsy. The wax men slowly go upright and Marina, looking over her shoulder, tries to find some surprise in Joseph's face.

"They're mechanical," he says, grinning.

Marina nods and tries again to govern her steps.

Now through circuitous rooms, each set with a stage upon which figures opulently rendered enact brief instances of history. Brass rails separate patron from the replicated; placards denote the players and scenes.

A wild-eyed Garibaldi raises an implacable fist above the table where he confers with Louis-Napoléon, the emperor's head swiveling in perpetual dismissal or disbelief. On the next stage the same Louis glides in a loop through the gates of Paris, both retreating and reclaiming. So goes clockwork history. Beneath the stage the hidden mechanisms drone.

A biblical wing: Joseph knows her ignorance of Old Testament scenes; he points, gives verses, directs her with brushes of shoulder. Jacob wrestled the angel out of ignorance; Joshua halted the sun above Gideon so that Israel could have more time to avenge itself upon its enemies.

Joseph likes this, telling her what he learned from his father—not only Protestant but a preacher at one time. She knows it makes him happy to remember obliquely the man he's told her shows up nightly in his dreams, just as she tells Joseph about the chandlery in Havana, about the sugar plantation her father managed and the stretch over the great railroad whose construction he oversaw.

Now scenes more to her knowledge: the Virgin flees with bundled infant Christ towards an Egyptian horizon toothed by pyramids; beneath a glittering crystal star, beasts and kings kneel before the manger; Jesus in full waxen-flower of manhood breaks bread at the Last Supper while a keen-eyed Judas looks on. There is no Crucifixion, but the trial of Christ is a massive affair of thirty figures—apostles mill; the Savior looks downcast; centurions spear back indignant Jews from Pilate's dais.

Mademoiselle waves them on into the Hall of War. Hitching, repetitive violence. Dull conflicts pass on. Here Joseph seems even more alive than at the biblical wing: his eyes are wide; he lingers at the ropes. Boys and war, always the same. With displeasure she remembers how, in San Antonio de los Baños, all the games where boys were concerned would inevitably become battles—sticks for sabres, stones for shot, cries to charge and slay. She remembers coming home one day furious and bloodied at the nose, her father explaining that it was in boys' nature to play at war. *And your nature*, her mother added as she tilted Marina's head back so that the blood ran down her throat, *should lead you to avoid it.*

A shrouded exhibit: musket barrels poke from sheet-covered figures. A battle of ghosts—one phantom side charging, the other turned in flight. Joseph antsy at the placard overhung with a sign stating that this exhibit has been: CLOSED BY THE ORDER OF MAJ. GEN. BENJAMIN F. BUTLER, MAJ. GEO. C. STRONG ADJNT.

The presence of Major Strong's name is still scarcely believable, though she's seen it many times at doors and shopwindows on printed leaflets, auction notices below red pennants signifying closure to the illiterate. And with the major's name comes his face: Americanly symmetrical, proportionate in the way common only to the soldiers in blue. Rare is a hooked nose or deep-set eyes or lips dark and overlarge; if they are what they appear to be—cast toy soldiers—Major Strong is the mold. On Ship Island, in the worst days of her suffering, he would tell her about Vermont, his home. Where, in winter, snow falls so thickly it covers your windows in a night.

"Manassas," Joseph says. He has lifted the order from the placard, plucks at the sheet of the nearest ghost and raises it to reveal boot and butternut knee.

She has heard this word before, spoken as a curse by the soldiers on Ship Island, bitterly invoked in the jagged way her mother would talk of Uncle Willie's women. For Joseph the word is breathless happiness itself as he reads to her from the placard: THE GREAT VICTORY OF THE SOUTHERN CONFEDERACY, LED BY OUR GLORIOUS GENERAL BEAUREGARD, DEPICTED HERE.

She searches the ghosts for the rebel general, New Orleans's hero, but they are each shrouded alike.

"We beat them at Manassas," Joseph says. "We could've gone all the way to Washington and it would've all been over."

She grinds her teeth. There is no *we*. I am not one of you.

He has caught some sight of her anger, a fiery inkling, when Mlle Pichon snaps at him to put the sign down and for them to come along.

A vast space is devoted to the Battle of New Orleans: General Jackson and his men crouch behind cotton bales, felling rows of Redcoats who are by gears resurrected only to be killed again. Joseph's father, he says, fought here, lost an arm here, saving the state and the country from the British. He clings tight to the rope and looks at the wax men as though he can see his father among them. Her hands, larger, rest beside his clenched fists. And what she does next is beyond her control; she might be a wax reproduction of herself who at the behest of clockwork bends to his face, meeting his widening eyes, and plants a misaimed kiss at the corner of his mouth.

Before either of them can speak—his mouth and hers moving, yes, but forming nothing like words—Mlle Pichon steers them by their necks, sighing. They share a look of mutual disbelief that crazes into a smile and there is no time to consider the kiss, for they are driven into the corridor of the Grand Aquarium.

Faint light plays in swirling mottles across wall and floor. Mademoiselle has let them loose, but Marina cannot tell how close he is. Around them fish dart and glide, alone or schooled depending on their nature. Sharks hang docile before signs directing you to mind glass smudged with a ghostly hundred imprints of fingertip and palm. She presses close, watches a devilfish roil its arms and pluck through a pile of oystershell. Now Joseph's reflection is beside her, then his person, nose doubled on the portal. Together they follow the intersecting paths of watery life.

The final marvel is an open tank of amphibious beasts. A swampy reek: the water murky with the creatures' leavings, patrolled by a pair of model steamships puffing smoke and occasionally menaced by the tail-wag of a small alligator or thudding off shells of turtles. Mlle Pichon is particularly tickled when the alligators are sloshed with a bucket of offal for feed.

The larger steamship nudges at one corner of the tank, a frog clambering atop its prow.

141

Like a drowning man. Like the ones scurrying up the sinking rigging until all they have to hold is water. She sees them from the lifeboat, waving just before they are pulled under.

When they have at last exited the museum and stand squinting for the sun, Marina is suspicious of the outside, the people walking by, the trundling carts, all seemingly motivated by the same hidden machinery, moving in predetermined paths.

Shouts and boos from down the way. Workmen and vagrants and gartered clerks and even women—their fists bunching skirt-folds, the veins at their necks where the white powder meets their true color—have stopped and turned their vicious attention to the street.

Joseph looks to her, his lip twisted, says, "It's them."

That voice again. The same drawled growl. His father's voice, his horrible inheritance.

Now Joseph's back is to her and she can see them too—soldiers riding three abreast, their faces obscured by the feathers of Mademoiselle's hat and the shaking fists of the crazed people. The soldiers halt before a turning cart. Joseph curses louder in his other voice, the voice of the low-tide-stinking people on the docks at Biloxi who shouted at—

Major Strong. Holy Mary, it is.

Stock-still seconds pass as through feathers and fists and rage-crumpled hats she sees flashes of his face—jaw upturned, utterly calm above these jeering beasts to whose voices she adds her own, only she is calling out his name. She jumps for height, to catch his eye, and whenever she comes back to ground there is Joseph, glaring. Major Strong doesn't hear. The cart moves on, the horsed men lurch forward. Landing, she darts for them but there is a hand at her arm, hauling her back.

Joseph's eyes are burning; his mouth slackens, lips skinned back from his teeth. She tries to pull her arm free, dragging him by inches into the cursing crowd but he will not let go and he will not stop shouting in that awful voice, now turned on her. His face is all anger and hurt; he wants to know: *Why*? They tug against each other in one motion, almost as if they were working towards the same end, until Mlle Pichon's voice sounds and she has them both by the backs of their necks again.

Mademoiselle steers them from the curb, prying Joseph's hand loose, and jabs a finger in his face, hissing to know what is wrong with him and why he's acting like he knows isn't right even for a child, which he's not. The hurt and anger bleed from his face; his chin sinks to his chest.

Now it is Marina's turn: Pichon whipping round so that the feathers of her hat take to the air and she is for a ridiculous instant holding down her hat with one hand while the other raises smartly to her shoulder, then whips round in a slap.

Marina staggers back. Her head strikes the window of the museum, knocking out a stream of explanation. If only she can make this woman understand—they are her friends . . .

"Shut your mouth." Mademoiselle casts a glance back to the crowd now surging on after the soldiers, and squares Marina in eyes that are all the more damning for how close they are to tears. "You don't know a thing, you silly little bitch."

Marina blinks, jams shut her eyelids over and again in hopes the world might change. But here still is Uncle Willie's zamba, regarding her with the same look of watery anger, and Joseph meekly approaching.

She straightens herself, wipes at her hips and legs and elbows as though she'd fallen to the ground. She reaches for the dull throb at the back of her skull and feels for a welt, but her hair—updone and piled with a rolled stocking for height, the long plaits themselves wound into a complex knot by the hands of Mademoiselle's girl, in a fashion more garish than she ever would have at home—has saved her.

The zamba says they should be going and starts off a few harsh paces past slump-shouldered Joseph, who avoids Marina's eyes so that she must bend awkwardly to confront him, the blow still sounding in her head. Or is that the whir of gears?

How many machines operate this boy? One to make him howl at her in that horrible voice, another to make him take her kiss—to take her hands, just as he'd done in what she is no longer sure was sleep, squeezing.

Mlle Pichon calls out for them to come along, these two now conjoined. And Marina wonders at the number of her own machines, for even as she wishes to throw his hands away, she does not let them go.

Two

A Matter of Business

In the courtyard of the Custom House, Admiral Farragut is shrieking:

"Damn the uniform! Burn it!" A sound of shattered glass. "Not water, you fool! Spirits! Spirits!"

The admiral, naked and raving behind an honor guard of aides who protect with unfurled horse blankets his flailing modesty, these parting briefly to admit a corporal rushing back from the medical stores with bottles clutched to his chest. Holding his end of a blanket high, a member of the honor guard casts a baleful look over his shoulder in the direction of General Butler.

At the open window of his office in the Custom House, he listens to the man who stole his glory hiss and spit geysers of grain alcohol. Evidently, when the doxies of a particular house had emptied the contents of their chamber pots down onto the passing admiral, his mouth had been open.

And he would be savoring a smile were it not for the presence of his older brother, redolent of distillation as no doubt our intrepid admiral is at this very moment. So he shuts the window, returns to filial obligations.

"So," says Jackson. "I made my survey of the saloons. . . ."

"Thoroughly, it seems."

"That's right." Jackson claps his hands to his knees, leans forward. "So, when do you give the order to shut them down?"

Some of the more puritanical officers have come to him bemoaning the men's slide into drunkenness. Drunk on watch, drunk on duty, drunk at mess and parade. *This city sweats spirituous liquors, General, and the weak-willed souls lap it up. There must be something you can do.* And, of course, there is.

"A few days at most," Butler says.

Jackson nods in mock thoughtfulness. "Now, I don't think we should buy out the larger, gentleman's saloons until—"

"I'll tell you again. We're not buying the saloons, Jackson," he says. "You will wait two weeks from the time I close them down, then you will buy their liquor." He pauses, allowing the order to penetrate the twilit depths of his brother's murky understanding. "You will buy their stores, and those of the importers. And three weeks later, when the owners are desperate, I will reinstate the drinking houses and saloons and you will sell their liquor back to them at double cost."

Elder brother huffs, looks about the office, readying himself to speak. And it is, the general knows, not the stupid man who is the most frustrating, but the stupid man who believes he is bright, strains his hamstrung faculties with overthinking, as Jackson does now.

"But, Ben, the money from the liquor's nothing compared to the real estate!"

"Real estate is a fool's game."

"You've made money at it before."

"Do you think housing values are due to increase in the South anytime soon? Or perhaps you foresee a rise in demand?"

"N-no, but right now we can get the places cheap."

"This isn't California—where you have to rush out and hammer your flag in the first mudhole you see." The general stops to watch his brother's eyes lower to the floor.

"It's an investment, Ben," Jackson addresses the boards. "An investment for the future. For when the war's over. I thought you'd respect that."

"When the war is over," Butler says, "any scrap of land or building will cost a quarter of what you'd pay today, you follow? *That* is when we buy property. So now consider liquor, which will only grow cheaper as trade is reinstated and Lincoln lifts the blockade, per my request. The liquor gives us a quick turnaround on a relatively small investment. A prospect I thought *you* would find particularly enticing, if not worthy of respect."

His brother has given up on the floor, looks now to the papers, logs, and inkstands that separate them and, yes, across the years and achievements, the inches of height and pounds of sinew, across the childhood battles for a mother's affections and the endless times when they would set themselves before her in competitions—who has drawn the better ship? who has leapt the highest? who has caught the biggest fish?—she was too much a mother to truthfully judge. Butler has learned the lesson from his experience of fatherhood: Of course a parent knows one child is more skilled or the better leaper, more intelligent or handsome, than the other. But you hide behind some false equalizing love: *Oh, children, I could never choose. I love you both the same.* And you leave them to fight among themselves, though each knows the truth.

Jackson's thoughts have taken another turn: "You know what one of them said to me today?"

"I can't imagine."

"I was at this run-down little shack of a bar, asking how was business, and this man—thickest drawl you can imagine, not a ball team of teeth in his head—called me, all Yankees, *indefatigable*. Indefatigable hunters of money, he said." Elder brother's face grows wistfully bemused. "You'd never think a man like that could muster such a phrase."

"And what did you say to this unexpected erudition?"

"Well, I was soreheaded I'll admit. So I said to him that Southerners were too lazy, too slow."

"And we're quicker, more industrious."

"Right."

"And that's what you believe?"

Jackson chews his cheek. "No, not really. I'd say, Reb or not, everyone wants money just as bad. Some of us just have the better method."

Like a pair of brothers holding up pages drawn with sailing ships to a mother's sigh-slung face, both wanting the same commodity of approval, dominance of the heart. You do not shout and mawk and beg the way your brother does; you know you've drawn the better ship whether Mother says so or not. No comfort, though, when brother can take you out back, knock you down, and pin behind your back the small, careful hand that drew so well, wrenching till you scream surrender in whatever terms he likes.

With a scowl he cannot fight, Butler says, "Well, we agree on this point, at least."

Three

The Arteries of the City

Legs of furniture pierce the surface scum of the New Basin Canal, and like the wrecked ships that haunt inhospitable coasts, in their brokenness the legs and arms and shattered ladderbacks reveal the reason for their abandonment as do the staved jugs and neckless bottles, the twisted kittens trailing placentae like shadow-selves, of whom dogs, barrel-chested with bloat, bob in slow pursuit. The results of city policy both official and unwritten: mass-poisoning of strays, violence and waste, inveterate carelessness.

The New Basin runs the western edge of the city, through the American reaches of the First District and northward into the sparser immigrant huddles where pigs root beside sooty children, and from there on into the lake. To the east its sister artery, the Carondelet, cuts a miasmic swath through the Second District, the Creole quarter, and on into Bayou St. Jean.

Now the veins of New Orleans, long riddled with rot, will at last be purged.

Among the discard and flotsam, burnished in the red haze of afternoon, Dr. Sabatier watches a pair of Yankee engineers slog along the banks with poles and equipment, the lips of their high boots marked with grime as the ebb-rimed grasses they part. The engineers, Massachusetts sublieutenants, prod the clotted waters with an almost student-like intent, scribbling notes. They have the doctor's figures, his information, and they are aware General Butler has appointed him their *guide*, but they would like to draw their own conclusions, thank you. Fine enough, he thinks. He knows what General Butler wishes, what he has ordered and approved.

Behind the engineers, on the opposite side of the canal, the line of the Jackson Railroad stretches towards its ultimate westward bend. The last cars that traveled these cold tracks had carried the Crescent Guards. He's heard spare news of them: billeted somewhere in Mississippi, to reinforce Vicksburg, which, unlike New Orleans, is readying itself for a siege.

"Even the scavengers here don't do their jobs," says one of the engineers, poking at a dead buzzard.

The doctor huffs a laugh. The nervous jabs of these boys in sweat-darkened blue are no different than the whispers, the suspicious glances of his fellows on the council; now they are aware that he is engaging with the enemy. Only on matters of hygiene, he'd assured Pierre Soulé after their last meeting. Pierre, grown more and more haggard in the time since their audience with the general, took the words numbly, saying, *I would be mindful not to seem too helpful to them, even in the interest of the city's . . . hygiene. . . . It won't look good when the tide turns.*

"Like Hindoos," says one of the engineers, loudly. "Filling their bathwater with corpses."

More than you know. In his years of efforts to convince the council to have the canals dredged, the doctor has made this walk many times, finding on more than one occasion the bundled body of a man or woman festering along the waterways. Generally ignored, these corpses would now and again be reported to the police inspectors who ledger them unseen as "drowned," though whites sometimes bear closer scrutiny.

But there is life here too: fry flicker at the edges; a neighborhood of mud-pat crawfish holes; a blue crane delicately balances, watching the mosquito-danced open water where catfish roll and peck; deeper, gar traverse the wreckage of object and corpse with prehistoric disinterest, sometimes rising to the surface, halved by snappers; and deeper still, in the microscopic dominion of pathogens, lives cholera, waiting, enriched by the endless fecal source. Disease in every molecule of water, death in every droplet.

Cyanosis can have no rival, and a population safe from corporeal disease will be all the more accepting of the societal sickness. So the canals will be dredged, by some fifteen hundred of the unemployed citizenry (to be paid out of our most magnanimous occupier's pocket at first, then by the seized assets of citizens now at arms against the United States), and the first strong wind from the south will flush all the filth up the arteries and out into the lake.

With the city and his troops delivered from fever, Butler may focus his efforts on other issues. The women, for instance. General Butler is much disturbed by their lack of docility, to which the doctor (when asked for his medical opinion) offered a diagnosis of contagious hysteria—a maddening of the female organs. The general had held up his hands to the members of his staff waiting in the doorway. *Go on, doctor.* And so the doctor spoke of the much-debated clitoral node, by which the Greeks considered all female passions governed and termed the House of Uterine Fury.

Uterine fury. Butler savored the sound, forced a chuckle from his throat. *I don't suppose it's too many patients for you to cure, eh?*

The sun has lowered behind the immigrant hovels, and the engineers have pulled themselves messily ashore, where they sit smoking pipes. The doctor thinks of the women in the shacks hereabout, of the women in the city who, just as they love clawing at a pimple or a boil, worry cyanosis and unknowingly inflame the disease. He wonders what the general might have in mind for them. Whatever it may be, they are as unknowing of the purge to come as the foulness that gluts the canal. As unknowing as Elise, with whom he meets this week to discuss Woolsack's will.

Elise. The way she looked at him during the funeral, the twist of her mouth speaking only refusal. Standing with her feet pressed tightly, as he imagines her legs, her thighs, bound in black.

He'd made no mention to General Butler of the current methods. The fashion in London is to use a crank-handled instrument to scour the offending node to insignificance; in Paris they have made great strides in curing female rages with the process of clitorectomy, as demonstrated by our own Dr. Sims in New York. He sees himself beneath a modesty-curtain, bent between the arched legs of a thousand women, turning and turning, grinding pacification into their flesh.

No need for such methods with Elise; he has just the instrument for her.

Joseph

Four
Wicked Youth

'Ti Poucet, tall as your arm, treads quietly through the ogre's halls. A clever boy, he has a plan to free himself and his seven brothers; but if his plan does not succeed, in the morning they will be consumed.

Sooner, if he's not careful.

Joints of leg-of-man hang curing from the ceiling; he hears them dully thudding high above as he goes, shuddering for the rumble of the ogre's drunken, meat-glutted snores. Holding close the mean wool caps he's taken from his brothers' heads, he stalks to the bedchamber of the monster's daughters.

They sleep all in a row—blonde, immense, and you might say cherubic if it weren't for the sharp teeth that show in their lolling mouths or the knowledge of just what diet makes their arms pinch-rolled with fat. Each massive head wears a golden crown, and like their father they are deep sleepers, in full grunting dolor from midnight raids of the larder. A gob of *enfant confit*; thin slices of smoked buttock. He thinks of the greedy things wiping fingers on their nightgowns leaving splotchy yellow stains of grease.

One by one he replaces their crowns with caps, and with the crowns slung across his neck and shoulder like sashes he pads away to wait out the night with his brothers, the ogre's daughters' crowns atop their heads.

When the ogre awakes, mind and sight still clouded by wine, he comes to the room of Poucet and his brothers, reaches for them, and feels the crowns upon their heads. A monstrous love-grumble, a butcher-block-smelling peck on blanched cheeks for his mistake. Then off the ogre thumps, to the next bedroom. There he cuts the throats of his own children. And it is only when he has the last of them by the ankles, letting it bleed out, and the blonde locks spill down from a mean wool cap does he realize he's been tricked into infanticide. By then, Petit Poucet and his brothers have escaped.

One of his mother's stories, now called to mind as Joseph makes his own trek down darkened hallway. A mission of a different kind this late hour, the devil's span of clock. And it is no ogre he fears waking, but the mother who gave him the stories; no woolen caps in his hands, but a nubbin candle and the key to his father's room, taken earlier this evening from the hook in Ligeia and Bernice's quarters at the back of the house.

So he treads, sockless, down the stairs.

When he was small his mother would sit beside his bed and tell stories of Poucet. There were many; the clever boy was always in some sort of trouble. Once, marked by a rogue wolf, 'Ti Poucet sheared off his own hair and placed it on the head of his sleeping father, who the wolf—obtuse as the ogre—unwittingly devoured.

Poucet's means of survival came always at the expense of others. When Joseph was small he took the stories without question; now he understands that it's the way of clever boys to leave bodies in their wake.

Here is the door, the jamb where he clung that night. To stand here is like approaching a tent at some carnival; behind the canvas you know there is fear, but you are drawn inevitably in.

He is grown past the grasp of fairy tales, but still he wants a story. Marina has her own—the book of Shakespeare, the enchanted isle. So he means to have one for himself, and like Poucet who finds escape in others' guises, Joseph wants his father's papers. The record of his life.

He turns the key, a metallic clack, and passes through the open door.

The room is not so different than before. The same weapons on the walls, silent, aimed at each other. Menacing lengths of dragoon pistol, the comically bulbous barrel of a Turkish shotgun. Here a fan of bayonets, there a curia of miniatures, not full-grown.

A tightness in his throat. Of all these, Joseph thinks, he chose mine.

No, he didn't choose. She gave it to him.

Wax runs and coats his fingertips as he cups the shivering flame and moves towards the desk, now at the center of the room. Darkness slinks away at his approach, not far but circling him like an animal frightened of fire.

The broad pine field of the desk, whose nicks and ruts and empty ink-hold keep little bites of shadow, is cleared bare and gives off a cold whiff of antiseptic. A scoured emptiness.

Pages frill the partly opened drawers. She's been rifling through them. And for a moment he is afraid that his mother has taken the manuscript, taken it away so that he can never learn. Squatting now, he slides open the drawer and his father escapes like a djinn in wafts of tobacco and whiskey, ink and gun-oil. Joseph rocks on his heels, breathing, for a moment embraced. He takes the nubbin from the desktop and holds it to the pages, which lay facedown as though examined and casually tossed back in. Unnumbered, but covered in his father's thin, slashing script—without figures or tabular notations, packed tightly as a letter but with no signatory, no address but chapters and dates. He resists the temptation to stop and read, draws the pages out, piling them on the bare desk until he must pinch the last away and his fingertips, checking to be sure there are none left, feel only wood grain, flecks of tobacco, dust. He gathers up the papers under the dark-eyed glare of barrels, the glint of blades.

Upstairs now. He hurries, the manuscript at his chest heavy and unwieldy as an ogre's head. He doesn't care that his speed, his swinging arm, snuff the candleflame and he's forgotten the thuds of his footfalls in his eagerness. He can see in the dark now, he knows his way back by instinct, and after putting the papers in his room he will leave the key before the door to Ligeia and Bernice's room. Clever boy, he jogs a bit.

The last step grabs for his toe and sends him tumbling forward, arms outspread to catch himself, thumping to the carpet, the papers and his breath knocked loose. He strains for either, fumbling, wheezing. The nubbin has rolled away, the key gone to some corner. He scrabbles for the slips of paper, listening above the blood-drum in his head for a sound from his mother's room, accepting the inevitability of her appearance: face masked in Gottlieb's Ointment, voice like tearing silk. She doesn't come.

When he has the papers bundled in his arms, he toes for any strays, which might be found in the morning. He will have to wake early, earlier than even Ligeia and Bernice, and slip the key back. He cannot sleep tonight. He paws the paper together and goes to his room.

Past the moonlit mosquito netting of his bed, parted curtains show the black rectangle of Marina's bedroom window. She is asleep, curled maybe with her Shakespeare. He lights his bedside lamp and her window is gone.

In bed. The lumped papers lay like a drowsing pet before his lap, white within but anciently yellowed at their edges from his father's smoke. His clumsiness has confused the pages, so he shuffles his father's life until he finds a hint of date scratched amid brown stars of coffee or whiskey: fall 1800. His father is a boy not far past Joseph's age, scrabbling on the western plains with the man who made him eat coals. Father and grandfather, in a hole dug in the turf. Living underground like rabbits or moles. He sees their faces pale as icing. There is a friend called Samuel, who his father fights and merrily cusses the way Joseph has seen boys in jean shirts do on the street, and a girl called Emily. But the disordered pages sabotage his understanding and now his father must be older; he rides down a lane towards a man he owes some vengeance. Father enumerates his hate to the hoofbeats, shoots the man, and cuts out his tongue.

My father cut out a man's tongue.

The page is bent in Joseph's hand, the cutting of the tongue not yet done when his father's words reach the end of the page, and on the next the girl, Emily, is reappeared. She too lives in a hole in the ground; she has ringworms at her neck and she is beautiful. Another stria of time invades; his father sets fire to someone's house, rages about the Negroes and the Spanish. The friend, Samuel, is still there. Jumbled time again, and so Joseph spreads some pages out. When he sees the words *Wife* and *Son* he stops, heartbeat quickening at the thought that he might grace these pages. But father calls his wife Copperhead, Red Kate, and the son is not him but some child of another time. Joseph sets the page down with both hands, as though to keep it from standing upright. A brother. A brother who would be an old man now. His throat is choked, tears run heedless, and time circles him like impermeable darkness. The only way to save himself is to read, to order and reconstruct. Shuffle the pages, make little stacks of years. So Petit Poucet reads on. He has slipped into his father's skin, to confound an agent of destruction he can't yet name. By morning he will be consumed.

Five

Mutatis Mutandis

Dented tin, light in his gloved hand, painted with crude flowers crowding round the scrawled name of the chamber pot's owner, one Shell Road Mary. General Butler tilts the pot to see his official portrait, printed as a handbill and circulated at the end of last week, staring back at him from where it is pasted in curved shadowy reaches that glint with a remnant trickle of urine as he angles for light. A grassy tang. He snorts to clear his nose.

Morning, the fourteenth of May. Two weeks into his occupation of New Orleans. In the courtyard of the Custom House he stands beside a growing pile of pots similarly decorated, brought singularly by orderlies or in carts, like waggish tribute. The offending items were taken, he's been told, from the whorehouses of Gallatin Street. The search for more is on, but, pardons, sir, it is feared that the practice has become popular and it may take some time.

Another armful clangs and up stamps adjutant Strong. And what is he to do with them, the pots? The price of tin is sound, but he can't very well send them North as he's done with Beauregard's bells. The bells, so he's read in a belated copy of the *Boston Herald*, have been sold at auction—to speculators of metal, to churches and schools, and even newly bred collectors of secessionist memorabilia. A lively event, the *Herald* claims, with thanks and praise to our most splendid general, may he know that the schoolchildren and parishioners of New England will be called to their duty by the tolling of his triumph.

Triumph to have his face the object of a thousand whores' expurgations, his troops the subject of constant feminine insult. The low women only do as their highborn sisters, but, he must admit, with considerably more wit. In fact, this might be the very pot emptied on the head of Admiral Farragut, who he's dispatched to the ships to prepare for the coming assault on Baton Rouge.

Strong shuffles round the pile holding up his palms, obviously disturbed by the proximity to women's secret things. Tibbets, the orderly, follows.

"Should there be an official statement? An order, sir?"

"Dear God no," he says. "Let's not make minor farce into high comedy. The papers would never let it go."

Strong frowns. "I'm afraid word will spread regardless."

Says Tibbets: "Seems the boys are wagging more than their tongues."

"Quiet."

"What would you have me do, George? Let this lie or shout so loud that Horace-goddamned-Greely writes an editorial about it?"

At the end of a rage-stretched arm, he has Shell Road Mary's pot aimed squarely at his adjutant. Strong closes his eyes, puffs his moustaches. Tibbets sidles the pot and comes to stand behind him. General

Butler lowers his arm, but does not let go of the damning, pitiful thing. Instead, he admires it. The childish brushstrokes forming a flower that exists only in the poor girl's mind, the nominal scrawl claiming ownership of such a meagre possession. And, he thinks, Shell Road Mary's pot is probably not unlike one his daughter might decorate. Blanche's would be porcelain, her strokes sure from years of instruction, her flowers of a known breed, perhaps roses from the very trellis outside her window at the Washington boarding school she threatens in her letters to climb and effect escape. The other girls call Blanche an uncultured Yankee. They say her voice is shrill and she is clumsy. They wave their fans in her face.

He hefts the pot, peers closer at the flowers. From a distance, Blanche's wouldn't be so different. Girls are girls the world over, women of a piece. Prey to the same failings, governed by the same place. What did the little Creole doctor call it? Uterine fury. Shaking his head, Butler pitches Mary's pot to the pile.

"Some good news, sir," says Strong. "We have the fellow, Mumford, in custody."

"The one who tore down the flag, sir," adds Tibbets.

"Yes, yes," says Butler, the man's face recomposing itself in his mind. And how much easier it is to correct men. So another is added to his continuum of difficulties and tasks, all of which exist on a plane of his own devising, without antipodes or hierarchy: the price of flour, the poor, the fever season, the thieving banks and impertinent consuls, the city council who will not vote for a dollar-per-day wage for those he's employed in dredging the canals. He tells George to see that the man is well treated, his family notified of his whereabouts. And with a click of heels Strong departs, and so, Butler knows, should he be. He is supposed to take Sarah on a house-hunting trip, among the mansions of rebel officers. She has had enough of the cavernous hotel.

Clatter and tong, the pile rises as the minutes fly. His patience with them. The whores will be sorry when they're pissing in their cups tonight. And good God how many can one city bear?

He has turned from the pile, heading back to the dank confines of his office in the Custom House. Fingers rise to cap-brims, greetings issue, and he sees behind the soldiers' eyes a wink at his passing. He slams his office door behind, throws himself into his chair, and angrily peels the gloves from his trembling hands.

Mary: the name in his mind like a stone pitched out into the winter darkness of an ice-mottled Lowell canal. Wind seethes across the sooty snow, the malformed ice, and in the sundown bluster and coming darkness young Ben Butler, gaunt graduate and clerk for William Smith, Esq., pretends to be a Revolutionary soldier with tricorne pulled to arched lapels, patrolling riverbanks for a British crossing. Imagining dispatches, rather than evictions, in his pocket. But, as happens more and more, law crowds out this brief fancy. By the end of his first year of study Butler has read more widely than his masters. Ordinances ancient and new, cases argued in the courts of governments gone to dust. He trudges down an avenue of slatboard shacks tamped with newspaper and scraps of cloths. He is alone but, he knows, observed from every crack and greasy pane. He gives the door a rap and there is revealed a pale face, round, curtained in black hair. The woman stares, wrinkling the faint dark moustache at her upper lip when he says his name and who sent him. Stooped shoulders draped in a furred shawl bow further, allowing him in. Children skitter in the far corner, eyeing him with rodential reticence. Their mother offers him the household chair, which he accepts. And with fists on his knees, Butler says his piece, delinquent pay, eviction, apologies. When the woman calls for the children to go outside Butler does nothing. He doesn't see the children go, only hears their departure, the door slammed by the wind. She slips her shawl and hauls him up, works his hand until he understands, assents. He follows her to a mattress stuffed with cotton dross. A passionless transaction: her mouth is dry, her skin loose. And as hairy knees wrench at his ribs and she steers him through the brief and ungainly disposition of his virginity, he thinks of women, of a pretty cousin who stayed in his mother's boardinghouse one summer, of whores he's spied; he thinks of how he will fix the accounts, of the rat-bitten fur shawl beneath them, of an ordinance he'd read in Riley's *Memorials of London* concerning lewd women, common women, women of evil deed and life. By the end his thoughts are hemmed, his teeth in uneven clench. Buttoned and empty, he is ushered back outside, the pair of children shoving in the instant he opens the door.

The stone comes to rest, the churned mud and water-wilted leaves settle, and there is clarity at last. The London ordinance, stark in his mind. A cure for troublesome women.

As he recalls: In the early winter of 1351, common women had been so daring as to trim their clothes in fur (a privilege reserved for the dames and damsels of the realm) and perform debased acts in the guise of their betters, while ladies, rightful wearers of such garments, were themselves also behaving lewdly in the streets. This, of course, would not stand. And so, the law states, after the feast of St. Someone next ensuing, the common women must clothe themselves in plain raycloth hoods, on pain of forfeiting the offending garments on the spot, imprisonment, &c; and their highborn sisters, should they be publicly lascivious, will be treated as befits their behavior, on pain of &c.

Genius. No whore who dresses like a lady will retain her clothes, and no lady who acts like a whore will retain her honor. The perfect employment of womanhood's diametric stations, the threat elegantly implied. By governance of one, the other is subdued.

In fetid memory, he's found his answer to these New Orleans harridans. He will keep only the inspirational seed of the old ordinance. Change what needs changing. Mutatis mutandis.

Governance by implication. He drums the desk, finds a slip of paper, and in his excitement flecks ink in blue spatter across the blotter. As he writes, his wife's voice comes whispering, telling her dream on Ship Island.

Oh, Ben, you'll never really understand a woman's fears.

But he does. For men, the knowledge of the threat is inherent. We exist, and so must women's fear. The women of this city simply need reminding.

Head-Quarters, Department of the Gulf,
New Orleans, Thursday, May 15, 1862

General Order No. 28:
    As the officers and soldiers of the United States have been subject to repeated insults from the women (calling themselves ladies) of New Orleans, in return for the most scrupulous non-interference and courtesy on our part, it is ordered that hereafter when any female shall, by word, gesture, or movement, insult or show contempt for any officer or soldier of the United States, she shall be regarded and held liable to be treated as a woman of the town plying her trade.
    By command of Major-General Butler
    Geo. C. Strong, A.A.G., Chief of Staff

Having signed his name, George Strong will not look up from the page. His eyes flit disbelieving over the lines. He is the first to see and so Butler, standing in the corner of the room, allows him a moment.

"The order may well be . . . misunderstood . . . sir," George says finally.

"I won't deny the possibility."

"But if just one man were to act on it—"

Butler thwacks fist into palm. "Then we'll have *one* act of aggression on our side!" Striding across the room, he regains himself, seeing the worry in George's face. "And if one of our men happens to, I'll deal with him so that his act shall never be repeated. I want this on the streets tomorrow morning. Double the printing."

George still will not look up nor let go the order. "I worry, sir."

"Now George," he says, fatherly. "What do you do when a prostitute accosts you in the street? You don't very well bend her over and have her right there, do you? No. You either ignore her like a gentleman or you have her arrested."

Strong is blushing. "That might well be inferred, sir. But perhaps if we were to make the order more explicit we could save a lot of trouble."

Trouble? Trouble is the wailing of the Rebel gentry whose fortunes he's appropriated to pay the cleaners of the canals, and the foreign consuls who willfully violate the sovereignty of the United States and hide the same money in their offices where they think it will be out of his reach if only they shriek to Paris and London and Stockholm and Vienna loud enough, designing with locals and sowing discord among them. And by God trouble is what he is bringing down upon the heads, quite soon, of Mayor Monroe and his men, on the well-coiffed head of Pierre Soulé. All those who might see the order as an opportunity to mewl and stick out their necks.

"Listen, George: inference cuts both ways, and I won't blunt the blade."

Six

Inheritance

"So, is General Butler as ugly as he looks in the papers?"

His eyes make arcs of the Woolsack parlor. This afternoon Elise has already asked whether Butler does in fact collect "confiscated" silverware and Negroes, whether he means to stir insurrection in the poor, whether he really will enforce the suspension of President Davis's proclaimed Day of Thanksgiving.

Before he can answer she catches to another bit of self-satisfied brightness and adds: "Or at least how he was in our old papers."

The old papers, whose columns once reported the happenings of Boston or Chicago only in the snide and clipped way one might relate the doings of a former lover, are much changed. The *True Delta*, unrepentant to the last, is closed; the *Crescent*, the *Picayune*, the *Bee*, the *Catholic Reporter*, all have had their staffs replaced by Union men or by subtler means become convinced to print the news for Northern eyes. So we've come to find, battles believed won a month past are in fact lost, and those who were once heroes are made villainous in these playbills of the national stage with the ease of actors slipping back and forth from behind curtains.

The doctor runs a hand across the buckles of his portfolio, within which the will and testament of Angel Woolsack waits.

"Uglier than that, I'm afraid," he says, placating, his capacity for small talk flagging even as Elise takes this statement as invitation to inquire after the specifics of the general's hideous physiognomy, which he gives as best he can, occupying his mind with the London method. The crank between her thighs. And one wonders, at times like this, if women have even the barest inkling of what we really think.

Elise listens, never shifting in her maroon wingback, a triumphant drawl to her *ohs* and *ahs*. Oblivious. She's gathered some mourning weight, a babyish bulge at the corners of her mouth. See how she attempts to mask the doubling of her chin by thrusting out her jaw so that she must look at him from downcast eyes. Blessedly, they are alone; she must have dismissed the women who have for the past weeks made up her seraglio of grief.

"A shame Joseph couldn't be with us," he says, instantly regretting having done so, sure that he's flung open the trapdoor to the bottomless pit of maternal interest.

But here she winces; silk creaks with the tensing of her legs. "He's upstairs, and won't be coming down."

He has the portfolio unbuckled, the will freed. A single page covered in the tight script of Edward Purcell, Atty., signed with Woolsack's spattered scythe-blade scrawl, and witnessed by the same hand that holds the sheet.

"Nothing wrong, I hope?"

"Not at all," she says, her mood darkening swift as an eclipse.

Likely the boy is hunched over his father's crazed manuscript, or perhaps taking advantage of these motherless moments for more traditional boyish pursuits. The doctor grins, but then there is the image of himself, age thirteen, sweating while the priest behind the screen asks whether he takes undue knowledge of his private parts. Dear God. He wouldn't wish that age on anyone. Nor what follows: coming lankily into one's own, the awkwardness and fear you fight and banish in the moment that you take the hand of a girl who has just bitten off some boy's earlobe, leaving you to skulk off to the cold European capital where girls giggle at your accent and from which, girded in knowledge, you return and latch to the first eligible female who gives you time of day. Lydia. Her wealth, your due payment. And yet here you are, drawn back into Elise's orbit. A gravity you've denied for so long, unmindful as most laymen are of natural forces, only to find it is insatiate and of unspeakable strength.

Her gleaming black-capped scalp. Her black eyes bored into pale skull. Her person choked by black fabric from throat to heel, containing within her all the colors of the world in the form of slick shuddering viscera and shielding the path therein.

He drives fingernails into his palm, rights himself.

Elise drums the arms of the chair. Left canine flashes as it finds her lower lip, works a salivary gland perhaps, gnawing the wet little node.

"Well," she says. "Get on with it."

Elise

Seven

Patrimony

Look at him, seedily expectant. What Emile wants is right there in his eyes, peering up at her from the damned will as a child admires some lush dessert over the lip of the table: tears, pleas, a fit pitched so that he can sit back and savor it with Angel's ghost at his shoulder, laughing at what a fool she'd been to think her husband would ever let her loose. He leans close to her, tries to force a coverlet of kindness over his soul-dead doctor's voice.

She listens, amazed to find within herself no anger to stopper, no tears in need of fighting back; with Emile's every word—Angel's ventriloquized through him—the coalbin of her feelings is further emptied, black bucketfuls spirited away, and there is only the hard dry-heave sensation of wanting to expel but having nothing left within. Her vision drifts unsharpened as he drones on, and she sees in the space between them, somewhere on the rose-patterned rug, what her husband thought she was worth.

This house. The massive crumbling wreck on the coast at Berwick's Bay, one of the pediments still bearing the mark where the axe wielded by Angel's then-wife fell. A monthly allowance of no less than two hundred dollars for the remainder of her life, provided that she doesn't marry.

Fair. Very fair. To the one who accepted his shriveled manhood, who coddled him through all the nights in which he'd go crazed with terror or rage untethered to this world, who nursed his sickly desires and gave him the son he's made sole beneficiary of money hoarded in banks and a catalogue of stock and bond and city-lots and slave-pens. ("Sadly, under the current circumstances these may not be considered assets," says Emile in aside.) In estimate: two hundred and eighty-four thousand dollars, to be managed in trust until Joseph reaches the age of his majority.

"Managed," she says, smiling, for she knows the answer. "By whom?"

Emile inclines his head. Such a heavy task. How kind of him to accept the burden. And she sees him bent over enormous ledgers, noting the loss and accretion of the perpetual wealth that chains him, not so differently than her, to her husband. The wealth Angel never sought to display or spend in all the time she knew him, and in his penultimate act added eight years to its hibernation. Eight years. Not so long a time.

Now a twitch at his cheek as he starts again. Can she have surprised him? Can he have been so stupid as to think she would melt like wax and puddle at his knees, begging for more money?

He trips over the words *legal guardianship*, hurries back over them again, and looks up with his scum-green eyes. Legal guardianship of Joseph Samuel Woolsack until he reaches the age of his majority. And this bastard reading another bastard's words must see the look on her face because before she can say what she wants he is showing her his palms.

"A formality, I assure you." He keeps his palms up in postpone-ment of her opened mouth. "For legal purposes only."

She has no protests, no questions. Only a statement of fact she gives, sounding each word with coffin-nail finality: "Joseph will stay with me."

"Of course," says Emile. "I would merely be a guiding hand, taking care to see that when he comes into his own, the boy is ready. I don't want to interfere with your son."

She feels her lips curl backward from her dry teeth. "That's what you want, is it, Emile?"

A show of nerves; he crosses and uncrosses his legs, daintily main-tains the portfolio in his lap, as though to hide an inopportune bulge. He wants what every man she's ever known has wanted in one form or an odious other—with his cowardice disguised as gentlemanly tact. Poor Emile. Is he really too scared to say? And, with reason she cannot yet name, there is something attractive in his fear, his reticence. The prey-tremble in his voice unexpectedly deploys her blood to needful reaches.

"I want the best," he says. "For both of you."

Then it won't be today. He's too afraid. At least part of him is; and the other part of him is the one that wants to draw the whole thing out. She sits back, wishing for a fan or better yet Mamere's little leather martinet. Something to do with her hands, the flicker and flitting threat of the blood-tanned tassels to take her mind away. He might like that, the whip. She allows her mind to slip, along the pathway of her blood. The prospect of what Emile wants is hideously attractive, straddles obligation and temptation. She would almost rather have it done with now than endure the tedious play of power he undoubtedly envisions will culminate in her, like some operatic damsel, falling into the arms of him, the dark pursuer, the villain.

But you are no villain, Emile. No more than Angel was. In the same way some men set themselves up as heroes—the role of strong-chinned right and steadfastness though their insides are filled with maggots—others wish to be villains, brooding over their wounds and grand wrong-doings when within they are needy little things, moiling and terrified.

And by the time their conversation has turned again, both feigning gladness to be done with the "business," the thought of what she herself or poor Emile may want has faded, distant as the footsteps faintly sounding through the ceiling, coming from her son's room.

It might as well be Angel's ghost that paces, inaugurating his haunt, his possession of the boy at last, though she's seen this coming from the start.

Seen it when Joseph was not yet a year old and he startled her one day with a look on his face so fiercely his father's that she had to leave the room and him, glaring from his bassinet. She knew he would inherit from his father certain words and looks, but this was like a veil of Angel thrown over the boy's face. And she had seen no evidence of his father so strongly until yesterday morning when she found him in his room with the pile of Angel's papers and once he'd shaken off his surprise and she'd by then lost control of herself and was clawing through the blankets tented by his skinny knees and Lord knows what else to snatch up every single sheet belonging to the man whose features were his inheritance. *You don't want me to know anything, but I already do! I know more than you do even!* Babyish taunts she might have shaken off, as we must do with what children say when they are angry—for there couldn't be much for him to learn from those awful scraps besides that his father was a brutal man in love with himself and his own wickedness, and he would know that already from life—were it not for the last thing he said before she, bundling the papers, slammed his door and screamed for Ligeia to come and lock it. *And I know what you did, too!* Ligeia snatching nervous at the space beneath her throat where she wore the keys, saying they were lost and she'd been looking for them since sunrise.

And if all men are, like the nuns said, made in the image of God, then she supposes He in Heaven wears quite often that perfectly male expression, somewhere between contempt and benefaction. Wanting to be both punisher and savior all at once, but always, always with you in the palm of his hand.

Who knows what came first, the knowledge of the power or the need to exercise it? But lately she's been doubting her own. She hasn't even been able to do what she'd originally wanted with the papers crumpled that morning in her hands and bundled in her dressfront and now stashed away like misgivings or ugly thoughts in the back of her bureau, which was to burn them. Like women she knows have done when they've come upon a horded batch of love letters from someone else to their men. What good is the fire? The warmth of the flames will fade from your face as surely as the pages are licked to ashes, and then the only place the hateful thing can stay is in your own heart, where it can't be hidden or buried behind scraps of taffeta, but stays right there soiling your loves and hopes by its mere presence. And you can't very well get at it there; you'd have to burn yourself.

Marina

Eight

The Sewing Bee

This is an Andrew's cross, blue for patriotism and set in a field of red that means spilled blood, trimmed in white as are the stars that mark its bars, for purity—from her perch on a low padded stool Marina sees the eyes of Mlle Pichon and Joseph's mother jointly narrow at the word—and represent the states of the Confederacy, plus Kentucky and Tennessee and Maryland whether they like it or not.

Laughter. Womanly, dutiful, bidden by the old joke the ladies like to slip into the explanation they always give her of the flag they are sewing—"General Beauregard's flag," they call it, to be sent secretly to the regiment in which Uncle Willie, among other New Orleans men, serves—and repeat as though it were school and that by rote she might be made to understand. The joke subsumes back to murmur and the tick of needlepoints, the tinkle of a thimble fallen to the floor and: *Please, Miss Marina will you fetch that for me, dear?*

There is always laughter at Mme Frick's sewing bees, but today humor catches on something in their throats and the reused jokes don't quite earn their accustomed pitch. Only Mlle Pichon laughs as usual, and hers sounds more like a taunt.

Down she swoops beneath the great billowing rectangle that hangs by four hooks from the ceiling of the sewing parlor, down in search of what she pretends is an empress's signet ring or anything more magic than a thimble. Marina crawls over carpet and bare boards from which rises the smell of camphor and the hair of Mme Frick's innumerable cats. Her arms, bent at the elbows, are embarrassing saplings among this glade of thick calves rooted in high-heeled shoes and an undergrowth of ruffled silk. And how can she be anything but stunted here with them, overgrown by womanhood while outside boys stretch in the sun and seem to grow like shoots before her very eyes. At every chance she spies them from one of the windows that face the courtyard below, where Mme Frick's grandsons and Mrs. Thornton's youngest shoot goat's-eye marbles. Only Joseph seems not to grow, sulking in the shadow of a mossy brick cistern. She hadn't seen him for two days, the longest stretch since his father's death, until this morning when they walked together behind his mother and Mlle Pichon to the sewing bee. She knew from Mademoiselle that he'd been in trouble, but not what for. The first thing Joseph had said to her this morning when they were out of earshot was, *Guess how many men my father killed*. She'd asked how did he know and Joseph turned his face to the sky and said, *I don't even know if I could count them*.

Joseph's father had, in fact, killed his own father. He'd blurted this, just as he'd blurted the rest, without greeting or a single question about her or the allowance of a space for her to talk, as though he were matching her somehow. And Joseph seemed shadowed by the knowledge, not darkened so much as made starker. *With a shovel to the head*, he said. *My father was a little older than me and this girl he'd . . . loved . . . had died and his father said to bury her and my father . . .* It was then that Joseph's mother, who was not really all that out of earshot, whipped round and told him to shut his mouth about that or she would send him right back home where he could sit with Ligeia and Bernice instead of playing with the boys. And Joseph, with a newfound petulance, said, *That's nothing to hold over my head.* And just as swiftly as it had come the voice was gone and his own whispered from the corner of his mouth, *I don't really care about those boys. I wanted to see you.*

Suddenly she is aware of being on her hands and knees, the sensation of crawling itself calling childishness to her mind, and she is ashamed to have thought of an empress's ring. She squints for a hint of the thimble, slowly scanning, and finds it hiding beneath the lip of an embroidered cushion, doubled by a pair of black-shod feet. Joseph's mother, Elise. Her calves are thinner than the others, though this may be an illusion of black. The long muscles jump as Joseph's mother pumps her toes to some hidden beat. Marina watches the tension of the woman's legs, admiring, willing herself to that length and strength as she crawls closer and stretches out her arm, her ringless hands, to ferret out the thimble, which she, rising to the surface, presents to Mme Decorde across simmering sea of star and cross.

The ladies' talk is studded now with words like *assault* and *honor* and *outrage* all loaded so heavily with gasped revulsion it's surprising they can let them out at all.

This is the reason the old jokes stale and the laughter—of all but Mlle Pichon—fishbones in their throats: the order issued yesterday by General Butler. Like all the others, the order is affixed with the name of Major Strong. And the ladies have consistently poor-mouthed his orders, but this one is different, aimed directly at them. At all the women who have been unkind to the soldiers with their spitting and cursing and pulling aside of skirts and things she's never seen them do at home. And it must be a more general anger, she thinks, because Mlle Pichon was angry when Major Strong and the officers rode past that day, but now is the one who interrupts the discussion of the order with a contemptuous snuff.

A pair of needles clack to halt. Mme Frick leans out from her chair, says, "And do you think it's funny, Inés?" Further she leans and Mlle Pichon, still smirking, meets her eyes. "Do you think it's funny," urges Frick, "to be raped?"

The word cinches them all tight—Joseph's mother looks scowling to her feet, Mme Decorde and Mrs. Schmidt grit their teeth—all but Mlle Pichon, who simply stares back at her half sister. She runs her tongue, slow, behind her lips, checking the points of her teeth, and before she can speak Mme Decorde, delicate as ever, is saying:

"Should we really be talking this way in front of—" she cuts her eyes to Marina. "She's only a girl after all."

"Why not?" says Mme Frick, giving Marina but the barest flicker of her locus. "She's on her way to womanhood, and she'll be acquainted with the concept sooner or later."

"No," says Mlle Pichon.

All heads turn her way, and to Marina seated beside on her footstool.

Mme Frick, eager: "No *what*, please?"

"No, it's not funny to be raped."

Mme Decorde again: "Oh really, should we . . ."

"I know what it means!" Marina says in a voice she realizes is too loud only once it has escaped and cinched the room again.

And she does know what it means. She knew even when they were calling it outrage. She has heard of men being outraged, of outrageous acts committed, but there is only one outrage that is committed upon women. When Marina was seven there had been a week of talk in San Antonio about whether Doña Alphonso's niece had an outrage committed upon her by one of the railroad hands, until Don Alphonso had the man quartered and his head piked on the gates of his estancia. She remembers her father being cross because he had to square things with his bosses and the authorities, and how, after many nights of her asking why father was so angry and what had the man done to Doña Alphonso's niece, Marina's mother took her outside into the garden and told her plainly. What grown and married women do with men, and how sometimes not grown and unmarried women have it done to them.

"Oh you do?" says Mme Frick quite merrily, not taking her eyes from her half sister. "Living with soldiers in camp for all those months I suppose you would pick up a thing or two."

No groping for the meaning of Frick's words, Marina understands. But she will not let them hold her mind any more than she will let herself think of Mlle Pichon's silence now, how she looks at the floor with what must be embarrassment, not even giving one of those sly disdainful looks she seems happy enough at other times to throw her half sister's way. Not when you need it. Stupid to think she'd defend you.

Marina knows by the creak of their chairs that the ladies have seen her tears. And she can't tell them why—that she's thinking not of the puckered old thing whose house this is (and who never could hurt her) but her mother in the garden, calmly explaining womanhood horrors while running her fingers down an angel trumpet's stalk.

When she opens her spent eyes the women's chests are falling in relief. Marina sits, hollow, staring out the window and resolving herself to hate them all as they bend back to their work, and conversation soon is bubbling again. The question is raised as to who will be attending the ball for the benefit of Secession Ladies on the British man-o'-war next week; another wants to know as to how they will observe President Davis's Day of Prayer, Fasting, and Humiliation.

"A little fast might not be bad before the ball," says Mme Fricke, holding her waist.

Laughter.

"What do you think he means by this . . . humiliation," says Mrs. Schmidt.

"To show humility, I should think."

"To be humble before God and pray for success."

Mlle Pichon, she sees, is silent, ticks away at her corner of bunting. Beside her Joseph's mother for an instant outwardly assumes all the disgust and hate that Marina has felt churning in herself. As though she reached over and snatched it. Joseph's mother breathes loudly, her lips pursed as though to spit.

"My God," she says, not looking up from the flag. "Haven't we been humiliated enough?"

Nine

In Trust

"You were there again today," Lydia says. Cheeks that have never known concavity expand as she sighs out her knowledge, threatening the flames of the candelabra set between them on the short table they use when there are no guests, as is the case tonight. Though, he amends, there are always guests. Only they are not among the living.

The doctor's eyebrows arch; he plucks an olive from the platter, chews carefully flesh from pit. And just as Lydia might read his thoughts from the tintinnabulations of a ring against a wedding goblet, so he detects the little wriggle of jealousy in her voice. Pleasing, sounding for the first time in years, like the return of locusts one sudden night in the trees.

"There are things still to do with the estate, and as trustee"—he thickens his voice with consternation at his duties—"I have to keep up with the boy as well."

Lydia wears an unexpected smile. "I'm glad to hear nothing interferes with your duties to Mr. Woolsack's . . . woman . . . and their son."

"To the estate," he corrects. "The estate that your father left to my management."

Were the doctor only to turn round he could meet fleshly eye to oil-painted eye with the man he's just invoked. Lydia looks past him, to her father's gilt-framed enshrinement, then back. On his shoulders, sore and not a little stooped, the doctor feels the weight of the portrait's gaze.

"And why he ever took up with that awful man I'll never know," she says.

And how would you? You were only a girl then and in many ways still are. How could you, Lydia, be expected to understand that the money doesn't come by showroom magic and honorable sleights of stagecraft, but by marrying your interests and acumen of business, your knowledge of stock and bond, to those who are willing to be dirtied, to walk the rows between the pens and see the black faces peering out. Those who do not care what polite society thinks of them and their trade, though polite society depends on them, not to mention the endless bondholders and Northern stock brokers. The fortunes of your father and his fellows were made by awful Angel Woolsack.

Again, she smiles. "But I wasn't talking about the Woolsack estate. I meant today you paid another visit to the Beast."

The olive pit juts against his cheek. He can see it there, hard and imperceptibly dark within his own darkness. He is not used to being fooled or wrong. And in his wife's about-turn there is also the echo of Elise's voice, how she so calmly took the will, how she subverted him.

"The Beast?" He laughs.

"General Butler, if you prefer." Lydia comports herself. In the candlelight she is ruddier than usual. Her health might be called immoderate; her firm-fleshedness, her glowing skin only increased in the course of their marriage, the way other women sag or sallow or gray, so that for their first years together Lydia's friends would ask if she were pregnant, until time killed all questions or hope, everything but her glow.

She continues: "Now that the canals are dredged, and with this horrible order, I can't see any good reason for you to associate yourself with him."

The Woman Order has in three short days earned Butler the appellation "Beast." In three days the public's sentence has been chalked on walls and carved into counters and fenceposts. No riots, no grand disorder, but a seething undercurrent, the high fever of cyanotic infection. Though, the doctor imagines, the reactions will be different in the unoccupied zones. Effigies burnt, prices offered. A grand blood-yowl for impugned womanhood.

"That is not the point," he says. "And why we are discussing it is beyond me."

She makes herself small, shrinks her voice. "I know it's not my place, dear—"

"True."

"But how would you feel if I were?"

"This is ridiculous."

"Then you defend it!"

"No, I don't. If you'd care to know, I think it's stupid, bullheaded, and a product of the Northern natural inclination to make a law for everything." There again it is the same bullishness and surety or right that let Butler push through the ordinance to clean the streets and canals, to appropriate the funds by any means. And here today Butler's office sang with the order's true purpose—a stream of letters from Mayor Monroe and members of the government, threatening resignation and worse. Soulé in open defiance, begging for arrest. Butler meanwhile asking the doctor about the canals and the coming weather, the enforcement of shipboard quarantines even as he quarantines those who resist him.

Lydia spoons her gumbo, a thin dark trickle of which runs at the corner of her lip as though she has been struck. "I will be attending the benefit ball on Monday. At the British ship."

The Ball for Secession Ladies. "Really, Lydia, you need to think carefully, think of more than yourself. There's more at stake here than making a little show."

"I should say the same to you. What do you think will happen when they're driven out? When *our* troops return and *our* government and here you are resigned and publicly associating with the Beast."

He has made his choice, taken the path towards future gain. Animals in herd will shy away from those they sense are sick, and so in recent days the council has asked for and received his resignation, the hospital driven him out, the Krewe of Orcus dismissed him from its last meeting. René Armand, fingering a watch fob he claims to be made from the legbone of a Union soldier, barring the doctor from the door of the Gem, tossing his mask out into the street after him.

She will not make him believe he's being cruel, no matter how much she withers. And there is no lack of enjoyment on either of their parts for a little marital parrying with the foreknowledge of how simmering anger is on occasion vented. "But answer me this, if you're so shattered by the order," he says. "Do you spit on Yankees in the street? Do you turn your skirts when they walk past? Do you curse them?"

"Only in my heart," she says, with the pride of having voiced a line already novelized or petered from some huffing poet's pen.

"Oh, Lord," he says. Hearts. To those who've not been disabused of such notions by holding one or more hundred stilled specimens in their hands, the heart may yet be the organ keeping love and fealty and fidelity.

"Just imagine, Emile. Imagine if I were . . ."

It's not for empathy she asks. She wants to thumb the germ into his mind. She wants him to see her brutalized, and by his own visualization of it to be made culpable—her mouth a black gap of shock, her eyes boiling with tears and streaked. Lydia has yet to light upon their marriage, so concerned is she with that other object of fidelity, the Nation. She wants to be a figure in his mind, something beyond obligation. And she knows, as well as he does, that the easiest paths therein are dark.

He sees the row of bent backs at the train station, scribbling over their hearts. And will he join them? Their scrofulous suggestibility, how they brag about women or even wives who dress up and perform rehearsed acts preparatory to copulation. Or themselves, he knows of one at least, blackening face and hands with burnt cork and bursting at the expected hour into the play-squealing woman's room, playing the part of their twined greatest fears and pleasures alike.

Lydia peels back the skin from a quail's leg. And he is stirred outside his own control.

Awakened. He would like to blame the wine, but can't.

She will retire early tonight, soak not overlong in her tub. Then preen and dress and slip into her bed, and what she's planted in his mind to grow, buckling the hardness of his mind like live oak roots eventually unseat pavement. Her dark little seed. Until he can no longer contain it and he goes to her bedroom and commits the pantomime, made false and only satisfying when considered briefly. For what joy is there in taking by force something that is already yours?

A flash of eyes mock terrified, perhaps, a mouth gasping refusal. And when these brief sensations and small pleasures bleed away there will be the thought, *How stupid for you to say no, no, no and that I mustn't. You said yes once at the altar and in so doing abandoned any right to ever say different again.*

Hollow pleasure, yes. He drinks his wine. But it will do for now.

Ten

A Point of Vantage

Monday comes with what the grown call perfect weather, bright and dry as New Orleans gets, the strange low sky pressing down in cloudless blue; and after a weekend of imposed separation they are allowed together again. They sit in high iron chairs at the small table on Mlle Pichon's balcony, Marina and Joseph, a card game between them untouched and scattered with the rinds of fruit.

The streets have become so clean, gutters and curbs she's never seen. Horse-piss and this morning's rain and buckets of water tossed by shopkeepers and slaves run in orderly flush. The doctor has something to do with it. The dark little man from the funeral and who she's seen make intermittent forays to Joseph's house these weeks. When the old man was alive the doctor would be sometimes in a Confederate uniform, though since the day of the invasion he seems to have abandoned it. This at least is a mark to his character. He went in the morning after Joseph's father died, with a black bag in his hand. She knows somehow it was he who made the corpse acceptable, the short man with bristling black hair and no moustache to hide the sharpness of his mouth. Joseph says he is to be his guardian.

"Will you stay with him?"

"Oh, no. I'll be right here with you."

This accomplished, he returns to the subject of his father's book of horrors, even as Marina feels her arm begin to ache from crossing herself so many times; he brings out each shameful detail with the grinning expectation of a boy who thinks you are afraid of frogs and has a pocketful. Only she is not afraid of frogs and what he describes with twisted pride are mortal sins by the dozen. And it is one thing to hear of neighbor's misdeeds and tragedies—these may be borne with rectitude and even a little enjoyment—but this! His father's first wife was a prostitute called Red Kate; his father cut off men's ears. The only thing Joseph seems sorry about is that he wasn't able to finish the book, or have it in much order beyond his own rushed reckoning.

"But I will," he says. "She hasn't gotten rid of it. The doctor has seen to that. He says it's part of my inheritance."

She shudders a bit at the thought of a prostitute for a wife, a deeper tremor at the thought of her own father ever doing so, or Major Strong. These images need banishing, so she makes to change the subject.

"Mademoiselle is very bothered," she says. "Testier than usual, and *stranger*. She even went to market with one of the négresses this morning, but didn't take me even when I asked. Then the girl came back with her basket as usual but Mademoiselle didn't until an hour later."

"Have you heard from your uncle?"

In some swampland, she sees him. Mucky and filthy and fighting. "No," she says.

The look on his face is funny, like he is at the far end of a tunnel and trying to see her. All the while Joseph gets farther away, receding, pulled from her by these awful inveighers past and present. And there he goes,

185

drawn up a string from his chair to the balustrade going past the table and Marina so that she must turn around to look with him down the street.

He points, a block down, to the house of Mme Frick. A carriage is parked at the curb and two uniformed men, American soldiers, stand at her door. Soon the house admits them; they are gone. And she is close to him, or rather he to her. His head comes just past her shoulder, and in directing her sight he leans tight there and his hair scrunches against her sleeve. She feigns as though she cannot see. "No, here. Look." Now they are together, tight. Nothing to draw him away, and he sounds wonderful and awed, conspiratorial, whispering. Where? Without frustration or thought he slides in front of her and, shouldering, takes her arm and extends it with his own. Now she may look out over the crown of his head to the street, with no need to feign a squint. The street goes murky, an indistinct backdrop to Joseph's head, the smell of his hair and arching of his backbone. Basking, she wonders how long it will be before Mlle Pichon bursts out the French doors and yells for them to stop. Closer now and Marina is the one who draws him in; he's small and the prospect of him ever reaching the height of one like Major Strong seems bafflingly distant. She keeps the bafflement and the distance right here where he leans his neck, between where her breasts will someday be and she has already begun to ache. Time creeps and jags. Look there, there! Coming out the door of Mme Frick's house are the two soldiers, bearing between them the lady of the house. Frick clutches to her chest a square package, its hasty wrappings peeled back and showing a blue bar and a small constellation of white stars. The soldiers part, enclose; with deferential moves they escort her into the carriage. And Joseph gives yips of surprise, bounces on his toes, looking back at her to see if she understands, then arching further as though there were someone near to tell. His father's voice is back, but rather than fly she holds him close. She's too strong for his struggles; and he can't see that she is smiling for the proof of her strength and that, if she can hold him tight enough and let him thrash, the voice will go.

Eleven

Beauregard's Banner

"I understand you have something of a flag-making concern at your house, Mme Frick."

"As you see," she says, giving the rectangular package a pat.

The lady is not shrill, nor harsh. A contemptuous wince to the eyes, but General Butler can begrudge her that. Quite an inconvenience to be dragged across town to the office of the man you no doubt cursed with your every breath while stitching away at your little flag.

"May I take a closer look?"

She hands the flag to Tibbets, who has been waiting at her side and passes it to Butler.

"Ah, yes," Butler says, holding a corner of the flag absurdly close, as though he were admiring the craftsmanship of the lady sitting opposite him. "Splendid. Truly splendid work. Please give my compliments to . . . how many are there in your sewing circle?"

He knows the answer already, and is disappointed somewhat when she does not lie. She goes so far, this dame with a vicious twist of graying hair, to start telling him their names. They would all be glad, she judges, for their names to be heard as patriots or some nonsense.

Today he has sent Mayor Monroe, Pierre Soulé, the chief of police, two justices, and ex-general Duncan to the brig of the *Lafayette*. A chessboard suddenly swept of its pieces. These who muddled and annoyed his past few days with letters of protest, retractions, and apologies, said apologies themselves retracted—*General Butler, I will put my name to the document on the sole condition that you insert "only" before "the women of New Orleans who have been disturbing &c"*—and so forth through a thoroughly shattered Sabbath until even Butler's limits were reached and he drew upon one of his many scraps of intelligence: that six paroled Rebel soldiers had taken to calling themselves the Monroe Guard, parading in their old uniforms, and boasting that they would soon sneak the lines and rejoin with their fellows. Proving the mayor's knowledge and support of this sedition was simple, as was Soulé's supposed dealings with France, and so the six sit in parish prison in violation of their parole while their namesake and his compatriots, who whined so much about how they couldn't guarantee the peace and safety of the city should they support Butler's order, will rest in absolute security in the brig, then only to be troubled by mites and sandfleas on Ship Island. Now it's left to his judgment whether the six should be hung. Leave this for another time. He has yet to hang anyone, though the hour nears.

"That will be enough," he says, cutting short Madame's harangue and lifting the flag before his face again. He has never seen one of Beauregard's in person, and yes it's far finer than the other Confederate standards he's seen: better than the confusing Stars and Bars, like some child's rendering of the flag of the United Sates, and the "Stainless banner," which looks perilously like a flag of truce. This one, though, with its ferocious colors and broad saltire, does have some personality. Redolent of the crazed, gaudy South.

"Well, Mme Frick," he says. "You are in luck."

"And how is that, General?"

"It just so happens that I have been looking for a flag exactly like this one, to send to a friend back east." He slips the flag behind his desk. "And I'll be sure to let you know if I should require another." He lets this sink through her plaiting and powder, now tempers his voice with a little steel: "Though I very much doubt I will."

Her glare is broken by a rap at the door, open for the sake of propriety. An orderly begs pardons and says there is a queue of Negroes building outside, more than Saturday, sir. He checks his watch. Yes, we're nearing two o'clock, the appointed hour in which he receives those colored persons who might wish to pass on whatever intelligence they see fit and earn themselves a coin from Butler's hand. The money is more for his own sense of fairness. Not a few of the blacks have informed for free.

"That little snake," says the lady, rising. "I knew it. I knew it was her."

Butler pushes himself partway up from his chair.

"Oh yes," she says. "It was one called Lizzy, wasn't it? Lizzy? Little scar over her cheek? A redbone girl."

"I'm sorry, Madame," he says. "But I couldn't possibly say."

Twelve
For the Benefit
of Secession Ladies

Chinese lanterns sway from the riggings of the HMS *Rinaldo*, cast a reddened glow onto the deck alight with thudding heels, swishing skirts, chatter, and laughter. Punch bowl stations are manned like guns by crewmen with nervous peaks in their fresh-starched cottons, intently bunching their arm-muscles as they chip at ice blocks and pour ladlefuls into pewter cups. There you are, ma'am. Rum and pulped watermelon and cool cream flecked with ice, the punch rests oversweet and filmy on her tongue. Elise tilts her third cup, reasoning how many more she'll need to last the night.

She has stepped away, a dress-width from the crush of womankind who make circles of giggling awe round plumed officers with razor-burnt cheeks. The long and toothy aspect of British manhood, abutted by ladies in stupendous gowns and jewels, and those, like Elise, who wear the black. Her sisters in mourning offer glances they suppose are knowing. Brief upward juts of chin and smiles pitifully drawn.

Crow's-feet bunch in sympathy, radiating outward, like nets to catch her.

You're wrong, dear, she thinks at the sight of one who wears a broad black sash printed with the word SHILOH. *Your husband died on a battlefield; mine died on his office floor.*

Elise smoothes the punch across the roof of her mouth, feeling the flesh that keeps her brains from her palate.

Then again, bullets work the same in each, dear, and you didn't have to see.

Or am I the lucky one? Is it worse to imagine death?

The tethered ship nods with the current, and she against it, a movement of little impact but telling of immense and ceaseless force. Elise struggles to set her feet and stand straight while those around her sway grasslike and accustomed. Mmes Schmidt and Decorde, at the buffet, where the South in sugarwork sits, spun and crafted by the captain's own patisserie, shift their positions about Mme Frick, who has drawn a worthwhile crowd and presently breaks off a portion of the Florida peninsula, takes a bite, and chews through her story. She is today an official martyr for the cause, brought bodily to meet the Beast in reprimand of her patriotic act. *Our patriotic act, ma chère Elise*, she'd said. Watching her now—Frick flitting her Jápon and regaling a pair of British officers and a growing clutch of ladies—Elise must close her eyes for blossoming rage, seeing in her mind the thick-headed bitch who'd made the rounds of all their houses this afternoon, flushed then with a mixture of terror and absurd defiance as only high birth and money may account. Mme Frick with her wrinkled face and tear-tracked powder yowling that of course she'd stood up to the awful man. *Oh yes he asked who sewed the flag and I proudly, PROUDLY, said all our names. Don't you see it's an honor!*

Elise had been at an early dinner when Madame's appearance called her from an oily soup and a sullen son. The woman into whose sphere Elise has in ten years yet to fully understand (more accepted as a natural fact) why she has fallen, had thrown herself into one of the parlor chairs, and upon Elise's appearance began bemoaning the Beast, her day, her flag, her slaves. Her histrionics only broke when she came to the subject of blame. Her first instinct had been to blame the girl, Marina, *so sadly foisted upon my dear adopted sister, Inés*. After all, the girl stayed with Northerners, knows them by name and face—but she's never out of that house without Inés, never on her own. So Madame was left to consider her household. Lizzy, she'd decided, was the one who'd gone and told the Beast. The sneaking little négresse, Madame told, had been nasty since the Northerners' arrival. Tarrying on her errands and prone to backtalk. Wistfully she complained how *before* she could've sent her to the prison, put her on water and broth for a week, had those strong-arms give Lizzy her correction. But now, sadly, the correction had to be applied by old Ebenezer, tiring out the poor dear old thing so badly he had to go to his room and lie down.

A handbell sounds; cups are raised and toasts made: to the ladies present; to the gentlemen at war on land and sea; to the City of New Orleans, whose women are indomitable; to Mayor Monroe and the others now imprisoned. So those toasting turn to face the sloop, anchored across the river, where the mayor and his fellows are held.

Elise empties her cup, wishing Inés could be with her here. Where I can go and she cannot, because my people faltered earlier than hers, or were quicker to regain the path to whiteness. And being shipboard, Elise allows her mind adrift. To Inés at home and manless, with that strange little girl whose hold on Joseph has worried her from the start. And Marina, Elise thinks, is not long for girlhood anyway. Not so little. Soon she will bud and bloom, as sweet aunts and mothers say when what they mean is bulge and bleed. And will it be Inés who shows her how to fold the cloth? To wash and change it out? And though she knows damn well that all the girl has to look forward to is pain of one kind or another, Elise cannot ignore the strain of envy clenching at her throat—to be young and have the entire elder world to blame for the pains you know and those to follow—no more than she can help, when she is in the presence of the girl, feeling like the black mirror: dimly imaging her future. And, standing on this ship, she sees herself on the white and gleaming shores of the girl's island; only now it's hers alone. Crescent stretches of sand in moonlight, pocked with the holes of clams and crabs, the surf's organic rush and seethe to soothe her, like her heart used to when she would press Joseph to her chest and let the squirm and tension of babyhood upsets relax with the maternal beat. She hears the perfect surf-beat rather than the slop-bucket sound of river-wake against the *Rinaldo*'s hull; if she looks hard enough, squints away the lantern-light, she can imagine herself on the island, surrounded by a perfect darkness and expanse of sea to keep everyone away.

Now the crewmen sing for God to save their queen, and Elise thinks how her mother would not be gratified to find her in the company of English sailors. The ancestral hatred never abated, and Elise has carried it on, coupled with her own antipathies for these germinal Northerners—their armies of commerce, their fiscal wars, their need bred in the cold and damp to press bootheels on the hotter portions of the world.

But that need was in Angel too. In the American hearts of him and his friends who made their plays for Cuba, Yucatán, Nicaragua.

Still, Angel would curse and spit at this scene, make loud declarations of how many of these men's grandfathers he'd shot down in '14. Then perhaps he'd take hold of her hand, press it to his boney chest, say, *Feel that blood there, girl. That's mine and all the ones I ever killed, pumping. Everything I ever done was all leading up to you. All that blood*. She can't remember when he'd said this, how many times. In all the nights and years before he'd abandoned her bed for his desk and the re-creation of his former life, when he would give her murderous love-murmurs, pet her hair, unmindful of the knots. Ten years of this, until she'd come to love the horror of him. His monstrosity. Then he'd abandoned her, the living, for those dead backlogs of his past who'd accrued in his memory such awful interest as demanded, finally, rendering in print. Then he'd taken himself away, and now Joseph—her light—into the grave-embrace of his memory.

The wind stirs the red lanterns and the partygoers below, carrying their laughter off. Elise drags her nails across a length of rope the thickness of her arm, squints again to make a sea of the Mississippi, imagines dark expansive bounds. But who is it exactly that you want to keep away? You, who are loved by monsters. Who might've bred one. You who love them too if you'll admit it.

A voice at her back: "Excuse me, miss?"

Elise turns. The woman is small, hair red gold. She bulges somewhat from her pink silk dress, the glow of her skin offset by the darkness of her narrow almond eyes. A fine thing, she must make some man happy. The woman bows her head in ritual deference to what she imagines is Elise's loss. And Elise is about to disabuse her of the notion when the woman says:

"There's no need to be so alone, my dear."

Elise, taken aback: "I prefer it." Now go away.

"Then why come?"

"That's how parties are, aren't they? You feel you have to go or else someone gets upset."

The woman smiles like a priest. "Or maybe you want to show them you are doing well, considering . . ."

Elise shakes her head. "I'm sorry." She pinches at her dress, her black, and holds it up. "My husband didn't die in the war."

"Oh," says the woman. "But that doesn't mean you should feel any differently."

She finds nothing in the woman's face to curse, no annoying tic or twist of nose or lip to this lovely little thing. Nothing to summon the rudeness it would take to drive her off. Instead, she thanks her.

Now the woman has joined her at the gunwale, shares her vantage of the river. After a few moments, the woman slips a gloved hand over hers by way of introduction. She does not let go. "Lydia Sabatier," she says.

Elise's free fingers send her cup over the edge; she stretches after it into the dark where a pitiful plop sounds from below, and looks up.

His wife. This radiant plump little thing: Emile's wife. The one who talks to ghosts.

"Oh that's all right, dear. Let me get you another." Emile's wife pats her shoulders, accidentally tugging her veil aside.

Elise pulls back from the woman's touch.

The wife draws her fingers in. "Is something wrong?"

She has always imagined her heavier, dowdier, paler, and more freckled. Not like this—ripe, thin wristed, and assured. She has had no children. And her breasts will have faint veins and stand of their own accord, her hips of their original width, ready handholds for Emile.

Lydia catches herself midstride, turns: "Oh! How stupid of me. I haven't got your name."

Elise adjusts her veil. "Pichon. Inés Pichon."

"Pretty! Now wait right here. I'll be back in a shake."

She waits for Emile's wife to disappear into the crowd massed at the punch station, then slips through a web of rigging to the port side past couples broken off for privacy and, hitching at her skirts, heads for the gangway where knots of red crepe coil like her insides raw and unstrung in the night air.

Thirteen
Little Vengeance

"You like stories, don't you, Marina?"

Tongue burning from the first taste of brandy in her life, Marina nods to Mlle Pichon.

Called out of bed this night from downstairs, summoned through floor and wall like Mademoiselle said her mother used to, Marina sits before her keeper in the bright parlor and waits to be told. The lamps along the wall give off the comforting, oceanic drone of a conch-shell held to the ear. Marina thinks of tilting her ear to the mouth of her glass, but decides against it. Lately she aims for ladyhood, and ladies do not listen to their glasses: ladies hold them by the stem, cock their heads at an angle so that their unpinned hair darkly tumbles to one shawl-covered shoulder, and they sip brandy and ask strange questions, savoring the span of their pauses. Ladies sit in nightdress and shawl beside a little table where a decanter rests on a silver tray, eyeing you with an air of initiation.

Pichon empties her glass, smacks her lips. "Then I'll tell you one I think you'll like, all right?"

"All right." She has never heard Mlle Pichon so sisterly and happy. She was like this when Marina first took her seat; she needs someone to share her happiness with, and because all the rest are at the benefit ball, Marina will have to do.

When Pichon reaches for the decanter, Marina sees the laces of her dress are all undone, dangling from the edge of the shawl, which is all that covers her bare back. Pichon keeps an elbow squeezed to one side. Otherwise the thin nightdress would fall.

"When I was eighteen," she says, "I still lived with Mme Frick. She was twenty-two, then. Only a year married, but already with the first of her fat babies—"

"What happened to her husband?"

She looks confused at the question, says, "He died, of course. Fever. Eighteen . . . fifty-seven."

"Oh." Marina thinks of Frick, who'd come today to vent her rage at being *accosted* by her enemies. By General Butler himself. Listening at the head of the stairs, Marina had stifled giggles at the woman's frets. What the woman said the other day still weighs on Marina's mind, surfacing now and again in quiet moments, trailed closely by the thought of how silent Mademoiselle had been at that moment.

Now she's anything but. Pichon is as unstoppered as her brandy cask, and as her words have the same burning effervescence, the same intoxication.

"So, I've just reached my full womanhood, and I've been living under the same roof with Mme Frick for almost ten years, since my mother died and our father brought me to live with him. Now, here I am, going to balls—not the same balls as her or Elise, but still—I'm courted." She grins. "I sneak from my window sometimes at night. And all this time my sister does not say a word; she's so wrapped up

"The policeman tapped his coin to the bars again. Hard. Held it up for me to see. 'You know what this means, eh? You know how many strokes this is worth?' I knew. I knew he had paid for my, Corraline's, *correction*. But by then I wasn't looking at him. I was on my knees, crying, reaching for my coinpurse. I dug out a dollar and told him it was his if he'd only go to Mme Jeanne Frick's at 108 Royal. She would vouch for me. I told him my name over and over in my squeaky girl's voice, so that he'd remember what to tell her. Inés Pichon, Inés Pichon, Inés Pichon. The policeman, he just stood there. Looked up and down the row of cells. 'More,' he said. I skinned my knuckles on the bar I pushed my hand—the whole purse—through so hard. The policeman snatched it and he went. Then all the girls were yowling my name back at me: 'Ee-nez Pee-shon, Ee-nez Pee-shon.' So I went to my stone bench and sat down, telling myself it would all be over in a little while."

She can see the skin of Mlle Pichon's shoulders where the shawl has been rustled loose. And maybe this is how she looked, sitting on her bench. Marina is breathless; she imagines dungeon walls pargeted with white mold in the shape of skulls. But here are Mademoiselle's uncovered shoulders. The threat of the older woman's nakedness, her confidence despite or because of it, somehow reverses standards and makes Marina feel the vulnerable one.

"So finally the policeman came back. I rushed to the bars, into his smell of beer, and he shoves my coinpurse back to me. His face is grave. He's had his drink. He says that I only make it worse on myself, slandering a white woman that way. Now I'm hollering. I can't believe it. I'm asking, begging. Yes, he went to 108 Royal; yes he spoke to Jeanne Frick, who said she hadn't the faintest idea who I was. And now the other girls are howling with laughter and singing my name. The policeman has his key, unlocks my cell. 'I've worn my goddamn legs out over you,' he says. But I wouldn't come out. I'd gone back to my bench and there was nothing to hold on to there, when he came growling in to drag me out. That sour smell of beer. He'd got himself drunk on the way back, you see. And I don't know whether it was because he could tell Jeanne had lied or he wasn't used yet to doing what he was about to do to me. He never said. He just came growling into the cell and wrapped me up in one arm, in his reek. Now I wanted to stay in that cell just as much as I'd wanted to leave it. But there was nothing to hold on to. He had me out before I could even grab the bars and I was screaming, a maniac. He carried me over his shoulder like a sack of flour and I saw all the other girls down the row of cells making mocks at me."

Marina's jaw is clenched; she feels blood throbbing at her temples. She is about to say, desperately, *What happened then?* But Mlle Pichon puts up a hand for her to pause and turns, setting down her glass on the side table. And what begins with a strange wriggle of Mademoiselle's shoulders and the easing of her elbows from her sides, ends with the shawl slipped down to her hips, her nightdress sneering open.

Her back is worked with brown-pink scars, the color of rotten beef.

"Here's what Mr. Henry Waterson paid for," she says, turning over her shoulder to catch Marina's expression, which is gaping awe at the scars and, more, at the muscle and flesh beneath them.

"Come close."

She does. Closer to this side-mouthed whisper, closer to this woman's bare back, where scars are hatched and crossed as though Mlle Pichon were an errant mark in the ledger of the world. Pichon reaches back and takes Marina by the wrist.

"Go on, feel."

Fingertips run along the whipscars.

"Fourteen," Mademoiselle says, arching round to let Marina know it's all right, that she may feel the ridges of pain, the troughs of spared skin. Pichon is the first woman she has seen unclothed since her mother was alive. This woman who is now something of a mother, a surrogate whose beauty has oppressed her, made her angry and afraid until this moment—her bare skin, the flares of muscle in her back as much a revelation as her story or her scars.

She falls round Pichon's neck, oversized and clinging now to the woman she's cursed for so long, who, hugging, begins to laugh. Little bursts of mirth, both tearful and relieved.

"It's all right, girl. Be calm." She shirks Marina's wrists from her neck, pats her cheeks and straightens her up. "You see me? I am happy . . ."

"But why?"

"You should ask your friend General Butler," she says, and seeing the knowledge dawning on Marina's face, Pichon smiles wide. "I got her," she whispers. "Jeanne. The bitch." Her smile fades into a sigh. "And do you know what she told him when he hauled her in? She said, 'Oh it couldn't have been Inés, not my *dear adopted sister*. She would never turn tattle on me . . .'" Mademoiselle snorts, reaches again for her glass. "Well, it's only a little vengeance, but we must give our paybacks when we can, my girl. And I have waited a long time to deal mine. I only wish they'd thrown her in jail. I only wish they'd—"

Marina isn't listening anymore. She has her own wishes, knotted and struggling in her head: she wishes she could be angry that Mlle Pichon went to see General Butler without telling her, without saying a word to the general about her either—and she knows this will one day be a festering resentment; she wishes she hadn't heard the story, touched the scars, shared the liquor and the lap she's yet to leave. And that she now finds herself bound to this woman in a way she can neither deny nor name. She has been a daughter and a niece, and neither felt like this. She has been a friend, but women are not friends with girls.

"I was so tired of you hating me," says Mlle Pichon as she pets Marina's hair. Down and up, in steady, practiced strokes of the same hand she slapped me with outside the museum. Now it's soft and kind and wants me to stay, wants me to know. And where is Joseph? Maybe looking out his window or in bed asleep, dreaming heroics for his vile father while his mother dances at the ball that won't abide Pichon, whose happiness at her little vengeance seems to fade even now. Her face slackens and she searches the bright extents of her petty keep. And watching the woman's relief slowly replaced by an unknowable wrenching tension, Marina is overcome with a loneliness the likes of which she's never known.

Another brandy, then to bed. Mademoiselle gives this little admonishment. Any more and you'll wake to your first hangover in the morning.

So they sit a while longer. Mlle Pichon wonders aloud at the hour, and that Elise hasn't come calling yet. It's her friend's custom to come and talk with her after such events; though the last was so long ago she might've forgotten the practice. Then silence, as though she were listening for the springs and wheels and hoofbeats. And Marina, settling back with the warm fist of liquor in her chest, considers secrets of her own—she should share them in kind—but finds hers too small to match the revelations of the night.

Fourteen

The Woman in the Web

Picture yourself a corpse, suspended in a netting of fine mesh strung from hooks in a cool spare annex, hanging there while the seasons play their parts on a Paris that, like your corpse-self, goes unchanged, inviolate of time and weather. Some man, a professor, has made you so. Now picture a young Emile, going each night to visit you and look upon your features. You are Jeanne Martin, corpse, curing in the air. But you are not her; you are what Emile wishes to see: Elise Durel, preserved and inescapable.

In Emile's office the gilded clock strikes ten. A lone paean to its affixed statue of a woman in shining robes, herself beside a bottle somewhat less filled than it was an hour ago. Elise must look up to see the hands. It should be midnight, a more auspicious hour. Beside her, Emile makes dark pillow talk. Of his youth and the webbed woman. She listens, and still she can't believe the door to his office was unlocked, no more reckonable a fact than his appearance. She'd sat for an hour, drinking, fiddling with his charts and instruments as if to decipher within them the source of her need and the reason she had come here, to the den of the one who hunted her. She'd been sitting in his chair, swiveling slowly, holding up a vial of something noxious, labeled in Latin, when he came in.

She raised the vial to his bewildered eyes, saying, *What would this do?*

To you?

Yes. To me.

Kill you.

She cupped the vial. *And what would* you *do, Emile?*

Bewilderment rusted and fallen from his face, he smiled, stepped inside, and locked the door behind him.

Pretend to be a corpse. Stiffen yourself on the cold parquet floor of his office, your hands resting at your hips, where his sharper blades have bruised them. No color yet, but the ache is there. Emile lays alongside, in a tangle of his own clothes across his lap, his arm stretched out to prop your head. Muscle smooth as a boy's, a fluttering fascination compared to the fleshy knots you've known. He has given you his handkerchief to squeeze between your legs.

He goes on about the woman in the web, how he saw you there in her. Sixteen years ago.

And they called *me* a ghoul. Is this supposed to be a compliment, Emile? He says he doesn't know. He's not practiced at compliments. Only his mouth moves, and even this stops and he stares up at the dappled ceiling. He's so close your smell on his lips mingles with that of his pomade. You want to kiss yourself from him, but you are dead and so is he. A children's game. The first to move is the loser.

They lay on the floor in the space where the pair of rococo chairs had stood, now kicked to the far corner and ornamented with her clothes. The same chairs in which she and her mother had sat so many years ago, when Emile had taken down her racial history, noted her down to the last speck of blood, white and black. Somewhere here, in one of these cabinets among the vials and jars and bones and ribboned portfolios, is her chart of descent. Remember Maman so nervously delighted at the sight of Emile. What a shame it's not him, she'd said. But you'll see, dear, an older man is no bad thing.

Angel. For the first time since his death, her husband seems truly gone; here in this cramped little room where she'd signed her life away, he is exorcised. If only for a moment. She knows that when she goes home, a distant consideration, Angel will reassert his ghostly presence in the form of their son. But for now he's gone and she has shed her black remembrance in crumpled pile, her crinoline and hoop upturned, showing its cagework. Her corset sits stiff and upright in the chair, a phantom, overseeing self.

Once a nineteen-year-old girl sat in that chair, without prospects, hopes pinned to a hideous arrangement, listening as her mother enumerated their familial curse to a boy she had run from years before. Back then, Emile's look had withered her, struck her silent and obliging while he talked and talked about the arrangement, about his client, about her health and race. A fine initiation for married life.

Tonight she'd sat in that chair again, uncaged, in her last layer of clothes; the hoop cartwheeled to a corner, her legs free. This time it was she who did the talking. Sitting low in the chair with her hips outthrust, she told him how she'd met his wife. Emile's eyes alighting in his own corrupt thoughts. She's very pretty. Prettier than I imagined. He'd said nothing, stunned and trying so hard to maintain himself, to tell himself he hadn't lost. To convince himself this was still a conquest preordained, that he hadn't been preempted and undone, when it was she who sat and commanded. *On your knees.* She who directed him, with an incline of chin and the opening of her legs, to the split in the crotch of her culottes.

Elise lets a hand wander past the bunched handkerchief into which she leaks, down to her right thigh, where he'd wiped his mouth when she was done. There, a fine dried sheen.

On the floor he'd torn at the remainder of her clothes, wanting her in absolute nudity. His eyes darting, noting her like an experiment. So strangely silent. No matter. The air, the words, belonged to her. A sudden, dark incantatory voice whose every word urged him on towards furious, trembling surrender. His handkerchief a limp white flag she'd accepted between thighs that are stronger than she's ever known. When she had them round his waist and squeezed, she thought Emile's eyes might burst. So, harder. Her insides had been strung down the gang of the British ship, but now she's gathered them back and with them the strength required to inflict herself on him.

She breathes the chemical air, traces escaped from his vials of poison and cure. He doesn't move, so nor will she. Desire dispatched for the moment, and in its void she feels arise a nameless dread. Of the future, of herself, of this man beside her with his slowly rising chest, his pale green eyes lighting on her, keen as one of his knives.

PART 4

The Gallows Season

Butler

One
Mercy

On May 31, he commutes the death-sentence of the Fort Jackson six. An uneasy pen-stroke deals life—at hard labor on Ship Island. The ink clots, the blotters' edges curl with damp. Butler brushes the crumbs of a working lunch from the signed order. George Strong is pleased, though withered somewhat by the climate, his bright eyes ringed, his lungs rattling; Strong offers to shake his hand. In this way, we mark the end of the first month of occupation.

The city sweats and grumbles on as June dawns, mercury hitches up the thermometer's gullet and summer starts its broil. The women keep their heads hung now—no more emptied chamber pots, no more curses. His men may go in peace, and to their credit not a single complaint of misconduct has been received. Uterine fury is vanquished; so it seems.

Not to say we are without discontent. What passed for a police force resigns overnight, in support of their imprisoned chief, justices, and mayor. Within forty-eight hours he has five hundred recruits and a bronzer working overtime to hammer out stars. His fresh forces are ready just in time to meet a score or two of slaves escaped from northward plantations, marching into New Orleans expecting freedom and protection. His policemen know the sound a cudgel makes on flesh and bone; they are dockworkers and roustabouts, Irishmen and Germans who took their beatings from the local White-Caps. They are ready to deal out pain and establish their place in the new order. The riot lasts a quarter hour, Butler arriving afterward to see the brained facedown and the rest herded limping off to the contraband camps he's thrown up in different quarters of the city and its outskirts. He will not have the escapees be indolent, as is their nature; he orders his officers to put them to work. The stauncher abolitionists complain; he tolerates them. There are reports that Colonel Phelps, at Carrolton, drills his blacks like soldiers. Already the camps in New Orleans are overcrowded with those who sneak from their masters' houses late at night. There are reports of abominable sanitary conditions. Open latrines, flocks of flies and mosquitos. You can smell them for blocks.

The end of May sees the first case of yellow fever. The captain of the Bahamian bark who offloaded the sick man claims he had no knowledge. When they passed the quarantine station the fellow wasn't ill. Not my problem anymore the captain says, hiding behind the Union Jack. Butler would like to have him shot. The Creole doctor had agreed, before hurrying off to oversee the sealing-up of the rooming house in which the sick man lay, to make sure the barrels of tar were burnt day and night, and not a single occupant would be allowed outside until thirty days had passed. Meantime he puts in place a forty-day quarantine downriver for any ship wishing to dock at New Orleans. Any foreign ship, that is. The Creole doctor thought this a most admirable design, saying so on his last visit, when he pleasantly informed him that the feverish man was dead and as yet none of the other occupants were affected.

Lately he watches Sarah for signs of sallowness or discomfort. He hopes she doesn't notice his inspections, but the heat is coming and the fear is on. As it stands, she is healthy, if somewhat thinned. The food does not agree with her.

Parish prison has grown crowded. The usual thieves and brawlers are joined by more exotic specimens awaiting transport to Ship Island or the forts: spies; pass-forgers; the authors and publishers of seditious literature; the owner of a drawing-shop that sold unflattering prints of the general; a man who flaunted a watch fob made of human bones, claiming they were the remains of a United States soldier.

Exiled loyalists return, brimming with sanctimony: a dentist who harangues theatregoers about the playing of Confederate tunes; a clergyman, lately defrocked, wishing to enlighten the blacks; ex-councilmen and ministers who swear that Louisiana's secession election was rigged.

He receives them in parties at his new living quarters, the mansion of a Confederate general now serving in Texas, a veteran of the Mexican War. The previous occupant of the immense brownstone, the man's niece, made a great scene about taking with her an engraved sword given to her uncle by Winfield Scott. Butler, sadly, cannot grant this request. Before his and Sarah's trunks are unpacked, he has the sword sent to President Lincoln. A tribute.

In the mansion, bounded by neighbors upon whose backs he's laid the rod of tax to feed the poor, his life regains order and a semblance of peace. Now he rises at six, breakfasts in the palatial peace of the Confederate general's second dining room, talks with his wife and reads familial mail, frees his mind of all domestic snares before departing for the Custom House at nine.

The streets unpeel like giftwrapping, the benumbed populace going about their daily business or lack thereof. At the corner of Canal and Decatur, his red flag flutters from the empty shop of a cobbler who, in the first week of the occupation, refused to shoe a Rhode Island lieutenant. The owner is in prison, the shop's contents sold at auction and purchased by brother Jackson, whose hoard grows immense. He rides up a block, rows of businesses whose columns are painted with black squares. Marks of mourning by their owners who have refused to reopen. He fines them one hundred dollars each, but some are so flush from speculation that they pay the fine just to prove a point. They do not realize that the first step in a return to normalcy is opening for business. For America to reunite, to lift itself up from the chaos of disunion, we must get back to work. This city owes her very bones to business.

For in her earliest, colonial days New Orleans had no buildings of stone. This was a city of logs and mud—palmetto-thatch for the poor, rough board floors for the gentry. Then came trade: ships exchanged their ballast of stone and African bodies for the sweet weight of sugar, kegs of indigo dye, bundles of tobacco, all soon usurped by the rise of King Cotton; and it was from the ballast, from the measure of her trade, that New Orleans erected her first stone buildings. Know them by their pockmarked blocks, chipped away in holds and by the rain, quite unlike the newer, smooth gray edifices of Quincy granite.

Ballast has become his business, too. Now that he's freed shipping from across the lake, from Texas and from the rebel-held interior, there is an increasing flow of horded sugar and cotton coming to the docks. The outlying planters who wrote him so many seething letters now have felt the wartime pinch, and so they trade with him. They send their cotton and the sugar they've kept stored, and he sends them back ready money and their fleeing Negroes, when possible. So when his transports and the ships under Federal flag offload munitions and supplies and stone, he directs their holds to be filled with cotton and sugar, listed on the ships' ledgers not as taxable commerce or Confederate trade, but as ballast. A neat trick, a winking subterfuge.

And the city's walls, whether ballast stone or the yield of Massachusetts quarries, withhold whispers. For the first three days of June he hears them, reported back by his agents and officers, by loyalists and the continual flow of blacks, and even brother Jackson, who takes some pleasure in the revelation: *They're saying you're soft, Ben. All talk, no tack. All bluster, no muster. The Beast has no Teeth.*

Enough.

June 3. He signs the order for the execution of William Mumford. The man who tore the flag from the Mint has languished at his expense for long enough; he will be the next object in the city's continual lesson, another opportunity for the foolish to raise their voices, stick out their necks. Mumford's will be snapped on the seventh.

Before George Strong—looking more ill by the day—is out of the room, Butler calls him back to the desk. He has a change to make. Mumford will be hung from the parapet of the Mint, just below the Stars and Stripes.

"Sir?"

"After the old custom, George," he says. "Execution at the scene of the crime."

When Strong is gone, his orderly, Tibbets, gestures at the air, wipes his bald brows. "The heat's upon us now, sir. And only June."

It seems far longer than a month since he first set foot in the city. And the heat, well: the natural world is equaled by human devices. He sent the Confederate general's sword to Lincoln as something of a placation; Secretary Seward is up in arms, paralyzed with fear that he has impugned the foreign consuls, "whose neutrality we must preserve."

215

Secretary Seward is not gratified to hear that Butler has been condemned from the floor of Parliament by the prime minister of Great Britain for Order 28.

He'd like to see Viscount Palmerston try to bring a hostile capital to heel with so little bloodshed. But the British Empire has other methods, strapping sepoys across cannon-mouths and the like. The women of Bombay or Hong Kong or Dublin wouldn't have been met with such tolerance, nor had their behavior corrected with such ingenuity.

So five days until Mumford hangs. Five days of renewed bluster and groans. They will say that since I didn't hang the parolees, I won't hang Mumford either. They will dredge up precedent and legality of my order, wheedling and nettling while the scaffold goes up. They will—though they'll never admit it—see the kindness of my soldiers, that none have abused any women, and think I'll grant another reprieve.

He sees Mumford, wearing the scrap of flag as a boutonniere, shaking his fist at the window of the St. Charles that morning weeks ago. His black-red hair and florid face. His gambler's air. The fool, he'll be the one to pay.

That evening he finds in the library of the Confederate general's mansion an old edition of *Robinson Crusoe*, his favorite book as a child, one of the few novels his mother allowed, and only then because the minister acceded Defoe some instructive moral heft.

On Ship Island he often wished he'd brought a copy to accompany those days and nights of wave-rush and the rustling of sand and palm. He wished he'd had a copy to give the little girl. Marina. He hasn't thought of her in so long. How nice to have a child around that's not your own. And it is, now, with remembered childlike delight that he sits down in one of his enemy's overstuffed chairs and cracks the spine. As a boy he'd loved Crusoe's lonely industry, tried his own hand at hut-making in the woods up Beacon Hill, bemoaned the lack of palm-fronds for clothes and a black boy to play his Friday. He dreamed of warmer climes, as did his father. And more: reading over and again his favorite passage, when Crusoe, after much of the minister's favored moralizing, puts into action his plan to slaughter the savage cannibals of the neighboring island.

Finding the proper page, he puts up his feet and settles in.

Bloody schemes, bloody acts. What more can you ask?

Two

Eavesdropping

"How many nights is it?"

"Four," says Bernice. "Fourth night, fourth time. She skips every other night."

"Pretty soon she won't skip no nights."

"She'll skip something else if she's not careful."

Laughter muffled by the sounds of halfhearted kitchen work: Pot-scrape and clang. Pouring water. Steam. Listening, Joseph crouches in the darkened hall, waits until he can hear the slaves' voices again. 'Ti Poucet: that clever boy.

Ligeia: "And here she was, sulking round the house like a skinny cat."

Un chat maigre. Bernice does not reply, clicks her tongue.

"Not even a whole month since—" says Ligeia.

"I don't want to hear it again. Don't want to think it again."

He'd come down for something from the kitchen-safe. Bread or ham, a handful of dried shrimp. Now he sits and chews his inner cheek. They are talking about his mother, who left the house after dinner. When she was in the parlor, veil down, pulling on her gloves, he'd stood in his nightshirt at the foot of the stairs and asked where she was going. He could see even behind her veil his mother's eyes squeeze shut in annoyance. She flashed them open, said: *For the hundredth time.* Out. *You don't ask the business of adults.* She flicked her hand at him so that the half-filled fingers of her glove flapped. *Now to bed, my love.*

"I don't want to hear it."

Maybe Bernice worries about his father's ghost. She used to talk about ghosts, to sit him down by the stove and say how the Gros Zombi, who rode the boat over from Saint-Domingue, would reach his long white arms up to Joseph's window and snatch him out of bed that very night if he wouldn't behave. When he shuts his eyes he sees the pale fingers, many knuckled and impossibly stretched, rapping at his window, shudders as he had a few moments before when passing the door to his father's room. And was it Bernice or Ligeia who would say not to go out at night because a pair of alligators lived in the halls? At the time, when he was three or four, their story had backfired: someone would have to carry him about even before the lights were low. He remembers his father holding him in the crook of his single arm, kicking a heel at dark corners, whispering, *There. Got the bastard. We'll collect his teeth in the morning.* For years Joseph would feel the gators nipping at his heels. But not anymore. Now he's almost grown; now he knows true fright.

In the kitchen the work grows rancorous. Water scalds; grease pops. Objects are personified and cursed. He hears the slip and clap of their wet hands, smells the bite of lye and scouring powder. He waits, held in place by their gossip. They know where his mother goes.

"All I say is that I'm glad he don't come by anymore and ask me questions about Madame." Ligeia's voice growls into a man's. "'When she gets up?' 'What she wears, what she says?' 'How she spends her money?'"

"Like he wished he had a little eyehole in the wall . . ."

"What I wonder is how on Earth would knowing little things like that profit a man? You know? Not secrets or what she looks like with her clothes off, but what she eats for breakfast?"

"Maybe he just wanted to know."

"I say that makes it worse."

"Maybe so."

Hesitation. A wrung rag snaps wetly like a chicken's broken neck.

"I tell you what," Ligeia says. "I'm glad the doctor's got her. I wouldn't wish either of them on nobody else."

The doctor. She's with him. Joseph scratches nervously at his bare leg. Gooseflesh risen though it's hot here at the kitchen's mouth. His father would kill the man, run him through, pare off his ears and show them to him, stake him to a beach at low tide. And there is a part of him that says a dutiful son should do the same. He imagines the doctor pained and fearful, but the man's image is overtaken by that of Joseph's mother. She's the deserving one.

"Stop it."

A pot slams. "You gonna tell me I shouldn't hate 'em? You go on and tell me, Berry. They didn't take nothing from you."

Bernice's voice is small: "Shouldn't be glad about it. That's all I mean."

Ligeia snorts. "That man don't know what he's in for."

"She might not either. Trim that fire now."

The stove-door clangs; there is the sound of breath pushed out from between ballooned cheeks. Ligeia stands. "This mean you're getting cold feet?"

"No." Bernice sighs. "But they're still turning niggers away quick as they come."

"Then what's the worst? They send you right on back—"

"Wait," says Bernice. And when he hears her coming out the kitchen, her bare feet slapping the tile, he's already up and scurrying for the stairs, thudding off the arms of the couches. Crystal hums with the swiftness of his passage.

"You stay in bed now or—!"

Or what? Ghosts? The Zombi will reach for me with his long fingers?

Good.

He pulls himself upstairs. There is no ogre to escape, no gators waiting in the hall. That feeling of jaws snapping the air at your heels is the opening and closing of all their lying mouths.

Three

The Spirit-World

Candle-lit faces turn in surprise, regard the doctor with wide eyes and shadowed disappointment. The people, four women and two men, his wife has gathered in her parlor for this night's spiritual conference must have thought they'd summoned a lively one. They are holding hands round a small table covered in purple cloth, where wax runs in ectoplasmic rivulets and carefully selected effects of the dearly departed are arranged in the shape of a star. Unlike her guests, who bear expressions of idiot credulity, Lydia's lips are pursed, her eyes narrowed to aggravated slits.

He laughs: "From among the living, I'm afraid."

The guests frown. Lydia is seething. And there, on the table beside brushes snatched with the hair of the dead and tarnished saint's medals, is a small withered bundle.

"And what's that?" he asks.

Lydia starts up. "Really, Emile." But one of her followers, an older man with silver hair, says proudly, "It is the mummified hand of an Egyptian princess. Of singular power and—"

"Ah!" he says. "Well, must be defective if it summoned only me."

Lydia bunches a fistful of tablecloth, opens her mouth, but he is gone. "Better luck next time," he calls back, drawing off his gloves. And on the way to his room, Dr. Sabatier savors the moment: science striding in and scattering superstition.

He dismisses Francis, the old footman; he will undress himself and make his own toilette. Francis, who served Lydia's father in the same capacity, ancient as the princess mummy's hand, recedes. One by one the doctor drops his studs and links into a silver bowl, escapes his shirt and lets it fall to the floor imagining how Francis's joints will creak in the morning.

His own are somewhat pained. There are no soft spaces in his office; what he does with Elise is on the floor (thus the impressions in his knees) or standing, her palms at the wall or grasping the lip of his desk (thus the soreness of his iliotibial bands) or in one of the chairs, where she hangs her legs overs its arms and he envisions stirrups, examinations. Clamps.

She has an unaccountable appreciation for the more grisly aspects of medicine. But maybe he shouldn't be so surprised that Elise the Ghoul wants to know about scalpels and surgical saws, about poisons and ether-masks and disease. Perhaps now instead of biting off Claude Arnaud's earlobe, she would delicately pare it with a catlin knife.

When he found the copy of the *London Medical Gazette* and showed her the diagram of the British machine, the crank-handled instrument for pacifying the clitoral node, she'd laughed so that he had to stifle his surprise. He'd meant to frighten her. *Well*, she said. *It doesn't need to be that complicated.* Then she mimed how it would be to hold it in her hands, turning the crank.

And did she do the same with Woolsack and his guns? Hold pistols at her breast and lay rifles between her legs? For the doctor she poses in her overskirt and stockings, holding a tenon saw at the fat of her bare thigh so that its teeth make dimples in her flesh.

He, cautioning: *Any more pressure and you'll need stitches.*

And will you give them to me, Emile?

With pleasure, he says. *And silver thread.*

He has never spoken like this with a woman. Not with the Paris whores of his youth, and not with Lydia, though she has her own dark speeches. There's some liberation in these moments with Elise, yet with every word he feels a bolt unshot in his faculties, his reason.

From the moment in her bedroom, the day after Woolsack's suicide, when he touched her and there'd been that feeling of untrammeled possession, he'd known. But it was she who brought this about. And if he stops to consider it for long, he might feel unmanned—as though he were the one seduced. But he does not stop; he cannot or he will fail in all his aims. You are infected; now embrace the symptoms. Analyze them. Bear their contradictions, like the fevered's shivering sweat.

The symptoms of their encounters show on her skin. He can count her contusions—from the room's edges, the chair, his overeager hands. Eight as of tonight. Elise has left no similar marks on him. She is not like Lydia, who goes in claws-first.

He thinks of his wife. Lydia's desire is yoked to her anger; she might even come calling, after the little scene downstairs. He stretches out in bed, thinks how pleasing it would be to deny her. The look on Lydia's face when she sees he's not the one in need.

Need disarms us, robs us of our primacy and control. And which, between he and Elise, is the needier? He can't decide. Tonight she'd laid him out on the floor while she surrounded him with vials and jars and cylinders, expectorants and caustics and ameliorants, narcotics and poisons—*but anything, Elise, can be a poison if you take enough of it*—and with that acumen she'd said their names like incantations one after the other, until he was surrounded and couldn't make a move without upsetting something labeled with a grinning little skull.

Rolling her eyes to a double-lined jar of sulfuric acid, she asked, *Why don't they just spray it across the battlefields, or some other poison? That'd be short work. Short war.* He watched her register his delight. *But then,* she said, *you'd have to take your chances with the wind.*

In his dreams the doctor is visited by poisons and diseases in disguise. They assume the forms of women masqueraders, so that he knows their identities though their faces are hidden. Calomel in dusty white linen; Diphtheria in her gray slick shroud; Yellow Fever drips black silk; Arsenic tosses pale yellow frills; Strychnine writhes in bunched garters; Cholera in fouled umber crinolines; Consumption, dainty in her white housedress splotched with virulent red rosettes; and his very own good lady, Cyanosis, raven haired and decked in blue surcoat and robes, her midnight stole bunching at the edges of her Columbine. Passing nearer than the rest, she brushes his cheek with the back of her hand. He sees the bruises on her arm, her trailing black hair, and he knows who she is despite the mask. The beautiful diseases are gathered at his bedside; they twirl and glide, surrounding him. And it is the greatest dream of his life.

Four
The Eve of Execution

Mumford's children mill about their mother's skirts—three small figures wavering at the entrance to the library of the Confederate general's mansion. He marks them as between the ages of four and seven, the mother somewhere in her thirties. Sandy haired, her eyes dark. The small ones gawk at Tibbets, touch their brows. Butler rises from his chair, waves them in and the discomfited orderly out. The woman hasn't taken two steps when the children, as if on cue, rush past her and clamber at his knees.

He didn't want this: the weeping and mewling, the little fists tugging his pants legs, little feet stomping his slippers, their hiccoughing cries. He uses his palms to try and gently force the children back, but they are a swarming pair and on a mission. If you were sent to plead your father's life, you'd put on no less of a show.

"My father is an upright man—"

"Good-hearted man!"

"A pillar—"

"General Butler, sir—"

"We shall starve!"

"My father is—"

And one doesn't have to be Sarah to hear rehearsal in their voices. He can spot craftily prepared testimony, knows such tactics well. When all else fails and the judge is eyeing you harshly, send in the begging babes.

He tries to ease them off and, failing, signals clench jawed to their mother for assistance. The woman hangs back. "Children," she sings, to no avail. And he has struck children before, though not his own: the unruly lads of the Lowell schoolhouse it was his twenty-two-year-old self's misfortune to teach for a year. They ran roughshod over him for the first few weeks of term; by Halloween he'd brought the rod and peace. Just like he will do in New Orleans. At his hips the children, who have their father's black-red bristly hair, jounce and wail themselves incomprehensible. When they are gone, he knows, he'll find silvery trails of dried snot on his trousers and cuffs.

"My father is . . ."

Your father is a professional gambler whose actions nearly caused this city to be shelled to ruins. Your father is a reprobate from North Carolina, not even from the city he "so loves." Your father is careless, and ridiculous. He should've thought about you before he climbed the parapet of the Mint while the guns of the fleet were trained on the town. Your father is a man who offered no apology or defense when brought before the tribunal; he knew what was at stake. Your father is an object lesson. And even if he were an *upright* man, he won't be so for long. By Saturday noon he'll be a prone man.

So Butler tells himself while he calls for his carriage, urges the woman and her sniffling children out, to take it and go to the prison, where they may stay with Mumford as long as they wish. At the door

The Five

Five

Execution

Morning, June 7, 1862. New Orleans turns out in full. Shops are shuttered, dishes left soaking in wash-pans, breakfasts abandoned untouched or hurriedly downed so that stomachs jostled in the omnibuses and cars streaming now in the direction of the Mint are alternately roiling and overfull. Their owners share condolent looks while others dab at encrusted eyes, at beer-stained shirts, reach for their necks (as many will today in instinctual sympathy with the condemned) and wonder where their collars could have gone to. The furtive resign themselves to swat their wives for making them late; the moony envision what descriptions they will give sweethearts whose mothers have banned them from attending. But these delicates are fewer than you'd think, for among the riders are wives in housedresses and others enhooped and used to wider berths, and crossing Canal, following the winding track of Claiborne in their carriages, are ladies, dressed for a funeral, and those who trudge behind husbands pushing vendors' carts or bang their pots and children both with the ends of long ladles, strutting roundheels with bonnets mismatched to their dresses, black nurses whose pale wrinkled palms are wonders to their white charges, and ex-slaves who now charge fees for washing. Freemen in Paris frock coats and shining kid boots go on horseback alongside cotton factors burping last night's turtle, trailed by sunburnt laborers from Jefferson and Carrolton; from across the river the Algiers ferry has brought its cargo of humanity, and at the point of the Esplanade and Good Children the faubourgs disgorge their inhabitants by every mode of conveyance: all closing in on the Old Quarter, on the Mint, until the infrastructure of the city can no longer bear the strain and at the intersections traffic knots into infuriating snarls so that riders must debark, make their way afoot through the thronging candy-sellers and coffee-stalls, shouldering yellow-fingered tobacconists and sneezing bookstore clerks who view the sun with surprise from beneath the visor of a hand, all hurrying faster as the hour draws near. And at the Mint another struggle: where to stand? A jostling scrum before the fences and the cordon lined with bayonets pointing skyward, at the Mint itself and the scaffolding beneath its parapet, so the spectators attain vantages not always suited to their ages, heights, and social stations. For this is not the theatre; there is no dress circle, parquette, or private box; and now the limbs of the oaks are fringed with the dangling legs of boys who drop orange rinds onto the hats of gentlemen below who look up, raise their fists, but just as quick reaffix their gazes to the gallows. No one wants to miss the martyring.

There is barely room enough for Marina to breathe. Farther back than she'd like, but the space before the soldiers is occupied by a crowd of men, friends of the condemned, swigging from bottles and throwing back their coats so that everyone can see the revolvers at their hips. Mademoiselle said last night it was an important thing to see, that her mother brought her to hangings at parish prison when she was a girl. Now, seeing the men with bottles and guns, Mademoiselle grows nervous: "We shouldn't have come." Marina isn't worried; the American soldiers are here. She searches the soldiers' faces for someone she knows. A Prospero or Ferdinand or Ariel, but they are so alike beneath their low-tugged caps. Marina sticks out her chin, as if to give an impression of strength to the men with their pistols and whiskey, to Mlle Pichon, and searches the crowd for Joseph and his mother. They were all together when they came to the Mint, but the crowd-crush has parted them. She wishes she'd been holding Joseph's hand; she wishes he hadn't seen, when the four of them were walking, her stop unconsciously at the window of a shop where sat a porcelain doll in medieval hood and pearls—that moment in which she wanted the doll, how perfect it would be for parts in the stories always forming in her head and begging to be played out—and Mlle Pichon had to say, *Oh isn't she pretty!* And before Marina could regain herself and laugh it off as silly and for little girls Mademoiselle asked if Marina would like to have her, and there was Joseph smirking and she had to scowl and stomp ahead, hearing from behind a sad sigh from Mademoiselle, who was only trying to be kind. Now the woman in her is embarrassed, the girl guilty. The crowd sways, exhales as one, and the friends of the condemned raise their hands and voices when the man is brought out. Their hurrahs are so strident you would think they want him dead. An officer she recognizes sadly as Major Strong steps forward to give a quavering read of the execution order, his bright clear voice melting like his fabled snow, then retreats as guards bring the condemned man forward. With his long black beard and wild eyes, hair tousled and hands tied behind his back, he reminds her of a pirate brought to justice. Her girl-guilted self reaches for Mademoiselle's hand, and is glad to be received and for the smile the woman gives her as she turns back to the scene. The condemned man speaks in a loud, commanding voice. He is saying his piece, striding back and forth on the scaffold, which strikes Marina as very much like a stage. A riverward wind unfurls the American flag, its edges flickering just above the gibbet.

Oh dear God, Elise thinks. *He's talking about the damned flag.* The man, Mumford, rolls his head heavenward and addresses it: he fought under this flag, he says, in the Seminole Wars, in the Mexican War, and did it proudly . . . Joseph nods along, little jaw jutting, lower lip stuck out in what he must think is a manly fashion but smacks purely of petulance. Elsewhere Mmes Frick and Decorde and Schmidt are sitting in their carriages, sipping lemonade. Emile, also, somewhere in this crushing crowd, she imagines him holding the hand of his red-dressed wife, who is so delicate she may faint but insists on being here to see patriotism at its height.

In a Paris museum Dr. Sabatier once saw an executioner's sword. Short, blunt tipped, and German, its blade inscribed with a verse: *When I raise this sword, I wish the sinner eternal life.* And, he knows, General Butler in his way wishes the same for William Mumford. Butler knows the names of dangerous men, men who threaten his life, yet Mumford is the one he hangs. Why? Because it looks better. Hang a man who threatens to kill you and you look like a coward, even to your home-front friends slapping with glee their copies of Beecher Stowe and their Protestant Bibles. But hang the man who desecrated the glorious symbol of Our Nation, and you have a ready answer for the platforms of the future. An electable answer: *I so love the flag that* . . . Because this order, this death, is only meant in part for now, rather it will exist in perpetuity in the minds of the Northern electorate, or so Butler hopes. The gaunt, sickly Illinois rail-splitter may not withstand the next election. And one day the people will ask, *Who can keep the South in line? Butler!* Butler, who is nowhere to be seen. He must be hidden among the officers at the foot of the gallows. Lydia flicks open her fan, bats gold chrysanthemums at her face. In her hair she wears a cockade of Confederate red and white. There is something beautiful in the stern set of her mouth, her unblinking gaze. The fan wafts Lydia's smell at him and, with it, memory. Hazy and disjointed: their wedding night. Had he pretended then that she was Elise? He envisions the low lamp, her bare chest and the Paris cold somehow still inhabiting his hands, so that when he touched her Lydia shivered. As Mumford shivers now, coming to the end of his ridiculous speech. The man's face is florid from shouting; see the penultimate flows of his blood. When he's hung, Mumford's blood, the color of Lydia's ribbon, will thunder downward, exploding arteries and valves, gorging veins and organs in stupendous rupture. The tongue and eyes will swell; the legs will kick even as they burn with the sanguine downthrust. The heart will halt. The genitals will grow congested. No polite person will mention this fact.

Butler's officers will tell him later that Mumford kept looking in the direction of headquarters, as though word of a reprieve would arrive at any time. A telegraph from Washington, a gunshot, a white dove, a burning bush. Butler cannot see for himself; he is in his office in the Custom House, alone. Outside his door a fifteen-man guard is arrayed, the cavernous building silent but for their echoed coughs. *For God's sake: talk*, he thinks, scratching away at dispatches to Secretary Seward, who is beleaguered with complaints from the foreign consuls. Seward and the consuls cannot hold his mind. He checks his watch. Ten minutes to noon. He has ordered that the execution be put off until the last possible moment. This might be interpreted as either mercy or cruelty, and he's glad to occupy the limn. Butler snaps the watch shut. Now it should begin, unless his watch and those of Strong and Provost Marshal Phelps, whom he allowed to dissuade him from attending with a fight he hopes they didn't sense was feigned, aren't synchronized and the deed is already done. It's growing hotter; sweat dots the page. He fishes out another smaller sheet, writes: *Dear Paul, I hope you are well. Today I had a man hung and didn't even show my face—* Now the paper is balled in his fist; he pitches it across the room. He's had no sleep in two days, and his greatest fear is not that some assassin will burst in, but that the men will come and find him with his head down, asleep at his desk. Just as the bastard humorists had him depicted at Big Bethel, dozing while his troops turned tail and ran. Later they will say Mumford kept glancing towards the Custom House and salvation through the end of his speech, and when the provost guard came to pull the black hood over his head, he was still looking.

The gallows is a scorpion, hunched and bristled. From its gibbet-tail the noose drips like poison. The rope writhes as it is looped over the man's hooded head, then takes on the motions of the quaking of his body. Joseph feels his own throat tighten. Beside him, his mother has her hand over her mouth. The liar. And he considers how his father, in his book, mentions hanging men. Joseph sees the lantern-lit trees, stout limbs slung with rope. His father, hauling two-handed. Now the crowd cries out, disjointed choirs of rage, contempt, and pity. Almost like a song. He must jump to see, and even then he glimpses only the gibbet and the rope, the noose cinched around the black hood. A flash of shivering shoulders. He springs upward as if borne by the shot-sound of the fallen trap: the black hood is gone; the poison rope swings taut.

Six

Adieu, Maîtresse

The moment Mumford's body goes slack all chance of riot passes on into whatever collective storehouse the people keep their rage. She can almost see it, rising up from the slowly dispersing crowd— now orderly, even polite—like steam off watered streets. She keeps her hand at the back of Joseph's neck, steering him in his surly jags through what has become a herd of sleepwalkers trudging back to their beds. Now and again she pinches his nape and Joseph turns, scowling. The sharper he scowls, the tighter she squeezes: little reminders that, dear boy, you are still mine. And he's been so angry lately, without a lone kind word. But this, she tells herself, is the way boys are. Mother, the first casualty of their ascension to adulthood. You are the first woman they will hurt. You're the strop, the whetstone upon which boys hone themselves into Angels and Emiles.

Now more than ever she will show him what women can do. Over the murmurs of the others on the street, she loudly tells her son what a waste it was. "What an awful, stupid waste." Neighbors filter back indoors for an afternoon of wound-licking, yet among them there is also an air of relief, as we feel when the most reckless child on the block breaks his arm or drowns and becomes a lesson to the rest: See, that's what you get. Now behave.

Joseph could have been such an exemplar. The occupation day, her frantic hunt, comes clawing to her mind. She folds his nape between the knuckles of her thumb and forefinger. When did you stop loving me? Answers peek round corners and quickly flee.

Just as well they've lost Inés and the girl. Elise is in no mood for the children's whispers, their secretive looks pregnant with the implication of childhood's end. She wants to say, *You have no secrets. I know everything you have done and will do.* But there it is, in Joseph's eyes: the look he's had since the night of Angel's death—that he knows something and saves it for himself while dangling the inference before her face. She lets go his neck when they come to the steps and he follows her up. All you can know, dear, is that I go out. Even with your readings of your father's filthy book, you aren't worldly enough to guess.

When she opens the door Joseph dallies on the steps, looking up and down the street.

"Dear Lord," she says from the entryway. "You'll see her later." For Christ's sake, should I have the rings sized?

Hands in his pockets, shoulders at his ears, Joseph comes. She goads him, shuts the door, and in this moment, hearing the empire of her voice over the all-too-silent house, Elise is suddenly afraid.

The jalousies are shut, as they should be, against the heat. The house bears its accustomed midday dim, as it will until late afternoon, when the sun sets and a measure of coolness returns and the lamps can be lit. It's not the dark that worries her. Like on the night when the curfew cannon didn't sound, silence fearsome as a shriek.

"Mother . . . ?"

She holds up her hand and strides into the parlor, heels hammering the boards. Through the sitting room, the dining room with its places set, her elbow strikes a chair and she curses for the pain, curses loud enough to make the windows sing when she reaches the kitchen, where the slats are open and light shines in from the cistern yard. Light to show the empty pots on the stovetop, a bowl of dry rice, the chopping block laid with a head of garlic, an onion, a green pepper, the tufted form of a chicken unscalded and unplucked. A knife rests alongside. Not as if work were interrupted, cooking abandoned in haste to some other chore, but like an illustration, a still life to show you what work needs to be done. And you'd better do it yourself.

She snatches up the nearest thing at hand. An empty crockery pitcher that would normally hold cool water and the canary-bright slices of lemon she likes to glimpse whenever one of the girls fills her cup. The pitcher doesn't shatter, rather breaks with an impotent pop into three shards on the tile floor. She kicks them aside, calling out the names of her slaves.

Joseph is in the parlor now. He says *mother* again as she goes past him and mounts the stairs, shouting. Their names are poor to scream, too ungainly for the resounding holler she wishes to emit. Upstairs, from one silent room to the next. And now she is slamming doors. Angel's office; Joseph's room; the girls' quarters in the back with its smell of coca-oil hanging from the furniture, the bare stripped beds. Goddamn it. Goddamn it. They bundled everything in sheets and threw them on their shoulders like beggars on the road.

In her own room, Elise scrabbles for her jewelry case, for the strong-box. Both are locked; both are full. And she too is brimming: with what, she cannot name. Her head is light; she staggers across the room and catches herself at the footboard, her face in the tangle of the mosquito netting. Somewhere on her way she's lost her veil; the fine fabric at her face is caught with last night's dead; a few still twitch, inching for her blood. Mosquito nets must be shaken out weekly, aired and sewn afresh each fall. She remembers doing it with her mother. Weeks hunched over, your fingers tensed with the fury of smallwork. Her sight sharpens past the netting, accepts the darkness of her room—the cave where she clung—and the shape of her made bed, where rests upon one pillow a small white square of paper.

Free from the netting, she has the paper in her hand. And if this had been the first thing she'd seen upon entering the house, you could say she reads it with disbelief. But there is precious little now she would find unbelievable, let alone that Ligeia can write.

Adieu Maîtresse

L.

Et Robert n'était pas son fils.

Her arm is trembling like the hanged man's shoulders when she sets the letter down. She should have, long ago, held the little bitch by her kinky hair and screamed in her face that she knew damn well that her brat—Robert, she writes his name as if he matters—wasn't Angel's. You could take one look at the little devil and know. Oh but how you must've hoped, Ligeia. You just loved to think that I was up here moiling over the thought of my man lurching after you. You pitiful piece of walking shit. Good luck. Good luck. I will not hunt for you. I will not call the police to haul you back. Pretty soon you'll be knocking at my door, begging to be taken back after a few days of Yankee hardtack and sleeping in a tent. And you've dragged old Bernice along with you. *Filles putains!*

She rasps a crazed laugh, goes careering out the room and back downstairs, where Joseph stands with his hands upheld. Now he is jabbering about hearing things and knowing things. *I* know, *mother.* His outburst is drowned by the roar mounting in her skull. She grips her skirts and looks over the room. Mantels rear up high and dusty, clock-hands grow fangs, and each trinket and stick of furniture waits like a snake for her to stumble on, coiled with the inherent menace of its care and operation.

Seven

Departures

George Strong in his sickbed. Not yellow fever, thank God, something respiratory. Troubling nonetheless to see a young man so laid out. Stubble darkens the hollows of Strong's cheeks, a shadow down his phlegm-rattled throat to the open collar of his nightshirt where someone has painted a plaster that smells of linseed. Still, Strong's eyes are bright, his smile winning, when he stirs awake and finds Butler sitting beside him.

George manages a limp salute and lets his hand fall to the bed, wheezing.

"I brought you something," Butler says, handing over a rumpled sheet of paper engraved with a scene of a tall, handsome Union soldier hauling a priest from his pulpit, subtitled: THE "STRONG" MAN ENACTS THE WILL OF THE BEAST. "Quite the likeness, eh?"

George first holds the sheet at arm's length, then brings it to his nose, as though unsure of his vision. What starts as a laugh ends with him rolled over, hacking into a pan. Wet gobs on tin. Quaking shoulders.

"No blood," Strong says, rolling back and settling in his pillows.

"Good, good," says Butler. For the better part of two weeks Adjutant Strong has kept himself going on coffee and nerves alone. His youthful energies failed him on the day of Mumford's execution. He has been abed for four days. The doctors say there shall be no improvement if he remains in New Orleans. The climate being disagreeable to his condition and, according to a current of wisdom popular among the ranker abolitionists who would have our soldiers replaced by armed blacks, the constitution of any white man. Butler has been quick to point out that the argument that southern climes are unsuitable for Anglo Saxon men is the same argument put forward by the slaveholders. Still they shout, *Send our boys home and give the niggers guns*. Strong is the fifth member of his staff to have fallen ill within two weeks. He cannot send them all away. They would have him officerless and with no more than three thousand troops fit for duty in the city, and all the while Secretary Stanton ordering him to send men north to attack Vicksburg. But George is the exception. He owes him that much.

"I've seen the news," says Strong.

"Oh yes: General Banks repulsed, McClellan's forces routed, Washington in the hands of Stonewall Jackson who is no doubt reading a sermon to his men while making them run barefoot along the perimeter of the city with Lincoln's head on a pike. It's not as bad as all that. The corrections are already coming in."

"I assumed the reports were . . . exaggerated. I thought I'd hear celebrations outside if the Rebels had taken Washington."

"Indeed," he says. "The capital thrives so well they're sending a man down to adjudicate the case of the precious foreign consuls. Do you remember Mr. Reverdy Johnson of Baltimore?"

George rolls his eyes to the ceiling. "That damned man."

Unlike Strong to curse, but if he hadn't Butler would do so for him. Mr. Reverdy Johnson, former attorney general, council for the defense in the Dred Scott case, and doddering old fork-tongued secessionist spy, and among the more odious and infuriating persons he encountered in Baltimore, will be dispatched by Secretary Seward to New Orleans within the month to arbitrate between Butler and the foreign consuls and the banks. In fact this will be an investigation of him and his department. The first step to removal.

"You've sent a complaint to Seward, yes?"

Butler nods. "But you know it won't do any good. They understand nothing."

The Sewards and Johnsons of this world could never do his job. Before he'd come to visit George, Butler had sat with the son of Commodore de Kay, lying now at the St. James Infirmary. A wound received on a scouting mission, gone septic. He'd visited the boy this morning, written his father a letter of condolence thereafter. He'd like to set Seward and Johnson beside a stinking corpse-to-be. See how they like it.

Strong runs a hand down his face. "Who has my post? Who's writing the dispatches?"

"Captain Davis, of the Eleventh Maine."

Strong is shaking his head. "Davis is a poor writer."

"I don't need a wordsmith, George. And besides, you're overqualified. Now you'll regroup and by the time you're well, have a command of your own no doubt."

Coughing again, George is careful to keep the pan out of sight. "I know I may have seemed a little schoolmarmish, all those hours going over the wording of orders with you over and—"

"Don't forget over and again," Butler smiles.

"But there's a reason for it, sir." Strong's face slackens; his voice goes soft. "Every word we put down will be printed. It's all going to be history."

"A man in your condition shouldn't be dramatic, George."

The coughs return and Strong speaks through his fist. "Mrs. Butler . . . Send her home?"

"She's already gone."

All his world is falling away, piecemeal departures and removals seemingly building towards his own. He saw her off yesterday morning at the Girod Street wharf in a manner hurried, tearless, and without ceremony. Sarah biting her lip. In her face remembrances of their argument the night before.

It's for your own good.

Fine. If you want me to go away . . .

A cold embrace despite the heat. She turned and stamped up the gangway and was gone.

Now as then he feels himself nearing the terminus of a dark passage, approaching not a point of daylight and open ground but nooses and gallows and the ledger-scratch of civilian commissioners, shadows in the weird angles of broken necks.

He tells Strong of the latest batch. Four men of the Fourteenth Massachusetts and two sailors from the same damned ship that brought him up the Mississippi have been robbing houses at night, turning the owners out with supposed orders from the general and helping themselves to the goods therein. Boys of Fort Hill, Back Bay, Boston dregs. He'll have them hanging in a week.

Strong sighs, shuts his lids. He stays this way so long Butler has risen to his feet when the bright eyes open and Strong takes his wrist, eases him back down.

"I'm worried you'll be rasher," Strong says. "Harsher without—"

"My two consciences—?"

"Your friends."

"I have too many friends. Every day I get letters from sanctimonious old college chums, railing at me over Order Twenty-eight." He thinks of one man who kept on about how disappointed he was. How

KENT WASCOM

he felt betrayed that his good friend Ben Butler would do such a thing. "But of course my business partners are happy." Jackson, running around the town buying up confiscated goods, packing the holds, Fray in Boston, Fisher Hildreth in Lowell. He looks to Strong, unable to help the touch of despair that creeps now into his voice. "I feel like the boy in the schoolhouse who everyone likes only on the day he brings a cake from home to share."

George, fists clenched, in surer throat: "And now they're sending that bastard Johnson. God Almighty. How will it end?"

"I should think poorly, for one of us. But I can't worry about that now."

"Bastards. Utter bastards."

He claps Strong's shoulder. "I haven't seen you so worked up since they shot at you in Biloxi."

For a moment George is laughing round his breath, but something has snatched his mind. His expression darkens. "You know," he says. "I haven't thought of the little girl, Marina, in so long. . . . She's somewhere here. . . . Been here for months . . . and I never once sought her out. Never once."

"You've been busy, man. Propping me up, dragging preachers from their pulpits . . ."

Strong pats the sheet. "My wife will like this."

"And besides see Miss Nancy, what will you do when you're home."

The ceiling has his attention. "I'd like to hike the White Mountains."

"The George Strong patented cure."

Strong shakes his head; other thoughts have him. The phlegm is shuddering in his chest, slime-fists slapping to be let out. "It just seems wrong," he says. "To be so . . . ghostly . . . in her life, then out . . ."

"You're no ghost." He squeezes a knot of muscle at Strong's elbow, thinks how he's never had one there himself. "Let's make sure you stay

244

that way, eh? We'll have you on the ship to New York by Friday. In ten days you'll be scaling the peaks or whatever you wish."

"I'm sorry to leave you here," says Strong. "I'm just so tired of being underwater."

Down here we all drown in one way or another. In greed or fear or in the lonesome encumbrances of power, George, it's all the same. Here and there, North and South, the waters flow the same. Deep and dark and ready for us all.

At the Custom House he dictates the order for the execution of the thieves. Captain Davis jots with cloying eagerness words George would amend for their harshness and brevity. George who fears for his commander to be friendless. George who never understood that all he does, all he's ever done, has been accomplished alone. He will preside over the dying lieutenant's funeral; he will share the Confederate general's mansion with the retinue of slaves, officers, and guards; he will have dinner with his damned brother; he will drink too much, by candlelight write letters to the bastards in Washington, letters he must ball up in the morning; he will await the arrival of Seward's spy; he will hang these four men. He will be the Beast.

Eight

Brave New World

The ceiba trees are fading in Marina's mind. Their limbs knot, trunks bloat and scale; they are becoming oaks. Sunlit rows of moro orange wither into urban groves reaching from the shadows of courtyards, bearing foul thick-skinned fruit. Coffee is not a tree with bright white blooms you can stretch your arms around or shake to make the petals fall, but dark burnt pills in a canvas sack and must be scooped and ground with care they are so dear. Even the scrawny pines of Ship Island thin to hair's-width fissures in a memory knit now by other landscapes, other lives. The clear waters of the Ariguanabo fill with mud, fouled and broadening into the brown swath of the Mississippi. And faces undergo like transformations: mother's and father's are drowned pale; Major Strong's twists into a mask of contempt before a hooded man kicking at the air. And here in the parlor of the Woolsack house she wavers half-formed and transient between the worlds, until Joseph takes her hand. He presses her palm down on the inky cushion of the couch, anchoring them both though their feet can't reach the ground.

Behind them, at the rear of the parlor, Mlle Pichon sits at the writing table with a glass of wine, composing another of her unanswered letters to Uncle Willie. She gives occasional coughs to remind them of her presence, and they test her earshot with simple talk until they find a volume that exists between suspicious whisper and outright speech. Elsewhere in the house Mademoiselle's slaves putter and scrub, clomp upstairs to beat and air beds untended for days. Joseph says the slaveless life has been fun but messy. Egg-scrambled rice for breakfast every day, dishes piling up, no one to check on you at night. When the war's over, he says, they'll be very sorry. He doesn't mention the hangings, as she fears, or ask what she thinks of her friends now. Anyway, she has her answer ready. Suddenly Joseph sits back, appraising her. His habitual way, as though he's just noticed you there.

"You look different," he says. And when she doesn't answer, he adds, "The good kind of different."

Marina with her free fingers pinches the pleats of her new dress. Cobbled from one of Mademoiselle's old summer numbers, the dress is of blue silk patterned with scallop shells. The morning after the ball Mademoiselle had come swishing into Marina's room with the dress in her hand. Shells and the sea, Pichon said, holding mothball-smelling and seemingly enormous expanse of silk to Marina's chest. It reminded me of you. So they spent two weeks of afternoons dismantling the gown, re-forming it into a more girlish cut. Looseness to wick the sweat, room in the sleeves to reach.

As she does now, guiding Joseph's hand to her leg.

Flesh exists beneath the silk and flounces and the underdress and scratchy shift and ruffled linen bloomers, but sometimes she forgets.

There are nights, more and more lately, on which she is amazed by what she finds when she is free of clothes. Now Joseph's hand is another layer, transmitting fearful life down to her through the artifices of cover. His eyes are frozen wide, his hand claw-tense. She eases his knuckles smooth against the slope of her thigh.

His hand is smaller than hers. She's never noticed it before.

Mlle Pichon coughs. Joseph's eyes dart to the side, but he doesn't turn around. He is breathing quickly, little jets through his long nostrils. He tells her that he knows where his mother goes these days and with whom. A hiss in his voice: he knows what they do. Marina doesn't blush or ask what; she tucks his hand into her lap. To feel his fingers she must press hard, as she's come to know. Press harder than you think you should, for all these layers are there to bar sensation.

It has not been long since she learned, sitting up of an afternoon at the edge of her bed, to press herself to the bell-shaped footpost. Rubbing, inching up and down. After a while you begin to feel on the edge of something wonderful and vast, yet distant, like wading through the shallows of the beach and coming to the sandbar after which, you know, the shallows cease and the true sea begins, but being too afraid to step off into the purchaseless deep. The feeling is good and strange enough that she has added the act to those for which she is nightly contrite. At her prayers, more than any other time, she finds her sinful self irreconcilable with the one who reads stories and plays and wanted the doll in the shopwindow.

New prayers will need inventing for this. For the first inching rub, which he does not resist but see his eyes, how wide and terrified. She moves his hand again and now in the rhythm she knows and cannot stop. Joseph is a doll she can move and make play. He bites his lip and cannot find a place to look. She sticks her legs straight out. Somehow this improves the feeling, brings her closer to the deep.

"I don't hear any talking," says Mlle Pichon, pleasantly.

Joseph jumps and Marina traps their hands between her thighs, cranes her neck to try and make him meet her eyes. His are slits fixed at his right leg, where the pale gray fabric of his pants is marred by a blotch of wetness, quarter sized. She holds her free forefinger to her mouth in the signal of silence and secret as Joseph covers his lap with a pillow.

Elise

Nine

The Ghoul

Emile, smiling, runs a finger down her calf. "You know I won't make you trustee."

"And you know that's not why," says Elise.

This evening he is in a reflective mood, sits up against the leg of his desk and like a dog going to bed makes worried little circles around questions the true answers to which would shrivel him. "Then why?"

He has bought a small pallet mattress, unrolled beneath them now across the floor. He has bought a new lock for his office door, ugly iron bolt shot tight and latched now with a chain as thick as the finger she holds.

She says, "Why, because you're so damned alluring, Emile."

"I told you—I won't."

She likes to do this, strip away his self-image, just as she likes to see him with his pants off. His thin jot of pubic hair, so spare compared to the curled fullness she sees when she looks down her belly, the weakness of his skinny, pale man's shanks—a precariousness she can only match in heels. In these moments she is greater than him; she can consume him.

He takes his finger from her and touches the lobe of his right ear. He says to bite him there, like she did Claude Arnaud.

"You'd have to do something rude," she says. "Something coarse. I don't bite unprovoked."

And it isn't in his nature, though he tries: reaches round and grabs her right breast, weighs it out, then kneads with his fingers as though probing for the gland that she has seen from his anatomical charts is like a hibiscus bud, wrapped redly in upon itself. Emile leans over her shoulder, fascinated by the indentations he makes, by the malleability of her skin and her resistance. Her refusal to whine. Her mind is on the anatomy charts in his collection, their long tan spines lining the shelf on the opposite wall; she sees the colored plates that may be peeled apart in overlays of nitrate paper, layers imprinted with tissue, muscle, nerve, organ, bone, so that you may see the woman in full, then dissect her with a flick of your finger. Flay her down to florid viscera.

He tugs out pinches of her, that wholly male touch intended, so it seems, to impart in the groped a sense of bovine acquiescence. In the corner of her vision, where he thinks she cannot see, Emile looks desperate.

She rolls her eyes. You don't have it in you, Emile. You're still the sort who asks permission, no matter how you cast yourself. Your gothic trappings, your high tight collars, your black coat trimmed in purple. Shed of these you are pale and puny, furtive on the floor of your office, where we meet because you are frightened of my house.

She nudges her back into his chest. He cannot be harsh with her; his cruelty is reserved for others. Earlier in the night she had gone to his instrument case and found a blue leather pouch left out as though put to recent use. When she flipped it open and asked what the twin steel prongs were for he said smallpox, and that he was afraid the city would be losing some of its recently acquired escapee population. Seeing the look of grim satisfaction on Emile's face, she shut the case.

Craning back, she scours her mouth across his cheek, lets her lips come to rest at his earlobe. Gently, damningly so. See the furor welling in his eyes.

He has not let go her breast. Now his hand is light; his fingertips ease back, feeling carefully until he has between thumb and fore one of the few dark lash-length hairs that sprout round her nipple. The look he'd worn when she asked about the case returns for an instant and in one savage wrench of his wrist he yanks out the hair and a yelp she can't keep back.

He is holding up the hair, examining it with one eye closed, when she breathes hot into his ear, sets her teeth, and buries them in his lobe.

Veins and sweat-beads stand out on his skin. He holds the hair to his parted lips. And she can't taste blood yet, nor will she. She doesn't want to sever, just to make him hurt. Pain communicates to her its boundaries and extents as his breath staggers in, still fixated on the hair. She takes the lobe, wet with her spit, between the tips of her canines and thinks of his ear pierced. What will his expression be? Will he command himself calm as he does now when he shuts his eyes and releases the hair to his outblown breath? Like a child making a wish.

Her own child hates her. Of this Elise is sure. He thinks she killed his father, wrongly. Rightly he thinks she has betrayed him. But how can you betray a ghost? And Angel was a ghost long before he put the muzzle to his head.

She hangs from his ear, a living decoration, tugs him atop her on the pallet. Enjoined now, inflictor and afflicted, there is the feeling of being at the calm heart of chaos. They are not starving, as the people do in Vicksburg; the city's not in ruins like so many towns;

there are no volleys or thundering cannons. Yet our lives may be crazed and dismembered by other means than violence. Means subtler and more insidious. Life sheared of certainty so that we are left to claw for freehold against the face of the black mirror, wondering whether it is worse to be loved by monsters, or to love them.

Ten

The Laugh

Royal Street: doused with sunlight from a widening rift in the low thin clouds. The shadows of passersby are lengthened; windows glimmer and stun. Squint and you can peer up through the breach and witness the hidden brightness of the sky above the cloudbank.

"You'll go blind," says his mother. Mlle Pichon, seated beside her, in the rocker his father once would occupy on such an afternoon, agrees. She knew a boy once who sat out on the levee on the day of an eclipse, stared straight at it—just like you did—and was struck blind as a beggar. Marina, her paper tricorne hat aglow, leans at the rail near the hyacinth basket. And all of them in Joseph's vision are swarmed with orange splotches—the only ill-effects thus far. Another lie, he thinks. The splotches burn to yellow and fade, the clouds heal themselves and Marina must think he's looking at her—her smile drops—rather than at his mother who, in her black veil and blacker dress, is the very image of eclipse. Likewise he is suddenly conscious of his own costume: his trousers rolled to calf length, the cloth tied round his middle, and his own hat, an athwart bicorne of newspaper—last week's *Bee*, somewhere within whose folds lies the report of the four robbers' execution at parish prison, which he'd read with relish and made a keepsake. That was until Marina came today with a mind to perform her play and impressed his newspaper into service of the show. As in all things, he had neither the wish nor the means to refuse her. When she first declared her intentions, he thought it would be from her precious Shakespeare, not something she'd written herself. But here are the sheets—*The Pirate-Witch:* act 1, scene 1—clutched in his hand. Marina, it seems, already knows her lines.

She clamps the tricorne down on her outspread, winding hair, tangled for the purpose of realism. (No pirate witch would go around well groomed.) She asks if he's ready and before Joseph can answer skips down the balcony, a bizarre lope for she wears a discard pair of her uncle's riding boots, and tells Mademoiselle and mother they are ready to begin.

Oh, they can't wait. Bated breath. His mother looks no more pleased than she had when Marina suggested they go and take swords from the office collection, a fancy swiftly quashed. She lifts her veil and raises her eyebrows, looking over the shoulder of the striding pirate witch, and glares at him.

Marina sets the scene: the *Midnight Queen*, flagship of the pirate witch's fleet, has come upon a lifeboat containing one Captain Poucet, her former pursuer and sworn enemy. She claps her hands. Begin!

He looks to his script; he has the first line. His voice cracks; he bemoans cruel fate to have fallen into the briny clutches of that wicked dame.

He feels a blanket of absurdness thrown over his shoulders; he reads on, thinking of other times. How at first Marina called what they do in secret *games*, and now there is no special name for those moments when they are alone and touch, besides sin, and the act that never seemed like a game has become a grim compulsion.

The pirate witch is so delighted; her cheeks are biting at her eyes. She cuts him off and charges into her own soliloquy in an unexpected voice. Not a crone's croak but bright and clear as the sky had been in the rift, and ringing so that for a moment he forgets to speak, looks to the balconies down the street for if any heads have turned.

And so they have—across the street at no. 208, down to Mme Frick's and on to the blind bend where Royal meets Conti—but not in the direction of their play. Instead the people look towards the bend; even those in the street begin to halt and stare in that direction.

"And what have you to say to *that*, eh?" prompts the pirate witch.

"I don't know," he says, peering now.

Arms folded, mother shakes her head as Mademoiselle rises, stretches out over the rail. Practiced, she waves to the old couple across the street, calls out in French to know what's going on.

"Well," says Marina, turning round to see. "You're spoiling the play—"

At the bend, the shadows mass and rear up frontages, followed now by figures in file. Soldiers—the call travels from gutter to balcony and down the street—stamping a slow pace at the heels of their penumbrae. They come on, unbunch, regain their rows with none of the usual jauntiness he's come to expect from these displays, and so the drummers rap a solemn rhythm, like whiplashes on the skin.

"I know that tune," Marina says, drawing off her hat.

Now rows of officers on horseback, sternly correcting mounts who wish to jostle and nip one another. And round the bend comes a carriage decked in black crepe and white flowers, a clutch of sailors and Zouaves its honor guard.

"Someone's died," she says.

Joseph grips the railing, struggling against a feeling of satisfaction and sadness. Even the war, his hatred for the occupiers, has lost its sting somewhat in the face of what he and Marina do.

"We can see that, thank you," says his mother. To Mlle Pichon: "And who is it? Butler himself?"

"The boy they brought back from St. Francisville, I bet. The one who was a commodore's son. They've been talking about him in the papers for days."

The procession yields to nothing in its onward drudge. At the intersections carts pull rein; a little dog jets out and is lost in a dark forest of boots, reappearing on the other side of the street. They are past Mme Frick's, and what at first had seemed a plodding progress has become an inexorable flow, strangely swift.

The cortege draws near. Marina turns, motions for Joseph to take off his hat. Without looking from her and the street, he reaches up, and when his hand finds the delicate edges of the paper, he shoves it down. Her lips bulb; she snorts, turns away. The drummers' strokes grow louder as they pass beneath.

"Fever, most likely."

"No," says Pichon. "He was shot. At least the boy I'm thinking of was shot."

"Shot? I hadn't thought there'd been any action nearby."

The mounted officers are clattering past. Pichon drops her voice to a whisper: "He was with the fleet, going upriver. He got himself shot by an old man while trying to liberate a chicken from its *coop*."

His mother laughs. Her voice is brighter and louder than Marina's had been when she was the pirate witch, and it is as though the laughter is unraveled from inside her, endless handkerchiefs from a magician's sleeve: she cannot stop. Mlle Pichon looks on, amazed, tries to put a hand to his mother's shoulder and she is stooped, bowed with mirth that shudders out from her in ecstatic uncontrollable peals. And her face at this moment, rent in gaping joy, is more beautiful than he has ever thought. Marina looks back and forth between them, aghast. Still, his mother laughs. Gouts of laughter, painful now. And he knows she isn't laughing about the dead soldier, but at some internal calamity, something deep within and wretched.

The procession does not halt, but there is the barking of orders. An officer has ridden back. Joseph flings himself forward; down the sidewalk an officer is pointing in his face, shouting to a pair of soldiers to by God guard this house and see that none leave. Cursing, the officer struggles to dismount; Joseph feels a hand at his back and he is collared, hauled to ground. Mlle Pichon has him and Marina by the necks.

Pichon's color pales, and with a wind comes the rich smell of her hairdressing, her oils. "Be still, now," she says and snatches away their hats. Past Mlle Pichon's affrighted eyes, his mother hunches, a fist pressed to her mouth. The sound of the door slammed issues from below. She shakes herself. Her throat is jumping when her eyes turn to the house. Movement, footsteps from within. And just as suddenly as it had come, his mother's laughter dies away.

Butler

Eleven

A Scratch of Your Pen

"I'm afraid," says General Butler, "there's nothing I can do." He waits for the doctor to speak, and, when he doesn't, wrings his wrists and worries braided cuffs. "Nothing *more* than I have already done—for you *and* Mrs. Woolsack."

The way he says Mrs. Woolsack—a hint of implication, of supposition, that tone of clubroom complicity that men level on one another. Dr. Sabatier stares at the general, feels the browless orderly lurking somewhere at his back, the *scritch* of weight shifted on the stone floor.

The general's bald pate furrows in thought, an expression likewise assumed by the new adjutant seated at a secretary to his left. The previous adjutant struck a finer figure; this one, though, with his sharpness, the schoolmasterly sternness of his insipid chin, the long thin fingers drumming on his kneecap, fits the punitive air it seems has overtaken Butler's office in the time since the doctor's last visit. Now sorts of trophies are hung on the walls: the star-scrap taken from

Mumford's lapel; an array of swords; plastered broadsides giving off a lacquered sheen; and directly behind the general's head hangs a four-foot banner embroidered with the words *THE SHE-ADDER'S VENOM IS AS DEADLY AS THE HE-ADDER'S*. Butler has always seemed a man who bluffs his way through the game, but now he wears it on his sleeve. He has become an etching of himself, a cartoon. And it is this cartoon of a man who the doctor must now entreat, to keep Elise from Ship Island.

"Six months, and at the heat of the summer. It's no place for a woman."

"My wife," says Butler with a wince, "spent three months on Ship Island and was no more the worse for it. And Mrs. Woolsack will have company. I've sent a half dozen women that way."

"She's not well," he says. "Not in her right mind since her husband's death."

"I don't know a woman who is. And that changes nothing. She will go: for gross disobedience of Order 28, for attempting to incite a riot—"

"By laughter?"

"By laughing at the funeral of an officer—and for keeping a trove of illegal arms."

"Antiques, sir."

Butler aims a finger at him. "Is a flintlock more frightening than a Colt when it's aimed at your face?"

He grips the arms of his chair. There is no reasoning with a walking aphorism. Elise is arraigned on charges of inciting riot against the army of the United States, of possessing an illegal trove of arms for perhaps nefarious purposes—all in violation of General Orders 26, 43, 99, &c.

Butler continues, "No, my friend. Her house will be confiscated, her hoard of weaponry likewise. And I repeat it is only out of my personal favor and the fact that her husband's estate is in your hands and was never proscribed to the Confederate cause that said legacy remains intact." The general knits his fat fingers together, affects a ponderous solemnity. "Be grateful, sir. I have indulged you before, but there are limits. Mrs. Woolsack is being dealt with very lightly."

Indulged? "House arrest, then," the doctor says. "She has a child who will be harmed by the absence of his mother."

If Butler could roll his strabic orbs, he would. It seems he's heard enough about children. "As trustee of the estate, is the boy not to be in your charge should any misfortune befall his mother?"

"Yes."

"Then, knowing you as I do, I should doubt the lad will come to anything but benefit from being in your care for a few months."

Blood thrums at his temples. And is this cyanosis at its peak, or some mutation, heretofore unknown? Is he so infected that he cannot remember what it was like before the symptoms took hold? His teeth groan. All his life is symptomatic now. He came to this, to cyanosis, believing that he could discover some truth, some viewpoint upon the profound functions of human wickedness, wipe away the old world like he did his friends in the Krewe of Orcus, and thereby stake himself a place of mastery in the newborn system. But here among the flag-scraps and cartoons, the doctor is struck by the loneliness of what it is he truly wants: Elise. Their doom-fraught moments on the floor like dogs in heat crowd out the doctor's thoughts. He had wished to hurt her, to punish her for breaking away and leaving him alone on the cold floor of the alley all those years ago. He'd been wrong about his own desires, and now she won't even be here for him to hurt.

"General," he says. "You've proven your sternness. Now you may show your mercy."

"I show my magnanimity each day New Orleans stands unburnt."

261

The doctor cannot stop himself: "This isn't a newspaper. This isn't a platform. I've helped you."

The adjutant's eyes widen.

Butler rears up. "I would advise you, doctor, to take your leave."

Already on his feet, he hears the browless man take one pace forward, ready to manhandle him. He pauses, glaring at the form behind the desk.

Butler affects busyness, papers in hand, belly brushing other shrifts, great forehead glistening with oil. The general looks glutted; the drooping lids do not rise.

"Hm?" says the Butler.

"It would take only a scratch of your pen. . . ."

Without looking up, so that the last impression the doctor has before he goes is of those reddened puddled lids, Butler says, "With a scratch of my pen, I could put you in her place."

The adjutant bites back a titter, dips his pen into the well, and begins to scribble, no doubt preserving the witticism for posterity.

The sun moves through its stations and the doctor towards home, each indifferent to the courses of the other. The former's way is an empirical ellipse ended at the equator in fluttering blaze of red unnoticed by the latter, who ducks into a coffeehouse on the American side of Canal and finishes two bottles of wine before setting out again into the surprise of full-night.

Will, the carriage-driver, is asleep on his board. The doctor gives his knobby knee a swipe with his stick and doesn't wait for the old black to hop down and let him in. Home, he orders, as much to himself as his slave.

Lydia is waiting in her parlor alone, knitting piled in her lap. A death-shroud perhaps, to be imprinted with the summoned features of some neighbor's unfortunate son. The doctor lurches for the doorframe, steadies himself. His thoughts are unmoored. Years since he was this drunk.

"Been to see the Beast, have you?"

He coughs affirmative.

"I expected so," his wife says. "You're looking rather beastly yourself."

In the passageway a pair of girls swish by with brooms, and looking down the hall he sees others lugging pillows and linens upstairs. After all this time: the failed attempts, the guilt, the blame. To have a child in this house. Good God.

On his approach the room's assorted gewgaws and objets d'art become limber obstacles requiring of the most careful avoidance on his part. Steady now. He aims himself at the sofa, the bare patch beside his wife's rump. In her housedress Lydia's form is more plainly visible than otherwise; her bare arm, jiggling lightly with the ticking of her hands, is cool to the touch.

"Don't do that," she says, edging back.

He removes his palm, apprehends the dirtiness of his nails.

"I suppose," he says, "you've already started getting a room together?"

"For your ward? Oh, yes."

"Yours, too."

"Certainly."

He eases into the cushions, crosses his legs. "It might've been different, you know. I tried."

Lydia is the second person today not to give him their eyes. She focuses on her needles, her mouth barely open as she speaks: "I'm sure you did. I know how much you care for Mrs. Woolsack's welfare."

Acid rises in his chest; he lays a fist at his sternum as though to staunch it. "The estate. I care for the estate."

"Yes, dear."

He turns to her, squinting to focus. "You have no idea. None at all."

Her jaw unhinges, her open mouth black. "Do not be ugly to me," she says. "So when should I expect our guest?"

"Before the end of the month. The twenty-seventh? I don't know." The doctor rests his head in his hands. "El— Mrs. Woolsack will be on her way by then at the latest."

"I see." Her eyes flash. "Next time you pay a call to Woolsacks, I should come along."

"In God's name why?"

"To meet the dear boy, of course. I won't have him just delivered like a package. I want to meet the poor thing."

"Oh," he says, shaking off the jags and confusions of his mind. "We'll have to see. The house is under guard, you know." He pats her leg, envisioning for the moment a meeting between Lydia and Elise. A confrontation between lovely—yes, she is lovely in this light and so well made and curved even in her housedress—wife and the woman who has jabbed like a splinter in his mind for half his life. "We'll see. But there isn't much to meet. He's just a boy, you know. At the age where he's hung up on a girl . . ." Memories of his own time in that station threaten to choke him.

Lydia cuts her eyes at him. A little smile. "Is he?"

"Seems so. His mother's disturbed by it. Do you remember Willie Fandal? His niece. Lives next door."

"But Mr. Fandal left with the army, yes? So who does the girl stay with?"

"Fandal's—" he begins to explain, but thinks better of it. "A woman named Pichon."

Now the needles stop and Lydia looks up. "*Inés* Pichon?"

"How should I know."

Lydia leans forward, eyes boring into him. "Mid-thirties? Straight black hair? Pale? Skinny? A type Spanish maybe?"

"Lord no," he laughs. "The woman, Pichon, she's colored. Free, of course, but . . ."

Lydia's expression sucks the words and humor out of him. She pauses for a great while, staring at him, before returning to her needles. Her voice is terribly composed.

"Oh," she says. "I must be thinking of someone else."

He watches his wife resume her work—downturned eyes, tongue pressing at her bottom lip, how the flicker of her hands and the quiet fury of her grip causes veins to rise at the undersides of her wrists. Fine blue veins, the faint threadwork of her life.

Twelve
Distant Shores

The soon-to-be-parted pass flowers back and forth, bow, salute, or curtsy according to their sex and occupation; the departing are beset by fatherly handshakes, women's wrists draped round ramrod necks, guffaws and rude jokes from fellows-in-arms, for this transport bears travelers of all kinds—soldiers, sutlers, speculating businessmen, the condemned. A fat woman plants a delicate kiss to the forehead of a shackled man with a gray-flecked moustache; one young man holds another's hand, not wishing to let go. For a long while the prisoners mingle with the free and might be indistinguishable if you did not look to their hands or take undue notice of the strain at their eyes. The few guards stationed at the launch stand far off, prodding garbage with their bayonets.

Marina alone goes untouched. Mlle Pichon has Joseph's mother in her arms; with foreheads pressed they share some words in French. Taut flanges of spit cling to the corners of their mouths. Mademoiselle wears her habitual yellow; the other woman glimmers in unpatterned white. Joseph's mother has been granted a reprieve from her black, if not her grief. In mourning-clothes the sun would take the woman in its fist, wring her loose of sweat and consciousness. So she will wear white and hope for coolness out there on the sands. Marina wishes it for her. She holds out her arms to take the measure of her distance from them all. From Joseph, who is held in place by the doctor's curled thin fingers. Joseph's mother lets go first; Pichon clings for a moment more, then steps back from her friend who amid this confusion of smiles and tears reminds Marina of a bride. The doctor in his dark suit, his fresh-shaved face still somewhat red, might be the bridegroom. See how the man never takes his gaze from her, even as he lifts his hand from Joseph's shoulder and flicks him forward.

Mother and son enact a sort of dance. She draws him near, his arms rigid at his sides, fists knocking a rhythm on his thighs. And Marina wants to tell him to hug his mother, to not let the moment pass. The guilt of passages and departures is too great.

Joseph's mother has him pressed to her and now his fists explode into fingers climbing up her sleeves, snatching at the white fabric. His sobs are silent, deadened by her body and her words. Marina looks away.

The doctor's eye is twitching. His eyes won't part from mother and son. A snarl inches at one side of his face. This is the man Joseph will live with; this is the man who will take him away.

Four shrieks of the ship's whistle, the gathered jump with each. And now the guards are calling out to finish up and board. The crowd jostles, rearranges. Separations of a few inches become feet and soon will be miles. A pair of men appear on the gangway holding ledgers and craning to look at papers produced by those who are already queued to board.

Pichon scoops her back. An oiled curl, smelling of coconut, lolls against Marina's cheek. The doctor has Joseph by the shoulders, and holds Joseph's mother in his pained stare. The sun flares, blinding, and in the flash the woman in white has become part of the crowd.

They watch her board. Mlle Pichon draws a handkerchief from her sleeve, dabs her eyes. Joseph stands dumbstruck, looking up at the ship until the doctor turns him round.

"All right," the doctor says with the awkwardness of a man unused to addressing children, loudly pronouncing each word. "We'll go home now. All right?"

He nods and the doctor turns his attention to Mlle Pichon. They are talking about when the two of them—Joseph and Marina—will see each other. Joseph, silent, pays her vacant notice. His eyes are glassy and the ship is shrieking again.

Thirteen

The Dark House

Sitting opposite the doctor in the jaunting shadows of the coach, Joseph keeps his distance. Outside the sun shines on green dung as it drops from under horses' tails. When they cross Canal, troops of small black boys appear and run alongside for a ways. Now the trees grow taller and fill the gaps between the great houses: oak-boughs make tatters of the light, bricked gardens disappear in oily magnolia-shade.

The doctor doesn't say they will be friends—that they shall get on famously and he will be quite happy. None of the lies his mother had said before she left, her voice filled with uncertainty and a tremor of disgust. The man stays silent, wrapped in his own thoughts.

Wishes are not real, but you wished her away. Because of you, your father is dead. Because of you, your mother might as well be. Gone, both of them by your own doing and it is not at all like the stories of orphaned boys. There is no freedom, no light. You are swallowed down a throat of trees and houses, and this man won't even speak.

Marina says she tries each night not to forget her parents' faces. And faces now rise up, like reflections in the pane before his eyes. Father's: scarified and eyeless, then inexplicably smiling, as in those times, when he was small and his father held his hand when the curfew cannon sounded and they pretended it was a war. Mother's: the gaping relief on the night she found him, her face tawny with dried blood, her stifled tears when—that was on a carriage-ride too—she said, *You're mine aren't you?* Joseph shuts his eyes, wills his mind to Marina but now there is an ugliness come over them, unshakable and unexpected as the ropy mess she urges out of him onto the cloths they hide. But irresistible and hideously nice, too. And what, he wonders, will happen to the cloths, stained and stiff and shameful, hidden in the far corner of his room.

He's jolted forward when the coach halts. The doctor throws open the door and steps out, revealing a path of moss-grown bricks leading to high steps of gray stone strewn with wet twists of leaves. Joseph slides from the bench and follows him down the path.

The man's back is thin, the high lapels of his black frock coat arch like wings. His heels clack crisply on the bricks, and Joseph finds their stride is matched now sound for sound, up the steps onto sweeping portico and sucked through doors opened by some unseen black hand into a dusky silent hall. The marble floor like a felled headstone. And this is the sort of house in which you'll never rightly see the slaves; the curtains are drawn, the corners deep caverns of shadow.

Joseph feels compelled to break the silence: "Shall I meet Mme Sabatier now?"

The doctor, plucking off his gloves, looks sharply at Joseph for a moment, as though examining his face.

"Another time," the doctor says. "I'm afraid my wife has taken ill."

Joseph says he's sorry to hear that, and he is sorry for so many things as the light from the closing door shears across the floor and disappears.

PART 5

"Thy Mission's Over Now"

Elise

One

Ship Island

Taken by the river down to where the land is drowned, past forts that teeter at the brink and anchored ships full of hooting sailors waiting out their quarantines, across the vast floodplain stubble of reeds and grass and withered trees, to the ruins of La Balize left over from the three hurricanes of 1860; there terra firma fades, the swirling outpour of the river's mouth pierced with the masts of centuries of wrecks, and islet slivers mirroring in miniature the place to which she's come.

Here sea and shore are in constant flux; by tidal invasion and retreat the land waxes and wanes, alternate glut and desiccation governed by the moon, while storms shape and decorate the island according to less knowable designs. An ever-present mystery and trial to Elise and the seven other female internees.

The island is the site of odd revelations. A dolphin deposited atop the dunes, flopping feebly, blinded and overrun with crabs. A copper fireplace spade hammered with the crude outlines of a woman's face. Century-old skulls bloom in tufts of grass; cactus tines guard rusted weaponry and broken tools. So she walks Ship's meagre span, popping the bladders of stranded gulfweed, awaiting a revelation of her own. Six weeks into her time on the island and her blood has yet to come. She missed it on the steamer, wished and prayed for it while above her rained the crackling spider-bursts of the soldiers' fireworks on the Fourth. The month wears on and she resigns herself to this punishment for being weak, for having ever let Emile near. For wanting him.

On a night in early August, she bolts up in pain—a wrenching of her insides she dreamily believes to be the tremors of some monstrous quickening—and finds the blood has come. Arriving dark and clotty, and with it an overwhelming surge of happiness that she's carrying no child of his. That she belongs to herself. The pain becomes the comfort of a strong and unseen hand. A confirming caress. Within days it too is gone.

So she clings to things that have no purpose or analogue in the world she now inhabits: the smell of perfume, like frozen flowers; the taste of wine and bread and cut lemons; the ease of a mattress on her back and not the cot into which she sinks to stare up at the sunlit canvas of the tent she shares with Mrs. Larue, a gambler's wife who wore a cockade of Beauregard's flag in her hat, both of them watching the fluttering material streaked with dried salt-spray; Elise remembering the smooth, yielding splay of her son's hair when he was small and she would run her fingers through it, his little forehead warm against the heel of her hand.

And yet, like the relief that came with the arrival of her blood, there are times when she finds herself glad at the thought of being liberated from the chore of caring for her boy. Hideous to think so, she tells herself. You're a mother first and always. So she fights the feeling off, and in spite of it knows her love for Joseph is not subject to any ebb or flow. You can love something and yet feel free to be relieved of it.

But our thoughts are never always in the light, are they? Our minds seek darker provinces in kind. So that when she is glad to be free of Emile, when she knows that she has killed any desire for him—buried any urge for his hands on her, for his legs parting hers and the loom of his shoulders above—revenant desire comes lurching urgent to the doorway of her mind. She shuts her eyes and there he is, clamoring for her with gloriously abject need. She shuts her eyes, imagines his mouth ajar at the moment he spends himself in her. When she has him utterly in her possession.

And there are as many eyes upon her now as there are ants and fleas and horseflies and mosquitos that never for a moment cease to bite. The eyes of intermittent sentries and guards; the eyes of the distant Louisiana men who trudge from their bunkhouse, some dragging balls and chains that make channels in the sand all the way to the fort; the eyes of the other women: Mrs. Larue, of the cockade; Mrs. Wiggins, who hid letters; Mrs. Jackson, whose son spit on soldiers and so, though she denies it, did she; Mme Aubert, who gave shoes (and a pistol) to a parolee; Mrs. Levy-Phillips, who claims her particular affront to be that she is a Jewess related to the Confederate secretary of state.

Together, the women wash and hang monthly napkins for soldiers and sutlers to laugh at, scour their pair of pots, turn down cots and sweep the endless sand, for supper trim the green rind from spoiled roast beef in New York–stamped tins, hoard together compressed cubes of dried vegetables and drop it all into the pot to stir and watch and ladle out in glops. A grinding monotony interrupted only when Mme Plaisance arrives in late August, bearing with her news of the battle at Baton Rouge, and more importantly a pouch of dried cayenne and a willingness to share. That night there is a small celebration on the dunes. Mrs. Jackson disappears with their communal waterbucket and a length of twine tied with salt pork, returns in the evening, bucket rattling with crabs. Sitting with her plate, Elise can't help but think the other women's excitement is all playacting—their squeals and claps when Plaisance shuffles over with her pouch and dusts the plateful of crab-strewn mush with an ocher cloud of cayenne.

She dislikes their happiness and feigned sisterly posturing. She does not hate them; only there seems to be no point in liking them either. Step back far enough from any group of friends and you will realize the arbitrariness of why you know, visit, care for them. As it stands she is too tired, sun wasted, and bug maddened to allow these women to draw on her limited reserves of care or to fit comfortably in the hierarchy they establish. She is an unwilling participant in the morning discussions of dreams, a topic suitably insubstantial and disconnected enough from their lives on the mainland to become popular for a time. And gathered to this purpose in the predawn dark they might be mistaken for a circle of white-shrouded oracles, yawning as they read divinations in their chicory grounds, when they have them, or the tart shreds of redbrow steeped in hot water when they don't. And while conversation tends to sputter and subside into the sound of wind and waves, the ritual blatting of the soldiers' bugles, still the other women muster daily talk. Home-side chatter. On rare occasions, as though possessed by phantom drunkenness, they share secret pieces of themselves. Trysts. Thefts. Slights given and received. Elise, for her part, tends towards quiet. There are parts of her that they may never know. That other island in her distant familial past. She watches them chatter, wonders if behind their ever-burning skins they could guess. Better yet, could she? They might all be alike, by black droplets afflicted and meanwhile, beknownst or no, moaning over the loose mouths of the niggers back home while Elise keeps hers shut.

But there is a moment when she does join them, loses herself in the company of others. It is the moment she takes the crab claw in her mouth and looks around, sees the pleasure dawning on the others' faces and, tasting, shares it—the tingle on the tongue, the joy of forehead pinpricked with sweat not because of sun or heat but spice.

Spice, you can control. And, suddenly empowered, the women laugh and touch their tender faces with awe, where despite bonnets and broad hats woven of palm-fronds the sun has laid its hand upon them by degrees. Their faces, necks, arms, hands, attain experimental shades. Mme Aubert continually blisters. Mrs. Levy-Phillips's freckles crowd together. Mrs. Wiggins goes gold. Elise at first burns in tomato-peel splotches, but day by day her skin evens to a raw reddish gold, pink where she peels back sheets of dead skin, plucks a quarter-sized flake from her scalp, parchment scraps minutely awled by hair.

Flick away the dead bits of yourself, insubstantial as the days you count until December and release, give them to the wind and sand and surf. Let the flakes float through the air as do you through sweltering days where you take only a few steps and months that see no letters from home. All correspondence must pass through General Butler's office, and when the first batch does arrive (on a day in September when there are three waterspouts) Elise snatches hers and goes off alone to the dunes. Squatting in a bed of sea oats, she studies the trio of envelopes—addressed from her son c/o Dr. Emile Sabatier and illustrated with a patriotic eagle—for a long time before she opens one and draws out a letter so brief her heart rises to her throat. So foreshortened she must invent the world that lives in the blank spaces Joseph has left on the page. A blinding whiteness like the sun's glare. Blinking, she seeks meaning in her son's rote phrases. *Dear Mother, I am well. I hope that you are too. The doctor is teaching me chemistry, and says I am a quick study. Mme Sabatier is ill since June, but isn't she lucky to have a doctor on hand?*

Elise digs her heels into the bed of sea oats, looks up from the page and under the gaze of a storm so distant she can only feel its thunder. And when she shuts her eyes she sees the labeled bottles in Emile's office roll by like pictures in a Magic Wheel, knows that in the later pair of letters she will read of the woman's death. She folds the first, secrets it on her person; now weighs the next two, turns to the purple clouds roiling over the water and savors the cool wind. In the distance, the day's third waterspout comes careering out of the storm.

She sees Joseph and Emile. His hand on her boy's shoulder, watching as he makes experimental incisions into a chicken or pricks it with a needle. Joseph and the girl, Marina, alone unwatched, making guilty messes of themselves. Or it could be they're kept apart, sulking for one another across town. Emile will want his privacy. He'd grow angry with a boy in constant tow. Angry and harsh. He might be anyway. At the least he will be cruel in unexpected ways. But boys crave harshness, need it in order that they might become men. The way obsidian stone needs volcanic fire to become the sharp and impenetrable surface of the black mirror. She tears open the next letter, and there it is. *Dear Mother. . . a tragedy*. She can see bereaved Emile bravely spelling out for Joseph the words *hemorrhagic fever*. She crumples the page and its edges jab her palm. And it's not the thought of Joseph subjected to harshness or cruelty, hating his new life, that makes her bolt up dry mouthed in the night, but that he likes it and will flourish.

The storm is gone, September's heat returns to swallow her, and she slips back to the tents. To this knot of women ringed by battlements of watchful men. The loafing soldiers, the prisoners allowed to dally from the barracks of a Sunday. Some sit and ponder; others devise a game with their shackles. Still others shout to the women. And the shouts of men are ominous, no matter how much they are chained. She lays in her cot and stares up at the wisps of salt in the canvas and remembers the black mirror. How when Mme Frick's husband was alive and talking about what kind of fire might have formed the obsidian stone, Angel reared up in their parlor, giving his lone hand a dismissive flick, and said, *What does it matter which? It's all because of God*. So it is, she thinks. And how Angel must be glad to see that his God of tests and trials, a Protestant American God who molds us as we live and breathe to fit within and animate His schemes, has her pinned to this dot in

the Gulf, trying her

shadowy at first,

She sees his pr

gown. And does he t

allows his words to tric

Before, when they were tog

stood him. She looks back v

the floor. *The floor*. On your h

and even when you sat up in the

all the same. You were kept; and ev

it will be to a kept life. His grip on yc

ball, when he dragged you down the st

wouldn't let go then. Why ever would he

Late September. An officer comes with

The women are allowed to write letters of the

Joseph's birthday, but she writes him as though

another to Inés on the back of a requisition slip.

taken off. They wait.

Night falls faster; October rolls ghostly by.

She is among the lucky few to receive replies, but th

Inés. Her man, Fandal, is dead. Measles. Vicksburg. The o

people in that city aren't eating, it seems, are the dead. *We*

New Orleans, I suppose. In her accustomed space between th

Elise feels her cheeks for tears—finds none.

The cold comes so suddenly the women give off steam. She se

rising misty from her arms and she is like steel taken from the forg

and quenched. And so her purpose has grown stark. Clear as her eyes

now they are accustomed to staring across miles of sea. Hard and defi-

nite and dark as her person.

She will make him let her go.

Joseph

Two

Convenient Graves

A ll Saints' Day. The gloves on his hands, the stockings doubled in his shoes, do nothing for the chill that seeped this morning from the deep corners of the doctor's house and took ahold of his fingers and toes and hasn't yet let go. Not when he, dressing for the day's duty of visiting graves, held them before the fire stoked by one of the doctor's aged slaves. Not when he rubbed his hands together on the ride across town, back into the neighborhood where he used to live, kneading and pinching so much that the doctor—mistaking the chill for nervousness—said, *Come on now. It's not as though you haven't been here before.* And not when he stopped at the cemetery gate, feigning that his laces were untied and, while the doctor strode heedless ahead with the beaded immortelle wreaths and bundled candles tucked under his arm, Joseph touched the sun-warmed leather of his shoes and tried to mash the heat into his stiffened toes.

Now, dragging feet that might as well be asleep, he hurries through the gates into the cemetery. Like all grounds in the city holding Catholic bones, Saint Louis no. 1 has undergone its annual transformation from a rank and weedy collection of monuments occasionally strung with flowers and haphazard mementos into a wildly bedecked shrine. Today the living pour into the cities of the dead and offer wreaths and light, favorite treats and articles, maintain vigils over souls both saintly and not. High-hatted men hang back from the flocks of black-veiled women knelt before the tombs. Joseph hears their murmurs, their clockwork prayers, the chewing noise of hundreds of feet on the oystershell walks as he and the doctor near the Sabatier tombs. He keeps his head down to avoid the sight of the veiled women, all of whom, give or take pounds and posture, could be his mother. If she were here and wearing black, not on an island in the Gulf, her dress white as the sand.

This is how he imagines her: white and furious, immutably blanched. And imagination is all he has—for his letters go unanswered. The doctor has written to the commandant of the island, who vouched that there have been no deaths among the female prisoners and the dearth of mail is inexplicable. A matter for the postmaster.

Unlike their neighbors, the Sabatier tombs are not freshly whited, their roofs—steeply sloped and pintellated with cruciform spikes—are overgrown with weeds. The doctor throws open the low iron gate and steps into the familial ground. Joseph looks to the downspouts at the feet of the tombs—grotesques whose open mouths are gagged with wet leaves. Glancing up from the hideous faces, he watches the doctor hang upon each house one of the ready-made immortelles he bought this morning on the way. This accomplished, the doctor turns about without a moment's pause and walks out. A pair of old women crouched at a nearby obelisk scowl and shake their heads when the doctor loudly heels shut the gate. Dusting off his hands as though from a great labor, he nods Joseph in the direction of the ovens. The beads of the deposited immortelles are still clacking against the moldy faces of the tombs when they set off.

Through corridors of crypt where families share pieces of chicken from wicker baskets and solitary men sit on the steps of graves slowly swirling bottles between their knees. Beneath bright garlands stretching from statues to stone urns, and miniature Parthenons whose columns writhe with blooms. Narrow vaults whose doors are embossed with swords or cannons. The tomb of an actress who died young, its pediment piled with roses and slips of poetry.

"I wonder," Joseph says. "What sort of grave I'll have."

Lately he's grown accustomed to voicing his thoughts to the doctor, who claims to enjoy them. What the doctor truly likes is to hear in Joseph's voice an echo of his own. A tone or turn of phrase Joseph never knowingly assumes, yet there it is all the same. He opens his mouth and there is this man's voice, where once had been his father's, sitting like a coal-fleck on his tongue.

"A little premature for that, my boy." The doctor smiles. "You won't have to worry about graves for"—his eyes glint—"no. Go on wondering. When I was your age, or maybe younger, my father would tell me not to think darkly. Dark thoughts, he believed, were unmanly. Of course, that was on the rare occasion I spoke in his presence."

Joseph knows what it means to occupy a corner of silence at the dinner-table, as was the rule when his father sat down with them. But he didn't hate his father for it; nor does he hate him now. At least not the way it seems Dr. Sabatier hates his.

"My dark thoughts served me well, and I believe you'll profit just as much from yours." The doctor taps his brow, a knowing nod. "You have the mind for them, you do."

Passing now twinned plinths bearing the names of pairs of husbands and wives, he sees Marina laid upon a bier, the way she likes to do when they act out death-scenes from her play. The pirate witch is always dying, always coming back to life. Only the death of Marina's uncle put her away; and then but for a time. Now she is the pirate witch in black, even their acting must be quiet so as not to disturb Mademoiselle. The pile of stiff rags remain still unfound.

At the stretch of ovens bordering Bienville they must shoulder through the crowded mourners to reach his father's home. In the time since the funeral his name has been etched in a brass plate along with his impossible years: 1784–1862. The doctor waves to be handed the wreath slung over Joseph's shoulder.

"I can reach," Joseph says, more than a little proud. The doctor is not a tall man, and in the last four months he has grown within an inch of his height. The spurt began with pain, bone-deep, on the first night he spent in the doctor's house. And for a time he thought his aches were in sympathy with the coughs and moans of the sick woman upstairs. He felt himself changing apace, his spurts attuned to rustles and agonies of the doctor's wife as summer wore into fall. By the time the woman died, Joseph's ankles showed past his cuffs. The bottom has fallen out of his voice, like a rotten floor. He is beset by an oppressive need for sleep. Easily attained, for there are so many cool dark places in the doctor's house and no one but the occasional slave with a duster to disturb him. And it is as though he'd needed the house in order to grow; or that it needed him to raise up and fill its emptiness. But there are times at night and even midday (the shadows do not care) when he isn't enough, and his fresh height, what he can encompass in his new arm-span, is not enough and the house swallows him. And when he feels enfolded by that vast darkness, he understands what it means for a house to have wings.

Now whenever he meets Marina he must look down; Mlle Pichon he may look in the eye. And if his father weren't encased behind these bricks with so many others, he could meet his eye too.

To hang the wreath he must get so close to the tomb that the smell of charnel, even deadened by the weather and stone, comes alive in his throat and lightens his head.

"Your father wouldn't care for this," says the doctor. "The flowers. The Catholic ceremony."

Father doesn't have much say in it, though, does he? The wreath catches firmly to the peg and he falls back from the stench of rot into the elbows and hoops of the crowd. Coughs and grunts from the men. Women tisk. A flicker of flame appears in the doctor's hand as he lights the candle he will set atop the tomb. One candle among the many, already yielding up their wax and throwing light that competes with the sunset.

"You may pray, if you wish."

On the street the soldiers seem more at ease, as though the cold has loosened their bones. And still this morning's chill clings to Joseph's fingers and toes. The doctor, unprompted, says that he will visit the grave of his wife tonight. Alone.

Joseph nods, tries to summon an image of the woman but can find none. He knew her only by her groans; by the decreasing depth of her coughs as the blood filled up her lungs. At night he could measure the hour by the sound of her torturous and protracted passage into the next world. The doctor, being kind, sent him to Mlle Pichon's at the end. And now Marina's uncle, too, has joined the dead. She and Mlle Pichon will be keeping their own vigil over the entombed corpse that was so rotten by the time of its arrival in New Orleans the coffin was kept shut.

Decomposition. Gaseous buildup in the tissues. Such are the things he has learned. There has been no talk of school these four months and he won't be the one to broach the subject and spoil his shadowy holiday. The doctor seems content to apply his own tutelage, which commences for an hour or so each day on subjects chosen seemingly at whim. Latin one night, Greek the next. He graduates from cutting earthworms to dissecting fish and piglets. A complication or organs spilled under the watchful eye of the doctor.

Near the end of this evening's lesson, Joseph looks up from the open book that rests between them and asks, "Do you miss her, your wife?"

"Yes I do," he says, drumming his fingers over the pages. And just as suddenly the annoyance is gone, his voice a rasp: "Do you miss your mother?"

"And my father," Joseph says, but the doctor doesn't seem to hear. His eyes are far away.

"She'll be back very soon," the doctor says. "Now back to work."

They return to the lesson, a fat volume of zoological curiosities, where the Compte de St. Claire tells us how certain beasts excrete a chemical compound that weakens their sensation of pain.

Three
Thanksgiving

The carcasses are picked clean, and the pie dispensed in slices to diners whose appetites are far past slaked. It is agreed that Southern pumpkins do not match their Northern cousins, which are far nuttier and more sweet. The uncomfortable prayers have been hustled through, the chatter of here and home suspended. Evening smears the panes of dining room, blots out the garden-pathways of what could rightly be called the Butler plantation. The shuffle of servants, the clack of bone on china, the dribble of coffee being poured by black hands now paid a wage. The sounds of things ending.

Fifteen miles downriver from the city: Vacherie, sugar country. Here the citizens have signed the oath of allegiance almost to a man, the lone exception being the former owner of this house, who abandoned the property and sent his family to Texas at the time of the invasion. So, with the cane ripe and the hands escaped or idle, the situation begged for an able man to be sent. Brother Jackson, needing diversion and to be out of New Orleans, fit the bill. He has driven crews of California Mexicans and gold-field Chinese, so why not Negroes? And the place is profitable, even with the hands being paid for the first time in their lives—lives the general has glancing observed from the dining room window this day of Thanksgiving. A different breed than the city blacks. Darker, leaner, troublingly quiet. One sits in the far corner, a withered manikin just behind his brother's head, basket of napkins in her lap.

From the opposite end of the table, General Butler watches his brother lean close to the loyalists, to Creole planters by whose expressions you may know the shallowness of their esteem. Each time they call his brother Colonel Butler, the general feels his wife's nails root deeper in his thigh. The clench of Sarah's fingers and the corner-cut of her blue eyes that he has learned in the course of years of parties, holidays, and visits, unmistakably ask, *May we go now?*

He closes his hand over hers; the nails stay planted.

After months of vacillation, arguments by packet, her letters, at first filled with reasons not to come back to New Orleans (to which he would, by silence, agree), turned gloomy and sulkier than their daughter's missives from boarding school; when he asked that she send photographs of her and the children so that he could have the family's portraits painted on china plate, Sarah's looked like a memento mori; when he wrote asking for new pairs of his favorite merino winter underwear and shirts, she acted as though the letters were lost; and finally her tone turned furious—livid lines screaming to know why he wasn't *asking* her to return. He tried to show his wife her autonomy, the ease of his hand, but she wanted to be told. And so he had, scribbling one late September morning, by turns ebullient and begging. A sick Ben in need of his Sary.

In his letters he joked that he wanted her happy and glad, so she arrived whittled and bitter. She begged for him to beg her to come, and now that she's here, Sarah is misery incarnate.

She said, *You want me fat to make yourself feel better. You want me fat and happy, to be like you.*

I am, he wished to say, far from happy.

Those who left him in the heat of the summer have returned: Sarah, spite-thin, who scrapes the tines of her fork everywhere on her plate except the slice of pie; George Strong, who days before rode off to Pass Manchac in hopes of earning his spurs in what guerilla contests pass for combat. All safely returned. Yes. Wonderful. They have come back just in time, to see the stripping away of everything he has accomplished.

Seward's man Reverdy Johnson did his master's work well. From a little office on the opposite side of the Custom House, sending notes back and forth to the general, Johnson made his sly "mediation" of the case. Obfuscation, threats, and gall—nothing more. And if he can be proud of anything, Butler is of the tolerance he showed the man. Various diplomats' trinkets seized by overeager soldiers were sussed out of pawnshops and whores' parlors, and most importantly all one and a half million dollars of seized specie was returned to the esteemed consuls, an order with which Butler graciously complied, adding only that he wished the esteemed consuls would also take the dies for making bank notes and the crate of plates for printing Confederate treasury notes that were found along with the kegs of silver.

"Cream, Monsieur?"

He says nothing; stares into his coffee. Sarah answers for him. "Oh, yes, cream and four sugars, please. He likes it sweet and fatty."

It's come to this. Treacherous foreigners are given a carte blanche by Washington, so terrified is Mr. Seward and his creature Lincoln of the prospect of European discomfort or, God forbid, intervention. He can hear them: Butler riles the Europeans—we must put a stop to it or this emperor or that king will be at our throats. Let them be treacherous in secret rather than open enemies.

Cowards. Goddamned cowards.

Since the judgment and Johnson's swift departure in August (fanned by rumors that the Rebels were planning an assault), such imagined conversations have held dominion over his resting mind. When not at some task, the voices come to gnaw at him. Seward yipping for his removal, Lincoln's drawl, the lazy chuckle only a drayman would mistake for wit. Stanton bellowing fruitlessly is his favor, drowned out by the chorus of the cabinet that is managing to lose this war. Butler is a liability. He (not this summer's failures in the field behind beauty McClellan) turns the European powers (ha!) against us at the moment we will need them most—the enacting of the president's proclamation to free the slaves in all territories not in U.S. hands. Butler is a liability, they say. Rash and impertinent. A thief along with his brother who calls himself colonel though he holds no commission. They have enriched themselves to the tune of millions. They buy cotton from Confederates and sell them salt and sugar. And worse, he is a Democrat.

"Gentlemen?" says Jackson, rising from his seat. He has in mind cigars and brandy and escaping the company of the women.

Sarah gives him a pointed smile. All her perfect teeth.

He is tired. He doesn't know which voices should have primacy—those he hears or the ones within. They seem equally unreal, equally consequential.

He has told no one of the news received today. The news that stabs his stomach. The confirmation of a summer-long conjecture, rumors dribbled southward in a constant venomous trickle: he will be recalled from his command. In August, hearsay had it would be General Dix, in September, General Fremont. He wrote the secretary of war, saying that if they had a replacement in mind, they should send the man soon so that he could enjoy the full fury of the fever season.

But of course there is no fever in the city. Some deaths among the poor, immigrants, Negroes, but not the scythe-sweep dying of years past. He has beaten the thing that killed his father. Yellow fever, like a whipped cur, is skulked off to Havana, San Juan, Veracruz. And no one will give him the credit. With less than ten thousand men he has held this half of the state, made incursions into Mississippi, bolstered the siege of Vicksburg, while with a hundred thousand McClellan and Burnside have their heads kicked in and lose everything up to the gates of Washington.

Now it has come to him by way of a spy among General Polk's officers, who saw it in a cable from Richmond, that General Nathaniel Banks, fresh off his "victory" over Stonewall Jackson's maniacs, is sent with thirty thousand men on an expedition against Texas. It is not without rage that Butler contemplates the fact that Jefferson Davis knew about this before he did. Banks. Nativist, Know-Nothing—hater of immigrant Catholics so long as it won him elections, and lover of nigger freedom providing it did the same. Of all the men they could have sent. Banks, who, within a year of Butler's age, has served as speaker of the House and a term as governor of Massachusetts. And in their acquaintance, on opposite poles of politics, still Butler has never been unkind to the man. Never noted, as do many others, that he started life as a bobbin-boy, threading the empty spools of mill-women in Waltham. He holds meagre beginnings against no man. Certainly not against Banks. Tall Banks. Dashing Banks. Banks with hair on his head to spare.

Butler rubs the graying tufts that cling above his ears—his tonsure—looks to Sarah and sighs. "I won't be long. Just a drink, then we can go."

From across the room: "Come on now, Ben. I need a smoke!"

Sarah shuts her eyes, waves him off. He will pay for this on the ride home, and at home he will spend the night at his desk to avoid his wife's boundless ire. He will sit at his desk and work. He will write directly to Lincoln, demand an explanation. He won't allow them to hide their designs. The Illinois rail-splitter will know his feelings, and be forced to make his own plain. And isn't that what our beleaguered president, who mortgages a war on political favor and thinks more of slaves than his soldiers in the field, likes best? Plain speaking. Plain dealing. Plain shit.

In the staggering powerlessness, Butler feels himself receding. Growing smaller. There is no maneuver to be made, no legal wrangling, no law to bend or mold. The judgment is out of his hands; all he can do is wait.

mixture laced with dulling morphia anodyne, for he never intended to be cruel. He intended to be rid of her.

Lydia, feeling the chill of the mixture as it climbed the tree of her veins.

When he has the stove lit, the doctor sits at his desk and opens his diary to today's date. The fourth of December. This day or the next Elise will be released, packed aboard a steamer and hauled back to the city under the parole that she will no more trouble the occupying forces. If all goes well, she will be here within the week.

Not *here*. They won't need to use his office anymore. When he looks back on their nights spent on the floor, among his instruments and files and collections, Elise arranging vials and jars, it is with disgust. Disgust at having rutted on the boards. And more, that she could so easily urge him to his knees, guide his mouth against her sex. The secrecy, the floor, the hiding, his desire, all of it had reduced him to boyhood self, echoes of which he sees sometimes in Joseph—whenever his charge speaks of the Fandal girl. He has done his best to temper the infatuation, spoken many times to the négresse Pichon, who seems content to abet their ruin. Though now they've carted Willie Fandal's body back from the Mississippi mudhole, he might take a lighter tone. The girl stands to inherit; and the matter of her parents' wealth is still unsettled in the Cuban courts. She might not make a bad match, but first he must get his hands on the figures. He has great hopes for Joseph, for his wealth-buoyed rise in the wake of cyanosis—so much that he's considered more than once making him his heir.

He is almost giddy, looking at his dates. Past his lamp and papers, his cigarbox and matchcase, over the lip of the desk, the carpeted floor stares back. He won't have her here again. He has unlimbered some of Woolsack's money and found her a house on the border of the Marigny, twice the size of her old one. She will have a cook, a washer, a maid. All paid. Prudent considerations, he thinks, for though Mr. Lincoln's coming proclamation does not include federally held territories such as New Orleans, it one day will.

Such are the changes wrought upon us by time and circumstance. Likewise, he is no longer aggrieved that Elise was taken. She had grown too strong, her hold over him too powerful. She'd clouded his mind, and now in these months as the heat bled out of the world his vision has cleared. She will return chastised and willing. Eager to assume her place.

Five

Arrival

Her father had a story of the songbirds in old Prussia. How in wintertime, before human understanding forced birds to take southerly routes, sparrows and swallows and redwings would flush from the trees of the Palatinate and dive in pairs down to the bottoms of lakes, and stay there, beak-to-beak, sharing air while their split-pea hearts beat a dirge for summer. Unless disturbed by the errant nets of fishermen, the birds of cold Europe would thus pass winter, even as frost spread over the surface of their lakes and their old perches bowed with snow. After the thaw, the birds would take one last gasp of each other's air and thrust up from the depths, feathery missiles shooting skyward. Then the birds would find a familiar branch and sit, sunning and fluffing their waterlogged pinions.

The widow Woolsack, flocked now with friends in the sitting room of Mme Frick, reminds her of the winter birds. Someone who has been driven to depths, held their breath, and waited while the season did its worst. Her face is dark, rusty, her eyes startlingly white as the sand of the place she left, some of which is retained on her dress. Marina knows it will take weeks to shake out; and even then grains will return like memories to nag you. Joseph's mother holds a saucer and cup, looking everywhere, carefully, encompassing them all. Knots of muscles jump at her elbow, in her jaw. The lines of care and age she remembers in the woman's face are gone, replaced by a smoothness not youthful or vigorous but burnished and honed, like a cast statue. And statuesque she sits, while all around her the ladies mill and primp, making passes to the buffet laden with an abundance of cakes and tarts and fruit, a trough of gleaming oysters. When a sample of each dandy is brought for her to taste, Joseph's mother gives her eyebrows an almost imperceptible lift, shakes her head so minutely you could blink and miss it. She can stomach none of the food. Coffee will be fine. Yes, a little cognac.

Of course, dear, they say, fluttering and almost dropping into curtsies. Joseph's mother surveys the room with her impossibly white eyes. Mlle Pichon is kittenish by her side, also in black, as though not in mourning but that black were the colors of her court; Pichon fiddles with her sleeves, strokes her friend's hair where it curls down in two black wisps before her reddened ears. Joseph's mother accepts the preening without comment or expression; she is one to whom dread honor is due. Even the normally haughty Mme Frick is subdued and attentive—after a showy burst of tears when they arrived from the landing.

Something nudges her elbow. Marina turns and almost knocks the punch cups from Joseph's hands. He gives her one, cuts his eyes motherward as he drinks. She still doesn't know how to stand near him; Joseph's new height, his odd mannerisms, his deepened voice have displaced her, forced her to be obvious, as though obviousness will afford her entrance into his now-guarded perceptions.

"Are you happy to have your mother back?"

He says, "It would be bad if I wasn't."

"Well, will you be happy to move to your new house."

He flicks his cup, screws up his lips. "It's just a new place. Another room."

"But you'll be closer—" She stops herself. The ladies are peeling away from Joseph's mother, gathering around the pianola. There is to be a song.

"Closer," he says, grinning meanly and affecting elegance. "To whom?" This is his new way, by turns enigmatic and snide. He's grown sharp points and doesn't hesitate to jab her. By turns she's cultivated her own.

"To me, of course," she says. "Or maybe you don't care about me either. . . ."

Joseph's grin grows sharper. Is this something the doctor has taught him? The mocking and parrying? These little tests to see how much she'll take? He is not the boy whose hand she took on the couch that night, whose fingers she pressed between her legs, the boy who shuddered and was terrified when the wet spot appeared on his thigh. The last time they were alone, a month ago, before Uncle Willie was brought back, Joseph had said words she'd never before heard, tried to hook his finger inside her. She, in turn, choked his part to purpleness.

The only other male fracture in this veneer of femininity is the doctor. A black ribbon on his arm in memory of his dead wife, he leans in the doorway, sips his drink, and stares at the back of Joseph's mother's head. For an instant the seeming vacancy of the doctor's stare is gone; he catches Marina's glance and she quickly turns away.

Someone clangs the keys of the pianola and the ladies test their trebles, call for Mlle Pichon to come up and join them in their serenade. So she does, leaving Joseph's mother alone.

"I should go over there," Joseph says.

She follows him, takes a place at the left wing of her chair. The ladies' voices join in concerted discord and the song begins. Marina keeps her eyes down, watches the fingers of the woman's right hand tap an entirely different rhythm. A song of her own. Before the second bar is done, Joseph's mother waves him close, whispers something in his ear. He nods and disappears in the direction of the buffet.

Now the tapping right hand turns upward. Forefinger curls for Marina to bend down. She does, the ladies' voices droning through a chorus about love. She has never been so close to Joseph's mother; she can feel her stray hairs and smell her breath—raw and metallic. For a moment she waits, then the impossibly white eyes roll from the singers to her, catch her up and fix her in place. The lips curl back and she sees the barest tip of the woman's tongue, red and darting as she speaks.

"Watch yourself, little girl; the world means you nothing but hurt."

Six

The House on Kerlerec

And she means to repay hurt in more than kind. She revolts from others' sense of equity, that punishment and pain are determined by some otherworldly score, and that we must smilingly endure whatever we are dealt. No. She will have pain dealt according to a scale known only to herself. A private criterion of suffering. And there are others now about who feel likewise. She'd met some of their number on the steamer back from Ship Island, when clutches of newly liberated prisoners were retching at the rails. Conversations between gasps, aching statements of intent by self-professed Southern men, saying they will inaugurate upon their return a system of recompense for the wrongs of the occupier and those who collude with him. Some of them were young, almost attractive in their rage. A few even asked to call on her.

She only wanted to warn the girl. A bit of advice while the ladies wailed their song. But when Elise spoke, the girl's face peeled back with fear and she lipped away, not reappearing until the party was nearly done. Poor thing, she'd do well to listen. There is no safety to be found in the world, and certainly none in the company of people. Starve your desires until they wither and are gone. Look out with clear eyes and take your mark through the hordes of the foolish and the cruel.

When leaving Frick's, her son in tow, she sees a jaunty man about to dart heedless from a tavern into the path of an oncoming cart; she says nothing, passes on. A crumple, snap, and scream that would be sickening were she not inured to nausea. She was so sick on the voyage back from the island that her insides feel as though they have been scoured out with wire.

The crushed man shrieks away his life, and Joseph yelps, asking did she see. Without looking back she snatches his arm, hurrying on to find a cab, and from there to the house secured for them by Emile. Two stories of pocked stucco on a lonesome corner of an ill-named street. Kerlerec, so Emile explained as he gave them the tour, was one of the first colonial governors of Louisiana. He ruled poorly, Kerlerec, but was a deft deviser of tortures. And when he couldn't be bothered to think up a new one, Mme Kerlerec would improvise the method, a genius in her own right. An extravagant woman: prisoners might be flayed alive or baked in clay kilns or nailed into barrels and cut in half, all in the course of a day. Just lovely, Emile. A fitting choice. Joseph, of course, had perked at all the storied gore, saying, *My father did worse than that.*

I'm sure he did, Emile laughed. *Maybe when you're governor one day you'll name a street after him.*

And the look shared between him and her son is the only thing in a long time that has frightened her.

That night, in her new bed, she is unnerved by the absence of surf, troubled now by the definite world and its bricks and wood cacophonous even in the early morning—cart-clatter, pans clanging, footfalls, shouts. The unfamiliarity of the house has her cagey; so few of her possessions are retained—she can see Emile at the auction, wondering whether to bid on this set of plates or that hairbrush, and did he even try?—the furnishings, no doubt purchased from some more economical confiscated estate, bear the smells and indents of previous owners.

Little here belongs to her, not even her son. She knew from the moment she laid eyes on Joseph that he has changed almost beyond her reckoning. More than the outward signs—his height, his voice—there is something else, and she senses the transformation just as she senses the remnants of the body of whoever owned this bed before. He is distant, gone from her. But that is what boys do, is it not? Grow further and further from the one who held them and sang and for whom their little body was the lone light in the world? Growth is one thing, she thinks, change another. The boy that was her son, brought up by her hand, could grow and become something to admire; but now he has come under other hands and begun to be molded by them. She's returned in time to take him back from Emile, whether he likes it or not. And judging by his silence, the tenseness of his perfunctory embraces, her son is far from happy to be in her possession. But, as Angel would say, it doesn't make a damn. Just as Emile molded sneers and coldness into her boy, so too will she reshape him into a more agreeable form.

Her son, redeemer of her blood, who says he only saw Emile's wife after she was dead, but heard her coughing every night. Who, when she asks what the doctor taught him, looks away and says it would be hard to explain. She has Joseph back, but in order to keep him and set him towards the future she intends, Elise must now take possession of herself.

Before they'd quit the party, Emile had whispered to her about meeting at his house tonight. She refused. Let him wait; let him tremble inside with want.

The noise outside worsens, life over-loud. The city seems ready to rend itself to tatters.

In the early morning she goes out to buy a copy of the *Bee*, wherein a columnist bemoans the city's supposed tranquility.

Won't someone please commit suicide? the newsman pleads. *A brazen robbery? A scandalous divorce?*

Can't we, please, have a murder?

Seven

Banks

Decorated-initial-D ecember 14. When George Strong, lightly scarred from his recent adventures at Pass Manchac, comes to tell him that General Banks's ship is rounding the riverbend, Butler doesn't blink. He's been anticipating this moment, gone to bed each night fitful and full of foreboding; each morning he has shaved his sagging face and brushed the gold embroidery of his uniform with the care of a condemned man. His belt and links and buttons have never gleamed so much. He has never cut a finer figure than now, at the end.

"Will we meet him at the landing, General?" says Strong.

The gewgaws and artifacts of his office crowd him in, the hanging swords and articles and drawings, the she-adder line on the wall. Everything will have to come down. He feels the aggregate pettiness heaped upon his shoulders as he rises, asking Tibbets for his sword-belt.

The orderly will not meet his eyes; bald brows furrow as he meekly hands over the sword and helps to fix it round the general's waist. A parade sword, its blade unsharpened and oily in heavy pewter scabbard. Butler, unbalanced by its weight, tugs his tunic down.

George's face is misaligned.

"Banks—he has a band on deck."

"Well then," Butler says. "Let's not be late to the party."

Going out down the rows of the petitioners lining the hall, Strong adds: "You can hear the music from the damned levee."

And indeed you can, jubilant and brassy even over the sounds of the ship's engine, the broad wheels chocking wake. At least the weather has become tolerable. Cool if not crisp. At least Banks won't be able to see him sweat. Others of his staff have come, unbidden, to the Bienville landing. Butler's shoulders are subject to friendly claps and squeezes. Like a lad being led to the altar. He watches Banks's ship grind against cotton-bale bumpers and crewmen scurry about to tie her off. The band blares the same old "John Brown's Body," but with added beats and a triumphal upsurge to each note.

The wind from off the river sharpens the cold. Now citizens have gathered on the levee, and because there can be no punishment, no confiscation or imprisonment, meted out for cheering a Union general, they hurrah out their hearts. They wouldn't whoop any louder for Beauregard himself, to whom Butler has made an offer of free entry into the city this week so that the enemy general may visit his dying wife. Of course, Beauregard won't come; he will allow his wife to die alone.

When Banks appears on the quarterdeck and gives them a princely wave, the people come apart. How many are here now? Hundreds? Butler swallows his spit; perhaps General Banks's command will be inaugurated by a riot. New Orleans greeting him with its characteristic scorn and discord. That would be pleasant, were it not for the fact that he has reduced the citizens' capacity for riot, bled them of their appetite for disharmony. Like all his other accomplishments, the man now descending the gangway flanked by his staff and trailed by god-damn trumpeters like some European prince will reap the benefit of the order he has wrought from chaos.

The river-wind only sculpts Banks's thick brown hair; stepping off the gangway he strides up to Butler, forcing gravity on a mouth that you can plainly see wishes to grin. Salutations; a handshake over-firm. The softness of Banks's palms belie his bobbin-boy days. Beside him George Strong shifts, for once not the handsomest man in the room.

Butler holds his replacement's blue gaze as the man fishes in his coat for the order. He hands the paper over and Butler slips it into his tunic. There will be time enough to moil over the wording later. For now he has a part to play, peculiar to our American system—the slump-shouldered and peaceable transfer of power.

He keeps his hand on Banks's back, leading him through the cheering crowd to the carriage. His mind lurches suddenly to boy-hood dreams of military glory. Of crowds, much like this one, calling out his name.

Banks, turning to him. His clear Puritan voice. "This was never my intention," he says.

Was the band, you prancing ass? Butler pats his back, absurdly consoling. "Well, it's never really in our hands, is it?"

Eight

The Women Who Hold Fire in Their Hands

The new house is no friend to secrets; within its bone-white stucco walls and behind the narrow shuttered windows talk is misdirected and projected into rooms as if by tympanum, so that Joseph can be (as he is now) upstairs in his bare bedroom, staring at the unfamiliar ceiling, and without straining hear—if not the substance, then the tone and the occasional word of—his mother's conversation with the man downstairs. At first he thought it was the doctor, went downstairs to see, and found instead his mother greeting a man she, after a moment's hesitation, introduced as M. Armand. A smile on his weathered sunburnt face, cherry-colored nose and ears gleaming with some ointment, Armand said hello and abruptly announced that he'd been a fellow inmate on Ship Island. When Joseph asked what M. Armand had done to be sent there, his mother cut him a glare and told him to go back upstairs. Muttering curses, he did.

Now their voices are forced upon him by the house's design.

In recent days the cold has retreated to the tips of Joseph's fingers and toes, in paradox with the worsening winter. He flicks them now, absentminded.

The downstairs voices drop to a murmur. Besides the women of the old neighborhood this Armand is the first visitor his mother has had. The doctor hasn't been by since the day they moved in, nor has his mother resumed her nighttime errands. So he has gone from the house that held the spirit of his father to the mansion inhabited by the doctor's dead wife, to still yet another house and a different kind of haunt.

His mother keeps the lamps low—the maid is always bumping into things—and spends most days asleep, or working at some household project: sewing new black clothes or instructing the cook. She sleeps in her room, in her chair in the parlor, and he has even found her curled on one of the sofas. These slumbers are deep and seem to him not due to exhaustion from her ordeal, but rather the gathering of strength for some great feat. The way cats laze and curl only to suddenly spring up all fang and claw when something weaker happens by.

Her focus is inward, this sleek dark thing his mother has become; she withholds herself from him, speaking rarely. Christmas is a week away and there has been no talk of gifts or parties, none of the excitement he recalls. Her behavior as mysterious as Marina's, who has become a hard thing to handle. Morose, difficult, and so very easy to hurt. Every word from his mouth sets her askew, sends her stomping off. No longer the pirate witch, she has packed away her play and they haven't so much as held hands in the few times they've been together since his mother's return. The woman-governed world has him entrapped, a tangle of lace and strange tempers.

Downstairs the door shuts, and going to his window Joseph sees the man, Armand, heading out into the street named for the devisor of torments.

Upon his arrival in New Orleans, so the doctor told, Governor Kerlerec held a grand fete. The dances and plays and feasts and music were inaugurated by Mme Kerlerec, who loosed a pair of tar-doused doves set afire. The sparks from the flaming doves ignited fireworks that rained over the city for three days.

Joseph wonders what Mme Kerlerec must have looked like, imagines a petite Frenchwoman, bewigged and powdered in the fashion of those times. It is dark—dark in the way that candle-lit world, the world before gaslight, could only have been. Shadowed, she cups the blackened doves in her hands and, impossibly, keeps them even as the taper is put to their feathers and they alight. The fire-doves jab and squirm and the flames flutter through the gaps in her fingers as she holds them up, and in the light of singed feathers her face is that of his mother, of Mlle Pichon, of Marina. Womanhood nascent or attained, ablaze with promise and threat.

Nine
The Witching Hour

What kind of woman walks at night, veiled, unaccompanied, and in black? What kind of woman seeks out darkness?

A widow belongs at home, a mother belongs with her child, and all women of character are barred from the streets at night. In her grandmother's day it was the law and superstition both that kept women behind doors after sundown. The old Latin law, which they feared less than the more ancient belief in the Witching Time, midnight, when the dead and daemonic were allowed entrance into our world. Dead women as well as men, she reasons, so it might be that we are judged equal in the end. May go in darkness as we please. Then again there are those of us the darkness itself seeks.

Down Dauphine she is mindful of every step, careful where she puts her feet for the shadows on the street are thick and pool in potholes and knots of roots and bucked paving like rainwater after a shower. You may step in and be up to your hips, with a broken leg for your trouble. And more than this she is vigilant for watchmen at the corners, for bodies lurking in doorways, for eyes peering out from trees, for alleyway whisperers and window-watching women who would carry the story of her midnight passage, and by gossip throw a noose around her neck.

But who can see her? Who can judge her features behind her veil of tightest tulle and her hat of jet mink? Know her form within the dress and the skirts upon which she must seem to float, draped in cape and coat likewise jet trimmed at collar and cuffs? She taps her hat down over her burning ears, rubs the fur at her wrists. The hat and coat, gifts from Emile, are the only way a watcher could mark her. No matter. Tonight will be the last time she wears them.

Thick clouds keep back the moon; there are no lit windows on the street, and rare the wisps of smoke from familial hearths. This is the cold hour, the black hour. She squints when she passes under the occasional streetlamp, smiles at the thought of the spiritual limn of her grandmother's time, one in which Emile's late wife might have even believed. The brief freehold of the dead.

Please, she thinks. As if the dead need a clock's permission.

A teat-slung bitch pads across her path, glancing back with shining eyes. Elise whips out her arm and with a snap of her fingers sends the bitch loping away.

She passes the alley from which she hears the clop and snort of Emile's hitched horse. Slats of light show through the shuttered window of Emile's office. He is upstairs, waiting for her. Grousing maybe, tapping his foot or smoking a cigar too fast. He hadn't wanted to meet her here again. When she told him she preferred it, his reaction was boylike gloom at the thwarted design of having her in his house, his grand bed. He said that she deserved better.

Oh? So you tell me what I deserve as well? And, she thinks, how to bend and move while you hunch into me heedless of my soreness or whether I'm wet. But now he's had to wait two weeks, denied at every turn, and his desire has won out over his newfound sense of propriety.

Something is scrawled on the street door but she cannot make it out, turns the knob and steps into the chill of the stairwell. She imagines him listening to the sound of her climbing the stairs, his anticipation mounting with her every step. What mounts in her is more akin to dread; winter-bleak, it tightens at her throat as she comes to his office and without pause lets herself in.

Emile sits at his desk, leaning back in his swivel chair. He has been watching the door, for his eyes, aimed at her, are the first thing she sees. His face is red; he's shaved this evening. He says her name, stands, and comes round the desk, hands outspread and eager for her. His thin fingers. Fingers to fit scalpels, fingers for needles, they dance over her now. And she has him by the back of his jacket, pulls him close so that their cheeks brush and her head over his shoulder. To the right of the desk, in the little stove, a fire burns.

While he watches, Elise draws off her veil and drapes it from the arm of a chair; he tries to help her from her hoop but she waves him back, writhes free like an insect emerging from its cocoon. She will undress no further; whatever happens will be through the split in her culottes. The underthings balloon at her thighs, swishing as she walks past him to the corner of the desk within the stove's partition of heat, and slaps her palms flat against the wood. Before she can look over her shoulder and give him the coyness, the wan eyes and the ridiculous open mouth that men love, he is at her back and his hands can't decide whether to touch her or hurry the unfastening of his pants. And he is whispering now, meaningless little grunts of word. His right leg slides hers out, heel-drag across the floor. She tenses her knee to give him the controlled resistance he desires. She cannot see but hearing the thud of his belt buckle knows his skinny shanks are bared, his pants in ridiculous bunch at his ankles; he shuffles closer to her, greedy fingers squealing the silk as he widens the split for no reason. Now he palms himself, and there he is, hot and twitching and ungainly prodding between her legs.

There is a moment of decision in a man's love, when he has you held or pinned or thinks he does, when he lays his thumb against your cheek and you can feel in his hands that he is considering his ability to harm you. He may press that same thumb against your lips, mashing, and allow his fingers to close around your chin, then turn your head and, squeezing, try to force out your tongue, which you stretch out absurdly to meet his. And all the while that tension in his hands, that trembling rapturous self-amazement at his strength, within which muscle speaks: I could maul you, but I won't.

Emile has been saving himself; before long he's on his toes and shuddering. Inside her stings the quick provender of man's shallow well. Sputtered breaths at her neck—how strange the exhaustion that comes over them after a few moments' hunch and thrust. But there it is all the same, the foal-wobble of his legs, his vacant eyes, the air sieved through clenched teeth, as though what passed between them were some great feat. It is all he can do to uncouple from her, fish out his handkerchief, and, after wiping himself, pass the tepid cloth for her to press between her legs.

They fall into the visitors' chairs opposite the desk, not facing one another, addressing absence when they speak, as though they've come to pay a call on an invisible.

"What would've happened," she says, "if I hadn't run from you?"

"When we were young?" The time is never far from his mind.

"Yes."

He shakes his head, laughing. "Good Lord. We might be married. Middling, not poor"— he stifles a cackle with his fist—"oh and some jealous neighbor would call your . . . heritage . . . into question. We'd go to court and—"

"No. I mean to say, do you think you'd have been different?"

"Different?" He looks to the ceiling. "No. Not in terms of character. From my experience a human being is molded and made before the age of sixteen. Everything after that is the embellishment of a fore-drawn design."

The stove is to her right and on that side she has the full benefit of its warmth. Radiant heat making her face feel taut while on her left, with Emile, the cold holds sway. She shuts her eyes and thinks of Joseph. Is he formed already? Does she have only three years to undo what's happened? Or is any effort merely putting off the settling of accounts?

"So you would have been exactly the same, done the same kinds of things no matter what?"

"What kind of things, Elise?"

"Like what you did to your wife."

His chest rises and falls. No surprise on his face, no outward denial.

He says, "If you mean care for her through a long and arduous illness, then yes."

"You know what I mean."

He has his hands on the arms of his chair, elbows bladed out. "And what about you? What would you have done differently, in imaginary circumstances?" He leans towards her. "Would there be a bullet in my head?"

Her mind darts; this is not really what she wanted to know. She tries from different angles to approach the same unfathomable thing. "When I was on the island," she says, "I dreamed of killing General Butler. Of how the shot would look in his belly. Of his whines."

"You might still catch him at the docks tomorrow," he says. "And would you, if you could get away with it?"

"I realized when I came back that he was unimportant. A figurehead."

"Your instincts do you credit."

"But not in the case of your wife."

He smiles, throws up his hands.

"Do you know that I met her—"

"On Her Majesty's Ship *Rinaldo*? Yes indeed, *Mlle Pichon*."

The pretty little thing who tried to console a hurt she didn't understand, who, even as she moved and danced and wiped cake-crumbs off her chin that night, did so within the tightening snare of someone else's story.

"Did she know?"

Emile muses, strokes his moustache. His expression takes on a darker cast. "In her own way, I think she did."

She says, "Did you do it for me?"

A crackle at the back of his throat. "I had you already. I could've gone on having you. . . ."

Yes, you could have. You would have me and keep me, dangle the money and my son out in front of me. And maybe if you tired of me or you worried what I might say, then you'd do the same thing to me as you did to her.

"And I will," he says to the absence behind the desk.

The stove has consumed its fuel; residual heat fades as the clock on the cabinet tolls two. Brassy tongs reverberate in the otherwise silent room, and in silence she rises and so does he. This time she lets him help her dress. The strangeness of clothes, that getting in is always harder than getting out. Emile's hands are the finest for eyelets and hooks. Particular and precise, almost ladylike.

He will be the first out. She holds up her hand for him to kiss. He does, and looking up the black causeway of her forearm the years drop from his face and he is very much himself at seventeen. All nervous deference and false-composure. She tells him good-night.

Releasing her hand, he goes to the door, dons hat and coat, and takes up his cane. He throws the bolt. Partway out, he pauses, saying, "We won't do this here again. All right? Next time we go to my house."

He stares at her for a long time, as though seeking something in her face. He adds:

"And that's final."

"Fine, yes," she says. And he is gone. The door shuts softly, and now she is the one listening to footsteps on the stairs. The fading echoes of his descent. Outside there is the clatter of a carriage rounding the near corner onto Dauphine.

She turns from the door to the increasing chill of the empty office. Listening to Emile's footsteps on the second flight, her arms shake and her hands ball into fists.

And this, she knows, is the point in the story where the world expects her, this tragic woman, sufferer of the supposed curse of Africanity, to go to any of the death-packed cabinets and draw out a vial or find a blade and surrender. To join the mass for whom redemption is attained only in death. Think of Angel, all the nobility of gun-roar and spattered brains and horror. A roaring death, a man's death. And hers should be womanly and quiet. A breathy acquiescence. What other way can such a woman take the course of her life into her own hands than to end the course itself?

The stories never say that there might be another way, though she knows it for a fact. When the counter comes, she won't be tallied alongside those who quit and withered.

She takes up her veil, hat, and gloves, listens to the carriage halt at the curb. Emile has reached street-level; downstairs the door yawns and slams shut.

At the window, she watches through the slats of the shutters: the sidewalk below, Emile coming down the steps, his head cocked in wonder at the carriage. Elise tugs on her kidskin gloves. She watches him look up at the coachman and back, arches her fingers as though for an invisible throat, makes fists so tight the seamed flesh creaks.

Ten

At the Curb

There was something wrong with her eyes. The look in them. He tries to place it even as he stands before the open door of this carriage that is not his. Nor is it a cab; it has no number. The driver sits unmoving beneath a heavy gray blanket, holding the reins taut as though he tarries here for but a moment; and where the driver's face should be, between low hatbrim and scarf, there is a grotesquely hooked nose and the jutting jaw of a Hapsburg, a scythe-sharp smile shears up to the pointed ears. A mask.

"What the hell is this?"

The driver does not move. Breath fogs at the lip of the mask, the inanimate face fixed in skinless grin.

The doctor hefts his cane, the weighted head of it, and starts from the carriage towards the alleyway and his horse. He goes quickly, feeling for the latch that releases the blade from the cane-sheath. It will take much more than masks to send him running. Rage unfurls in his chest; his steps are light; he feels purpose in the heels of his boots, the points of them, in the brutal weight of the cane. Whoever it is, they have no idea what he can do, what numberless bodies he will wade through, what blood. Nothing will stop him.

A man steps out of the alley-mouth. Another mask, one he knows. A red-faced devil of the Mystik Krewe of Orcus. Striding, a curse in his throat, the doctor shakes loose the blade, the cane-sheath clattering to the ground, and crosses the gap.

The first blow comes from behind and strikes fire in his spine and he is toppling to the boots of the man whose mask he knows. He jabs the blade out, whirls it round him as he falls. And he is caught by hands from behind, and a sudden, absolute darkness when the hood is yanked down over his head and cinched shut by rope.

A voice is saying to get him down, get him down. René Armand's voice. The owner of the devil mask.

On his knees and the blade is gone and he is fighting with fistfuls of trash. He hears his horse neighing and stomping in the alley. On his knees—goddamn it—no no no no. It will not end this way, with a boot pressed between the blades of his burning back, using his cracked spine as leverage to pull the rope tighter round his neck. The names of bones are dislodged from his mind as are the bones themselves. He cannot feel but hears the crumpling of his esophagus. He claws at his throat, forcing his fingertips over the rope. His tongue is filling his mouth and light bursts within the blackness of the hood. And they think they kill infection but infection never dies. It moves; it takes another form and life is infection, what you call a soul is a disease occupying an organism, a vessel of flesh that stands there and watches you go with that look in her eyes—of the most beautiful girl he's ever seen, someone's blood dribbling at the corner of her mouth, a lunatic serenity born of the knowledge that she will do anything, and can.

Elise, swaying there in her gown of midnight blue, red hawthorn berries coiled at her wrist. The crowd shudders back from her and the music stops; the dance will not resume. No one will go to her but him.

He holds out his hand and is almost to her when the next blow falls.

Eleven

The Body in the Well

From out of a dream of smoothness, curve, and yield, the brush of fingers across his forehead brings him awake. And if one can be wide awake, he is narrowly so; the reality of the hand, the bedside presence, is hemmed by dream. He keeps still before the human weight on the mattress, the looming form indistinguishable from the darkness, yet by its touch, by its smell, and by an instinct he cannot name, he knows it is his mother.

"You're back," he says, not lifting his head from the pillow.

She hums a note, strokes his head. He pulls the bedclothes into a bundle at his waist, suddenly aware of his embarrassing state, the after-effects of the dream. He tries to wish it away, as he would in church.

His mother speaks as though they have been talking for a while. "Do you remember," she says, "what happened to Mr. Fisher and his children?"

He doesn't hide his surliness. "*No.*"

"You must have been too young to remember." She pauses, gathering herself. "Mr. Fisher lived in the neighborhood. Close to the Esplanade. Mr. Fisher had a wife and two children. A happy marriage by all accounts. Then one day, when the children were seven and six, the wife disappeared. No one knew where. Except of course, Mr. Fisher."

"So?"

"So—Mr. Fisher never told his children that their mother had run away with a cardsharp from California. He never told his neighbors either. He didn't want the shame. Nor was he a liar. He didn't say she was on a trip or visiting distant relatives. He said nothing. And it happened that around the time his wife took off, Mr. Fisher was filling up an old disused well in his back lot. The neighbors watched and the children watched and no one could decide just when he'd started the project but all noted that he certainly finished it fast.

"Time passed and neighbors began asking his children questions. Idle little things about their father, and *especially* their mother. Then one day the daughters went to buy a dime of beans. The shopkeeper asked, as did everyone, about her mother, and the oldest out of the clear blue said, 'Oh, my daddy killed her and buried her at the bottom of the well.' The shopkeeper then turned to the younger one and asked if this was true and did her daddy kill her mother and bury her in that old well? The younger, maybe six at the time, nothing of a girl, said she thought so."

"But that wasn't what happened," he says.

"No it wasn't. But when the child spoke the neighbors went wild. Some called for the police while others stormed the house and dragged out Mr. Fisher, who told them at last about the cardsharp but by then no one believed him. The well was sitting there, calling to them. To the worst in them. The police had to hold back all the men and women with shovels and picks. They closed the street and started digging. Mr. Fisher by then was in parish prison and his children quartered with one of his charitable neighbors. So for a whole day and into the night they dug, newspapermen fluttering around, the coroner nearby at attention, everyone ready for the ghoulish reveal. Rotten flesh and bones. A skull split in by an axe . . ."

His mother begins again to stroke his hair; he snatches up her wrist and pushes her hand away. He sits up. "Why are you telling me this?"

She shifts, a sound of rubbing. She must be holding her hand.

"Because there was no body in the well," she says. "By midnight, when they came to the sealed base there was nothing to be found but dirt and stone. And before word reached parish prison that he was to be released and the neighbors were working on their apologies, Mr. Fisher had hung himself by his belt. To this day the youngest daughter—she must be around your age now, a maid in the house of the people who took her in—doesn't speak. Struck mute. The older girl ran away a year afterwards.

"Just imagine," his mother sighs. "Father dead, life undone, all on their own words."

He thinks to ask why the daughters said what they did, but finds the confirmation in himself that for certain of our deeds there are no explanations. Joseph wouldn't know what to say were someone to ask him why he climbed down the balcony on the invasion day, why he brought the pistol that caused his father's death; and now he feels something of a kinship with the daughters, the weight of consequence, complicity in a suicide.

He blurts: "You're not telling me why."

She inhales. "I'm telling you because I want you to understand that words can bring more ruin than you know. I want you to know that no matter what happens, no matter what is said or rumored—*there are no bones at the bottom of the well*. And no matter what, everything we do is made sacred by the blood we share. Everything is forgiven before it even happens. Nothing you can do will ever take that love away, and everything I've done or will do is for your sake."

He wants to crawl to the bedside, embrace her, feel her arms around him. But some adolescent instinct keeps him rooted in the sheets.

He says, "Why do you hate Marina?"

"What? I don't hate Marina."

"Oh."

"I only worry," she says, and then her tone shifts, as though she addresses herself. "I don't know. I look at her and see the ticket for your going waiting to be stamped."

He remembers his mother weeping in the carriage on the way back from his father's rushed funeral. The smell of the ovens lingering between them. Remembers her tears behind the veil, but not what he said to make her cry. *You're mine*, she'd said. You're mine.

She bends closer. "Be happy. See her. But you're very, very young, and your whole world can change in an instant."

He goes rigid, playing dead, when she kisses his forehead. She stays at his bedside, in silence, for a long time. Defiantly, he tries to stay awake. But time and quiet and tiredness and the comfort of the bedside presence, which he cannot deny though there are parts of him that scream for her to go, conspire to close his eyes.

"Tomorrow," she says. "We'll go and see General Butler off."

Twelve
El Vómito

His old complaint. Today of all days. To be sprung from bed impelled by the burning urgency of his bowels, scrambling for the pot and, while Sarah daintily plugs her ears, to squat tugging at the tails of his nightshirt so that they won't be dirtied by the foul and shameful evacuation lasting longer than normal and more painful; to dress in the sore emptiness and oversee the loading of their things as the hour of their departure nears and his gorge rises like the long hand of the clock ticking upward the contents of his stomach, bodily failures synchronized to coincide with the end of his administration; to ride to the wharves with a bucket between his knees and Sarah rubbing tight circles on his back, whispering, as she would to one of their children, for him to breathe like a puppy as he hacks and gasps and exhorts all his tried worn will upon this sabotaged function he cannot stop and must run its course as does the carriage through tightening flocks of onlookers to the Bienville landing. Today of all damned days.

The bucket sloshes as the car halts and he must dab his cheeks, draw on his cap, and hope the visor shields his reddened eyes from those who might mistake the cause of his tears. The door opens at Sarah's side: George Strong there to help her down. Now his door swings out and reveals Tibbets in salute. Lifting his leg over the bucket brimming with his shame, General Butler steps out.

The guards, among them his own men recruited from Lowell twenty-one months ago, have cleared a square. An arena at the foot of the wharf, in the shadow of the steamer that will bear him away, not unlike the one on which he dispatched brother Jackson not two days ago. Jackson, guffawing and patting his stomach as though it were a money belt and saying he would write you, Benjy, about the mantilla'd maidens of old Havana. His brother—his overgrown garrulous shade. At least he won't have to suffer Jackson's presence here today.

The other members of his staff stand in file facing that of General Banks, who waits at the end of the walled ranks like a bridegroom. Behind Banks there is a small plank platform, less like a place for a man to make his parting speech than a pillory of the sort where English kings would have the treasonous disemboweled.

He passes between the officers who murmur hails and farewells, sees out the corner of his eye George Strong leading Sarah to the gangway and the ship. (She will collect herself onboard, begin unpacking their cases and arranging things for the two weeks' passage to New York. More productive moments than witnessing his public debasement.) And when the cheers begin and he takes Banks's hand—the man trying to look solemn and grateful—he hopes she at least listens. He studies the cleft of Banks's chin, wishes him well, and goes to mount the platform.

Even this middling height affords him a view of the throng. Women with muffed hands, laborers and besuited speculators, the lean-faced parolees, hobbled veterans. Children everywhere and somewhere among them no doubt the girl who floated to Ship Island and made him play a Shakespeare part, to whom he showed the shapes of the beach sand under the lens of his microscope. For a moment, as he mimes clearing his throat and in actuality is fighting back the next upsurge of bile, he looks for her. But there are so many faces; she is a momentary fancy. The Union societies are represented in full, the men at their forefront holding banners of thanks and encouragement; long-bearded heads nodding with grave approbation for the man who restored the city to the Republic. And like the protoplasm making up the body of this cellular South, this minute cross section offered up to him for one final glimpse through the microscope, are untold blacks whose faces show their shared expectation of Mr. Lincoln's proclamation, two days hence. Not thrilled faces or heedless, gleeful faces, but solemn and stamped with what Butler wonders might be the understanding that no proclamation will unseat the inborn aptitude of men to hate those not like them.

Here he stands, raised above them all, at New Orleans's mouth in the moment before the city vomits him out. At the front of the platform appears George Strong. And looking up from his adjutant to the crowd, he begins. The speech is long and he knows it all by heart. The heart cursed by so many, the heart they wish would stop. As he speaks the soldiers stand taller, the Union Society men throw out their chests, and those who wish to pitch fistfuls of oystershell are still; no heckler's voice is to be heard. His final speech. That is, the last New Orleans will ever hear. This is an election year, despite the war, and there are campaigns political and military (each in symbiotic reliance upon the other) to be won. He is far from finished.

Bile reeks in his moustache; stomach acid rarefies the back of his throat. He gives his parting words and seeks out the scowls, the barely withheld derision of those who hate him now and will nurture in future generations the legend of his villainy. Delicious, the imagining of that legend passed down. It washes the taste of bile clean away. There is more than one kind of immortality, and who among the great fool mass of onlookers can hope to attain it? Not these paltry footnotes, these spectators of history who stand in idiot silence when he finishes his speech.

Now clap, damn you.

Thirteen

"Thy Mission's Over Now"

At the end of *The Tempest*, after all the other players have quit the stage, the sorcerer Prospero remains. He pleads directly with the audience, with you the reader, to applaud. Only by acclaim may he be freed.

Likewise General Butler stands alone on his stage, looking out over the people, expectant; and only when the silence is broken, at first by lone leathery whacks and then a rising chorus of whoops and cheers and fiercely slapping hands that know no rhythm, does he step down, disappearing behind the screen of adult backs now flaring with the motions of their arms, the twirling of their hats, that block Marina's view until the general is climbing the gangway, giving them all the back of his hand.

He is gone but the applause goes on. The people shout taunting good-byes and virulent well-wishes, hurrahs legitimate and not; those who think they can get away with it curse. On her right, Joseph folds his arms and glares, the same hateful expression his mother wears beside him. On Marina's left, Mlle Pichon looks almost happy, a wry smile inching at the corner of her mouth. And in this arraignment of emotion Marina cannot find her own. She is far from happy, but neither is she sad to have watched the general go, or his wife, the woman who called her Miranda and gave her the book of Shakespeare. She feels herself at the edge of something vast and bottomless she can't yet name. These people, the general and Mrs. Butler, are figures in her past, and thereby distant, never to be reached again. They never asked after her or called though they lived in the same city these nine months. And why should they have? She only knew them for a few weeks. A nothing span of time.

Now the crowd dissipates, and the guards are called to rank and march away. Above the hum of departure, a woman's voice calls out and begins to declaim a poem. Marina looks about for the owner of the prim shrill voice, but cannot find her. The poetess goes on in spite of taunts:

"And if in Hell there ever dwelled
A demon such as thou,
Then Satan yield the scepter up,
Thy mission's over now."

When the poetess is done the four of them set off through the remaining crowd. At Decatur they must wait while an omnibus churns past. Not two feet away, chatting on the corner with a handful of his fellow officers, is Major Strong. He is just as handsome as she remembers, his teeth just as perfect and white. White as the insides of one of his apples. Marina touches her face, realizing that she has her veil pulled back, and with a glint of blue he sees her, turns, patting one of the officers on the chest. Major Strong is bent now, hat in his hands, smiling at her.

"Miss Marina! It's you! How long has it been? My goodness!"

She looks from Major Strong to Joseph, who glares unremittingly at the man now repeating her name, and slips her arm through the loop of his cocked elbow. The crisp outlines of Major Strong's words begin to fail, and in the slackening of his smile, his eyes' confused dart, she witnesses the outcome of her repudiation. There are hands on her shoulders, a transference of womanhood from Mlle Pichon and, yes, Joseph's mother. Her past stands before her, asking what is wrong and what he has done, and she could no more tell him than name the gulf at the heart of herself.

"Marina?"

Beside her, Joseph is shaking; she sees her future written in the fury of his glare. His are the kind of eyes you'd want to watch you die or have a child. To encompass moments she can barely fathom and are sketched in her mind in vicious strokes, waiting to be made distinct by time. The women are going on ahead, a black vanguard that floats across the street. She tugs Joseph's arm and they follow the course cut by the women through the mass. She sets the pace and they stroll on, arm in arm, to the fading sound of her name.

Joseph

Fourteen

A New Year

The house on Kerlerec is alive with voices; its boards shudder with the weight of visitors, its air electric with the plucking of guitar and mandolin. The hired musicians occupy a corner of the parlor, the only males here other than Joseph. None yet dance, though some are deep into the punch, which steams above a low blue flame and smells of cloves and allspice. Joseph's mother had ordered the party to begin in her absence, overseen by Mlle Pichon. And when she returns from the court recorder's office, the year of our Lord eighteen hundred and sixty-three is being welcomed with all the joy the ladies can muster despite their whispered fears of servile insurrection and chaos caused by Mr. Lincoln's proclamation, made this day official across the warring South but not here. Cheering her arrival the ladies rush the door on the upturned cups of their dresses. And Mlle Pichon, at the fore, takes hold of his mother's hands, pumps them twice as if to shake the information out of her. Across the parlor,

Joseph can just make out his mother's voice above the music and the ladies' clamor.

"All of it," she says.

The inheritance, then, has been decided. After the doctor's disappearance sole proprietorship of the money is given over to his mother, to manage until the year of his majority.

Mlle Pichon lets out a yip and the ladies form a wave to push his mother forward. The musicians take this as a signal and strum louder. They steer her towards the punch bowl but she breaks away and makes for where Joseph and Marina sit. He rises to greet her and she takes his head in her hands and tilts it to her lips.

"Now it's done," she whispers. "Everything is safe."

Another kiss. She lets him go and follows the voices of her friends. Joseph slumps back to the couch. Marina pats his leg, lets her fingers linger there, and they both look to the far wall where hangs the obsidian mirror, a late Christmas gift from Mme Frick who said (while his mother was out) that she never could stand the thing and, well, Elise was always mooning over it.

Now that she and Mlle Pichon have come to live with them, Marina is a wild constant. Their days are spent in idle oddness, devising games known only to them, talking of a war fought in and for a dreamstate, and night finds one of them padding to the room of the other. Neither mother nor surrogate seems to care or take especial note their scrofulous doings. The women are tolerant of these two recent outcasts from what is imagined to be the Eden of childhood but the children rightly see as a tangled garden of poison flowers where the trees are heavy with deadly fruit. Soon they will both return to school, but for now life is pure and strange and they are twinned, their eyes bagged and their chests hollow. Willing victims of a wasting love.

Seated before the fireplace in an immense wingback, his mother smiles, talks, moves her hands as though she directs the flames. Her flesh retains its sunblasted color, but the fierce whiteness of her eyes is gone; free of the veil, her braids curl hornlike round her ears.

In the rear of the parlor hangs the black mirror. It looms above them, glittering with firelight and traversed by shadows. Now the party, one by one, approach, and the black mirror presents them their benighted likenesses. Its borders are thickets of razor-edged garland and inky thorn, and lurking there are other figures, shades dancing across its surface like that of moonlit water, the doorway to a drowned world within which lies a sunken submarine, perhaps, or the bones of a man.

Acknowledgments

My most heartfelt thanks go out to:

My agent, Gail Hochman, for being the finest advocate any writer could ever want, and for helping me through trial and travail with an ever-guiding hand.

That prince of perfidious Albion, that magnificent and unparalleled hewer of plot and prose, defender of my most serpentine sentences, my editor, Peter Blackstock.

Elisabeth Schmitz and Morgan Entrekin, who took huge risks on an unknown, unproven writer and a big, brutal book called *The Blood of Heaven*. And just when I thought y'all two had changed my life forever, Elisabeth invited a certain New England bookseller to dinner at Winter Institute '13, and introduced me to the love of my life. Such debts are beyond the realm of simple thanks.

The good people of Grove Atlantic: Deb Seager, who saved me from a particularly aggressive bootblack on the mean streets of Chicago; John

Mark Boling, who shepherded me through a tour which included my hysterical cancellation of "lost" credit cards, among other self-made catastrophes; the wonderful Judy Hottensen, who preached the good word of *Blood*; Amy Hundley, who brought it to the continent and the home of my ancestors; Royce Becker, whose beautiful cover designs leave me breathless; Jess Monahan, who I swear to get that playlist to eventually.

Eric Chadaille, ne plus ultra translator.

The Tennessee Williams New Orleans Literary Festival, the AJC Decatur Book Festival, and the Tampa Bay Time Festival of Reading, Northwestern State University, Louisiana State University, and the University of Massachusetts Amherst, for hosting me.

Jim Davis and the Louisiana Book Festival for bringing a prodigal son back within the wings of the mother pelican.

All the indie bookstores and amazing booksellers who hosted me, including but far from limited to: Garden District Book Shop, Square Books, Sundog Books, Malaprops, Politics & Prose, Books & Books . . . and so many more. And one huge wild yawp of love and thanks goes to Jeremy, Keaton, and all the fine folks at Brazos Bookstore.

Bob and Catfish for shelter, love, and understanding in the most trying of times. Words do no justice. And to my walking partner on many a roadside stop and chill mountain morning, Miss Emma.

Friends old and new. Y'all know who you are—and it's all of you. From the mountains of New Mexico to the coast of New England, no finer array of humanity exists.

Andrew Smith, dearest friend, scholar, fellow gamesman, for hours of unbridled joy.

Adelita Solorzano and Sanctuary Illuminarie, for giving Alise and me the most wonderful fairy-tale place in which to live.

The Hamiltons, Chuck and April, for welcoming me in and never for an instant making me feel like anything other than family.

My parents, Kirk and Patricia, whose love and support has never for a moment flagged, and without whom I would not be.

Above all, to Alise. My love, my life. You are and will always be *wondrous*. Every moment of the journey, begun in snow-shrouded Kansas City, encompassing months and miles and lovelorn hours, sleepy Carolina villages and southwestern peaks, has been a glory. May it never end.